KNOCKED UP BY THE MOB BOSS

A MAFIA ROMANCE (LEVUSHKA BRATVA)

NICOLE FOX

Copyright © 2019 by Nicole Fox

All rights reserved.

No part of this book may be reproduced in any form or by any electronic or mechanical means, including information storage and retrieval systems, without written permission from the author, except for the use of brief quotations in a book review.

❦ Created with Vellum

MAILING LIST

Sign up to my mailing list!
New subscribers receive a FREE steamy bad boy romance novel.

Click the link below to join.
https://readerlinks.com/l/1057996

ALSO BY NICOLE FOX

Kornilov Bratva Duet

Married to the Don

Til Death Do Us Part

Heirs to the Bratva Empire

Can be read in any order

Kostya

Maksim

Andrei

Tsezar Bratva

Nightfall (Book 1)

Daybreak (Book 2)

Russian Crime Brotherhood

Can be read in any order

Owned by the Mob Boss

Unprotected with the Mob Boss

Knocked Up by the Mob Boss

Sold to the Mob Boss

Stolen by the Mob Boss

Trapped with the Mob Boss

Volkov Bratva

Broken Vows (Book 1)

Broken Hope (Book 2)

Other Standalones

Vin: A Mafia Romance

KNOCKED UP BY THE MOB BOSS: A MAFIA ROMANCE (LEVUSHKA BRATVA)

By Nicole Fox

They're coming to take her baby. They'll have to kill me first.

She's an innocent maid.

I'm a ruthless Bratva boss.

She says she wants nothing to do with me.

But in my world, when I want something, I take it.

And I want her.

The problem is, Zoya is hiding a terrible secret:

A baby in her womb that was never meant to be.

And I'm not the only one who knows.

Our enemies are coming.

To hurt her.

To ruin me.

What they don't know is this:

I've found what I want in this world.

And they'll have to kill me to take it.

1

ALEKSANDR

I've been in the office for hours. Long enough that my eyes are burning, and I'm not sure what time it is. I could stand up and open the blinds covering the window, but part of me doesn't want to know. If the sun has set, then I've been here too long. If the street below is emptied of people, then I've been here way too long. If the sun is already coming up, I'll need more coffee to make it through another day.

"What in the hell are you still doing here?"

The sound of another human jolts me from my work, and I push back from the desk, my wheels squealing, prepared to fight off the intruder. It takes me an exhausted second to recognize my own face, standing in the doorway

My twin brother.

"It's after midnight," Mikhail says, checking his wrist, though he doesn't have a watch on. He pushes the door closed and drops down into the leather chair across from my desk. The focused light of my desk lamp means that he is half-hidden in shadow, but even in the dark, I can see how worn he looks.

"You came here looking for me. Why do you sound so surprised to have found me?"

Mikhail lets out a humorless chuckle. "Because I hoped I was wrong about you, but apparently your life is just as sorry as I thought."

He is only half-joking, and we both know it. It isn't healthy, how much energy I devote to the family business, but it is all I know. It is all I've ever known. From the moment I was born, there were expectations, and I've always been willing to kill myself to meet them. Not just to please my father and my mother—though that is part of it. Mostly, it is for me. Who am I if I can't live up to my family legacy?

Mikhail has never suffered under the same burden, even though he should feel it more keenly than even I do. Born two minutes before me, he is the heir to the family legacy. We were conceived in the same moment, but because he took his first breaths one hundred and twenty seconds before me, he has to inherit the business and command the small army my father has gathered. I don't envy his position, even though it doesn't seem to stress him the way I think it should.

"Crime isn't as easy as people make it out to be," I say breezily, leaning back in my chair and crossing my arms. I tip my head towards him. "Why were you looking for me?"

The fake smile falls away immediately, and Mikhail runs a hand through his hair. I'm not surprised. I could tell from the moment he walked in that something was wrong. Not to mention, he rarely visits me at the office. Though Mikhail and I are two halves of the same being, we couldn't be more different.

He may be the first born, but he likes to keep a safe distance from anything that resembles hard work. Usually, the only time I see him is when I finally head home after a late night in the office to find him passed out on my sofa. It is how he knows better than anyone the hours I devote to the family business. I've tripped over him in the dark enough times that he knows my schedule.

He reaches beneath his wrinkled shirt and pulls something from the waistband of his jeans. He looks like he could do with a shave and a shower, but I long ago gave up pestering him to take care of himself. That is our mother's job.

He pulls out an envelope, crumpled and damp from where it was pressed against his hip. "Father left me a message."

My brows pulled together as I took the letter from his hand. "He sent you this?"

"Left it for me," Mikhail corrects. "I found it pinned to my front door."

My heart sputters in my chest. In our business, finding things taped to your front door is never a good sign. It is a threat. It means the sender knew where you lived, and they want you to know they could access you at any time. Of course, Father knows where Mikhail and I live—he even has a spare key to my apartment—but the ominous undertones remain. He could've sent a text or left a voicemail. Instead, he chose this.

"Have you read it?"

"Of course I read it," Mikhail says, flinging himself back in his chair so it rocks backwards on the rear legs. "It was nailed to my fucking door. I couldn't exactly ignore it."

"Nailed?" I lift the flap, noticing the jagged tear where Mikhail had torn it open and, for the first time, the hole in the center. It really had been hammered in. Mikhail says nothing as I read the familiar, spiky scrawl.

Mikhail,

My grace is running out. I will not allow you to be an embarrassment to this family. Fail me again, and you will be out of our business for good.

-Vlad

"Signed *'Vlad'*," Mikhail says hollowly, his top lip pulled back in a snarl. "Like he doesn't want to consider himself my father anymore. Can you believe it?"

Truthfully, I can. Though I won't tell Mikhail that.

Our father has always preferred Mikhail. He has a soft spot in his hard heart for his eldest son, for the man who will one day take over his business. However, that spot has been firming up with each new indiscretion. For years, Mikhail's vices were relegated to his personal life. He spent his free time in clubs and bars and drug dens, having his fill of whatever sin was offered to him, but it didn't affect his day-to-day duties as the second-in-line to the Levushka crime family crown.

That has changed in the last few years, though. His nights out have turned into weekend benders that leave him unconscious and impossible to reach. No one can find him, and when they do, he is too sick to be of any use. Father has done his best to impress upon Mikhail the importance of his role in our family, but Mikhail can't see beyond the haze of drugs and women long enough to get a clear picture of his future. It appears that, now, Father has finally had enough of his games.

"I mean…" Mikhail says, standing up and fisting his hands at his sides. His fingers are trembling, and I wonder how long it has been since he's taken something. His blue eyes are the clearest I've seen them in the last few months. It won't be long before he'll give in again to the pull of the drugs, though. It never takes long. "It is bullshit. He can't kick me out of the family. We are blood. Flesh and blood. Doesn't that mean anything to him?"

"You know it does," I say gently, knowing my brother well enough to recognize that he isn't ready for a harsh reality yet. If he feels backed into a corner, he'll crawl into some hole, shoot up, and disappear for a week. "Father loves you, but he is worried. That's all this is. Just him trying to let you know he is worried."

"Worried about what? I'm fine." He reaches out to run a finger along a book on my shelf, but when he realizes how badly it is shaking, he tucks the finger back against his palm and lowers his hand.

"Your hands are shaking," I say. "And this is the first time I've seen you in four days. I'm not sure I'd classify that as being fine."

He spins around, and his face is red. I can't tell whether it is heated with shame or anger. "You are in your office past midnight. Again. Are *you* fine, Aleksandr?"

"If you're trying to prove you are better than me, I'd suggest you find a higher bar to jump over," I say. "Just because I'm fucked up doesn't mean you have free license to be, too."

"Sure it does," Mikhail says, his shoulders relaxing. Exhaustion seems to come over him all at once, and he moves back to the chair and flops down, the legs groaning under his sudden weight. "We're twins, after all."

"But you're older." He shouldn't need the reminder. God knows he hears it enough. And yet, the reality still doesn't seem to have sunk in. "You are the one who will inherit everything, Mikhail. That is why Father sent that letter."

He nods and runs a nervous hand through his blonde hair. It is cropped close to his head, a couple inches shorter than mine now, but his fingers still grab at his head like he expects to find hair there. "What if he does kick me out?"

I want to tell Mikhail that won't happen. Not only for his sake, but for mine. I've always had a desire to please my father and be a dutiful son, but I have no interest in Mikhail's inheritance. I don't want to be second-in-command. My entire life has been spent in the background of my family, and I've come to enjoy the shadows. If our father follows through on his threat, I'll be the new recipient of all of his attention. The hopes and dreams and expectations he had for

Mikhail will be transferred to me, and I don't want them. Not one bit. Especially if that comes with Mikhail's banishment.

I hold up the letter. "Then it means you fucked up again. The threat isn't a mystery. There is a clear action and consequence. If you don't want the consequence, don't mess up."

My twin shakes his head and looks down at the floor. "You say that like it is easy."

"It can be," I say. "You have to want it, Mikhail. You have to fight for it."

"You think I'm not fighting?" The chair he was sitting in is across the room and on its side before I can even jerk back in surprise. He leaned forward, his palms flat on my desk, and I met him head on, refusing to turn away. "You think I like being this way?"

"Yeah, I do." I stand up so we are the same height, my eyes looking straight into his. To anyone walking by, it would look like I was looking in a mirror. "Because if you didn't like it, you'd change it."

Mikhail's eyes go hard, and he leans forward until his nose is only an inch from mine.

"Fuck. You."

I sigh and sit back down, too tired to deal with him right now. It feels like I've been too tired for years. Mikhail wants my sympathy. He wants me to feel bad for him, but he doesn't want the truth. He doesn't want to hear how he is failing. Because honestly, I think he already knows.

Mikhail knows that he has a problem. He knows he needs to get off the drugs and get away from his lowlife friends and the women who cling to him because he pays for them to get high. He knows this life will kill him if he doesn't get away, but it is easier not to think about it and drown his worries in the bottom of a bottle or the end of a line.

"And fuck Dad, too," he adds, pushing off my desk and stumbling backwards. When I don't say anything, he moves to sit down, but remembers he threw his chair. He looks sheepish as he picks it up and sits it upright across from my desk. "Neither of you know what it's like to be me."

My brother is like a small child. Selfish and self-absorbed. He can't think beyond his own needs and wants. Even if he does get clean, he won't be the kind of boss our father is. People won't respect him. Still, I'd rather it be him than me.

"Maybe we don't," I say. "But we seem to be the only people who know what you could become."

Mikhail rolls his eyes, but I can see that my words are breaking through his wall. He is softening.

"You seem to think this is all you'll ever be," I say, waving a hand at his stained clothes and bloodshot eyes. "But Dad has always seen a leader in you."

He presses his lips together until they are white. Then, he looks at me out of the corner of his eye. "And what about you?"

"What about me?"

He folds his hands together in front of him, elbows resting on his knees. "What do you see?"

I stand up and walk around the desk until I'm standing in front of him. I rest on the edge, legs crossed at the ankles. "I've always seen my brother. My twin. And I have every bit of faith that he is in there somewhere, and he'll return one day."

He stares at the wall for a long time, his eyes flicking up towards the ceiling, and I know he is fighting back tears. "The ultimatum won't do shit for me," he says finally.

"Losing your family isn't enough motivation?"

Before Mikhail walked in, I hadn't realized how tired I was. Now, exhaustion seeps into my bones. I feel like I could fall over at any second.

Mikhail points a shaking finger at me. "That's why you don't get it, Alek. I already feel like I've lost my family."

"How?" I don't mean to raise my voice, but I can't take his victim act anymore. How he can think he has been alone when I've been covering for him with Dad for years is absurd.

"Because I'm in this alone," he says, gesturing down to himself. "No one knows how it feels to need what I need. No one gets the pull. And because they don't get it, they don't get me."

I think his logic is bullshit, but this is the closest we've ever been to a real conversation about his issues. And I can see that Mikhail wants me to get it. He wants someone to understand. For the first time, he is reaching out for help.

"I'm not going to shoot up so I can understand you," I say firmly. "But I will always have your back. Always."

He nods. "That is all I need. I need you to help me. Support me."

I run a hand through my hair. It is greasy; I desperately need a shower. I check the watch at my wrist and realize, suddenly, I need to be on a plane to St. Petersburg in eight hours, and I haven't packed yet.

"You need rehab," I say, pushing myself to standing and walking back around my desk. I grab my jacket from the back of my chair and shrug it on.

He snorts. "Rehab doesn't do shit."

"Doing nothing doesn't do shit," I say. "Rehab at least shows you are trying. It shows that you care. Go and get clean. Then, we start from square one. Together."

He has been to rehab before. Never consistently. Never long enough to clean himself up properly, and I can tell he doesn't like the idea even now. But I don't care.

"Is that your condition?" he asks.

I nod. "My own ultimatum. Go to rehab and prove to me you're serious. Then, I'll stand by your side. If not, you are on your own."

He sighs, and I can already tell he is going to give in. We have the same face, which makes him incredibly easy to read. "Will you at least go with me to check in?"

I shove my wallet in my back pocket and shake my head. "I can't. I'm leaving first thing in the morning to oversee a weapons shipment. You have to take this first step on your own, big brother."

I walk to the door and flip the light switch, plunging the room into darkness. When Mikhail turns around, I can see his blue eyes shining in the light from the hallway. He looks at me for a second before looking down at the floor and shuffling past me.

"Are you going to go?" I ask when he reaches the end of the hallway.

He gives me a thumbs up over his shoulder, but he doesn't turn around. I shut the door to my office and follow him out, hoping he's telling the truth.

2

ZOYA

My mother sits silently in the seat next to me, her gaze fixed on the blurry scenery passing outside the window. She hasn't looked at me since we pulled out of the parking lot. She hasn't *really* looked at me since I delivered the news a month ago.

Getting pregnant was not part of the plan. Eventually, sure. But not now. Not when we'd only lost my father a few months before, when my mother was mired in a dark pit of grief. And certainly not when I would have to do it all on my own. No, the pregnancy had been an accident, but my mother didn't see it that way.

"The baby seemed big," I say, my voice expanding in the tight space of the car, filling every crevice. I'd spoken softly, but it still felt too loud.

My mother hums in agreement.

"I think the image was blown up, though," I say, tapping the black and white sonogram image sitting in the cup holder. "I'm not showing enough to have a baby that big inside of me."

"They magnify it." She turns to look forward, her face pulled back in an expressionless mask. Her lips, which only a few months ago were constantly turned upwards in a smile, sag towards her jaw. She looks older.

"Did you have sonograms with me?" I ask. "When you were pregnant, I mean? Did they have the machines back then?"

"I'm not that old," she says, her voice filled with a playfulness I haven't heard in too long.

"If you say so," I tease back, but when I elbow her arm across the console, her mouth tightens and she pulls her arms closer to her sides.

I swallow back my disappointment and turn down the long road that leads to the estate where we both work and live. The Levushkas hired my parents as caretakers to the sprawling estate when they were freshly married and my mother was pregnant with me. They were young and didn't have any skills, but the mafia family found a rare bit of pity for their situation.

My parents were forever grateful to the Levushkas and dutifully held their position for the last twenty years. And now that my father has recently passed, my mother is even more committed to her employer, Boris Levushka. *Our* employer, really. As soon as I was old enough to work, I started alongside my mother as a maid in Boris' home. Now that my father is gone, however, my mother has been taking on his duties, as well, leaving more of the cleaning to me.

"We are running late," she says, glancing towards the clock on the dash and then back out the window.

"We said we would be back at ten," I remind her.

"Yes," she says with a frustrated tip of her head. "And it is five after."

"Boris knows how doctor's appointments can go, mother. He won't—"

"Mr. Levushka," she says. "You should call him Mr. Levushka."

My brows pull together. "I've always called him Boris."

Growing up on the estate, I had free run of the grounds. My parents kept me inside our cottage when important guests were staying in the main house or when a deal was being worked out, but otherwise, I ran between our cottage and the estate's kitchens as though it was an extension of my own house. And Boris was always kind to me.

He is a broad man with a thick neck and arms, and his shiny bald head makes his smile look menacing, but he always had a smile for me as a child. I'd seen him raise his voice to other household staff, berating them for simple mistakes, but even once I began working for him, he had a special fondness for me that I attributed to the fact he had watched me grow up.

"That was before," my mother says.

"Before what?" Before I began working for him? That had been four years ago, so if he minded me calling him by his first name, certainly he would have said by now. Or did she mean…?

Finally, my mother acknowledged the sonogram picture sitting in the cup holder between us. She pointed to it with a stiff finger. "Before this."

Before the pregnancy. Yes, many things were different before the pregnancy. For one, my mother would look at me. She would smile and laugh. She would pull me into a hug at the end of the day and kiss me on the forehead. Now, I'm trapped in the after. When my own mother is so consumed by disappointment that she can't even say my name.

"Why did you come today?" I ask, finally voicing the question that had been burning inside of me since she told me she asked Boris—Mr. Levushka—for the morning off. "Why did you come with me if you can't even bring yourself to look at a picture of my baby?"

She stiffened at the words. *My baby.* "You shouldn't be alone."

"I'm alone all day," I argue. "I spend hours cleaning rooms in silence. Not to mention coming back to the cottage at the end of the day to find you are already in your room. You don't mind that I'm alone then."

She crosses her arms over her chest. She is thinner than she was a few months ago, and I want to ask if she is eating. She hasn't had dinner with me for the last week, but I'd assumed she was eating before I came home. Now, I'm not so sure. "The doctor is different."

"How?" I want her to look at me. Being silent and waiting for her anger to pass clearly hasn't worked, so perhaps I should try asking her all the questions I've kept pent inside. Maybe I should force her to voice the thoughts and feelings she has been silently stewing over for the last month. Maybe it will help.

"They could give you bad news," she says sharply, her tone in direct opposition to the concern shown by her words. "You shouldn't drive after news like that. Someone should be there for you."

The stone around my heart softens, and I reach across the console to lay my hand over hers. "That is different," I agree softly. Tears spring to my eyes at the thought that my mother still cares. She still worries for me, still wants to be there for me. However, they dry immediately when she wrenches her hand away and leans into the passenger side door.

"And it shouldn't be me," she snaps. "It should be your husband. Or boyfriend, at least. But you do not have one of those."

Her words slithered down my spine like ice water, sending a shiver through me. "No, I don't."

"It should be the father of your child," she said, pointing again to the sonogram in the cup holder. "He should be the one here to take care of you. Where is he?"

We'd had this discussion too many times to count in the last month, and it always ended the same way. Me, closed-lipped and burning with shame, my mother marching off to her room and slamming the door.

I turn onto the gravel driveway that stems from the main road and wraps around the back of our cottage. It is narrow and bumpy, used only by the very few people who ever make their way to our house.

When I don't say anything, my mother sighs and shakes her head. As soon as I park our beat-up car behind the house, she throws open the door and marches inside. I know where she is headed—her room. She will hide in there until I go up to the main house to work. Then, she will emerge and go about her day, doing her best to pretend I don't exist. To avoid me. I can't live this way anymore. Losing my father was hard enough, but now I've lost my mother, too.

I follow behind her, grabbing her arm just before she can grab the handle. She gasps when I grab her, but I'm too angry to care.

"Why are you acting this way?" I feel more like the parent in this moment. Like I'm disciplining a stubborn child. "You cannot just avoid me until the pregnancy is over. You do realize that, right? At the end of this, there will be a child. A baby who will need to be taken care of. Are you going to ignore me then, too? Are you going to continue pretending I do not exist until you join Father, wherever he is?"

"Do *not* speak to me like that," she hisses, stepping forward, her nose inches from mine. We are the same height and build, though her body is softer, thicker around the hips and thighs. And her eyes are a deep, dark brown. My blue eyes came from my father. "I am still your mother."

"You haven't been acting like it." My voice is loud enough that she takes a step backwards, but she isn't giving up. Not a bit. Her eyes narrow.

"I've been your mother for twenty years, Zoya." It is the first time she has said my name in a month, and I almost sigh at the relief. Even in her anger, it feels good to hear it. "I have raised you and cared for you in the way I thought was right. I've cleaned toilets and scrubbed floors and dishes to make sure you could have a good life."

"I do have a good life," I say, lifting my arms to gesture to our modest, but clean cottage. There is a flower bed in the backyard where my father and I planted herbs and a few vegetables. Flowers bloom from the ground in colorful bouquets on the other side of the door. My parents built something here in this cottage, and I am happy to continue it. I had a happy childhood, and that is all I can hope for my own child.

My mother shakes her head. "A *better* life. I wanted you to have a better life than me."

My mother had never said so, but my father let slip late one night—after he'd had a bit too much to drink and my mom had gone to bed—that I was an accident. Not unwanted, he'd clarified. But unexpected. He and my mother had only been married a few weeks when they found out. There was no time to be young and aimless and in love. Suddenly, they needed jobs and a house and security. So, they'd come to work for the Levushka family and they'd never looked back. As a child, I thought their life was a fairytale. Love and a warm, cozy cottage, and laughter every night. As I got older, I realized nothing was that picturesque, but still, to hear my mother say she didn't want the same thing for me—it stung in ways I didn't expect.

"I didn't grow up wanting to be a maid," she says. "I married your father because he was young and handsome and smart. I thought he would go places. I thought *we* would go places."

"And I ruined that for you?" I ask, bitterness dripping from every word.

She looks me straight in the eyes and shakes her head. "You did nothing wrong. I gave up, Zoya. I gave up on my dreams and that is what you are doing now."

"What dreams?" I ask, throwing my hands up. "What have I ever done except be here with you?"

She flings her hand over her shoulder, pointing towards the cottage. "Your walls are covered with your dreams. Your father spent a month's pay buying you a laptop so you could pursue your dreams."

I sigh and run a hand down my face. "The graphic designs are…a hobby."

"They are your future," she snaps, pointing at me so forcefully I expect her to jab her finger into my chest. "Working here as a maid is a dead end. Who will care for the baby while you clean toilets, Zoya?"

I feel my face redden. I haven't considered all of the details yet. "Just because I don't have an answer, doesn't mean—"

"We can't afford a sitter. Not on our wages," she says. "I cannot afford to stay home with the baby while you work. We are only useful to Boris if we are both working. What do you think he'll say when you have to take days off to stay home with the baby?"

"He will understand," I say, regretting opening this floodgate. "Babies get sick."

"And maids get fired." She hurls the words at me like a slap, and I pinch my lips together. "You may call him Boris, but he is not your friend, Zoya. He is not your friend or your family, and as soon as we are no longer useful, he will find new employees."

Tears sting the back of my eyes. This is the most I've talked to my mother in a month, and all she can do is tell me the many ways I'm failing. I imagined she would come around eventually and offer to help me. Instead, she is simply pointing out the many different ways I am alone. The many different reasons I can't count on anyone. Not even her.

I push past her and into the house before she can see me cry.

"You can't run away from this, Zoya."

I let out a harsh, biting laugh. "You would know all about running away, wouldn't you? You've done an awful lot of that the last few weeks."

Before she can say anything else, I walk into my room and slam the door shut.

The pictures on my walls flutter in the breeze from the door closing. There are pen and pencil drawings hanging above the little desk in the corner of my room, but as the pictures begin to expand outward and take up more space, they turn to color—paints and markers—and eventually, computer animations.

Before I had my own computer, I spent as many free hours as I could find at the library. I used the software on the computers there, paying thirty-one rubles to print out what I made, and tacked my artwork up on my walls. I started by copying pictures I found in magazines or characters from television, but as time went on, I began to create my own. Aliens with purple skin and golden hair invading Earth, turtle-like creatures flying through space and playing soccer with the planets, and flowers as tall as trees casting shade over silver lakes filled with glimmering fish.

They were the imaginings of a child. Nothing anyone would care about. No one besides me, that is. Or my mom.

Regardless of what my mom thinks, my art is for me and me alone. Putting it out into the world—hoping for anyone else to care—is only asking for heartbreak. And life has enough of that already. No need to pile on.

I slip out of my flats and into a pair of cloth sneakers, pull my long brown hair into a heavy ponytail, and walk out of the cottage and towards the main house without looking to see where my mom is. I have to focus on my real life. On what matters: scrubbing Boris Levushka's toilets until they sparkle.

3

ALEKSANDR

I didn't sleep much after parting with Mikhail, and I feel the weariness in my bones as the plane begins to descend over St. Petersburg. It is early, fog rolling across the water that stretches into the horizon. It's a beautiful view, but I'm in no mood to appreciate it.

"Is there anything else I can do for you, Mr. Levushka?" the flight attendant asks, leaning forward to give me a straight view down the front of her button-down shirt. If I remember correctly, it was buttoned up to her neck when I arrived. Now, it barely covers her cleavage. She mentioned her name when I got on the plane, but I made no effort to remember it. We rarely use the same attendants twice. No one outside our operation should know too much about our movements. It is an unnecessary risk.

I shake my head and wave her away. She brought me coffee at the start of the flight, and I made the mistake of smiling at her. More than anything, it was an attempt to lighten my own mood. Mikhail's predicament is a dark cloud over my head, and I wanted just a tiny ray of sunshine. Unfortunately, life couldn't give me even that much.

The attendant may only be working this one flight for me, but that doesn't mean she knows nothing of my reputation.

She, like most of the women I come into contact with, knows all about my wealth, my family connections. If she was smart, she'd run in the opposite direction, but based on the way she has sashayed up and down the aisle of the plane the entire flight, doing her utmost to give me a peek at what is under her polyester skirt, she isn't smart. She does a poor job of hiding her disappointment as she sulks to the back of the plane.

The airport is small and there are no other flights taking off or leaving. I see my uncle the moment I step off the plane. He is standing next to a shiny black car, leaning back with his legs spread wide beneath him, his meaty hands shoved down in his pockets. Mikhail and I take after our mother's side of the family—tall and narrow—while my father's family has always been squarer in stature.

"I thought I'd be collecting Mikhail," Boris says.

Many people swear they can't tell us apart, but those closest to us can. Even from a distance, Boris has no trouble.

"Are you disappointed?" I ask flatly.

He shrugs, bobbing his head back and forth like he isn't sure, and then tips his head back in uproarious laughter. The sound feels too loud for how early it is, but that is how my uncle has always been. Too brash, too loud, too much. It is why he scares people. Not because he is scary, but because he is startling. Because he isn't afraid to operate outside the confines of normal human behavior.

He pulls me into a quick hug, slapping my back once with the palm of his hand, and then steps away. "It is good to see you, Aleksandr."

I nod. "We should go. The flight took off later than I'd hoped."

Boris raises an eyebrow and then chuckles to himself as he walks around the back of the car. "Yes. You are certainly nothing like Mikhail."

I decide to take his comment as a compliment.

The warehouse isn't far from Boris' home in the countryside. The gray metal building sticks up from the rolling landscape like a blight, but the benefit of the rusted old structure is that no one wants to go near it. Anyone who doesn't have business there will naturally do their best to pretend it doesn't exist, which makes it the perfect location to meet contacts and conduct exchanges. Plus, its location between the shore and an airport offers several modes of escape should things go awry.

As we pull in, Boris surveys the gravel lot, preparing himself for such a possibility. *Know your exit.* It was one of the first things my father taught me.

"Cyrus is here," Boris says, tipping his head towards a black truck barely visible beyond the corner of the building. He grits his teeth. "He arrived early."

Being the first to a meeting is beneficial. It is the same as being the host. You are there to welcome whoever arrives after you, and it ensures no traps or tricks can be laid before your arrival. Cyrus apparently understands this as well as we do.

I have a gun and a knife stored at my hip, and I press my hand against them as we cross the parking lot, ensuring I can access them easily. A quick draw is important. One second can be the difference between life and a bullet to the head. Though, I'm not expecting much from Cyrus. We've met with him before. As a longtime partner of our family, he relies on us to make up a large percentage of his business. Crossing us would be bad for his bottom line, and in the business of importing weapons, the bottom line is the only thing that matters.

The large space is dusty and dark as we enter, but my eyes adjust quickly. From the outside, the space looks like it could be abandoned, but lights flicker at half-brightness above our heads, filling the room with an electrical hum. Cyrus is standing at the far end of the warehouse, arms crossed over his chest. He is a small man in every way and the tall ceilings of the warehouse seem to only emphasize this fact. He looks like a child standing before us, though his face is grave. His brows pull together as we walk closer.

"You do not have a greeting for me, Mikhail?" Cyrus asks, chin lifted. "I thought we had become friends."

Boris laughs. "If you were friends, you'd know this is not Mikhail."

Cyrus creases his brow further, leaning forward to study me as though I might be a mirage. "Aleksandr?"

"Unless I have a long-lost triplet I didn't know about," I sigh.

Cyrus laughs, but the sound is shrill and humorless. "Even if there was a third, I'd still prefer Mikhail. He is good to do business with."

"That might be the first time I've ever heard that," Boris says mostly under his breath. Cyrus still hears him, though.

"I'm sure none of your other partners are as forthcoming as I am," Cyrus says. "They wouldn't want to bite the hand that is feeding them, per se."

The smile on Cyrus' face tells me he thinks he is being hilarious. I don't want to engage him. I don't want to encourage whatever joke he was telling, but the thought that he is having a laugh at my brother's expense makes me tighten my fists. "And what has Mikhail ever fed you?"

Cyrus turns to me and shrugs lazily. He has grown too comfortable here. He should be quiet, respectful. We are not royalty, but our business associates usually conduct themselves with a level of respect. Professionalism, at least. Cyrus acts as though he is talking to two friends. One thing must be made very clear: we are not his friends.

"Come on, Alek," he says, calling me by the nickname I only allow Mikhail to use. "You know your brother better than anyone. He isn't cut out for this business."

My spine stiffens, and I widen my stance, fingers itching to grab the blade at my hip. "You do realize that one day soon he will be the boss of the Levushka family? Mikhail will be the man in charge? Are you sure you'd like to speak about him like this? Believe me, I do not forget such slights."

"No slight intended," Cyrus corrects quickly, hands held out in front of him in defense. "Everyone likes Mikhail. He is a good guy. Last time he was in town, we—" Cyrus' voice cuts off, his eyes casting nervously up to me and then away. "Well, we had a good time."

I know what that means. They got high together. They partied together.

Father doesn't like when Mikhail lets loose in front of the clients, and I'm sure Mikhail told Cyrus not to say anything. Clearly, Cyrus doesn't know when to shut his mouth, though. If he did, he never would have opened it in my presence in the first place.

"It's just that Mikhail doesn't have an eye for details," Cyrus continues. "He lets things slide. Things that benefit me. I mean, I'm sure you can't blame me for not mentioning them to him."

Boris raises an eyebrow and crosses his arms over his chest, his stomach protruding out in a way that makes him look sturdy rather than fat.

Cyrus notices his change in demeanor and laughs nervously. He turns to me, head finally bowed low. "It is just that everyone knows you are the hard ass, Alek. The serious one."

"Don't call me Alek." I clench my fingers, my nails biting into the palm of my hand. I've always prided myself on my ability to marshal my anger. To keep my feelings close to my chest and focus on the logistics. On strictly what is necessary. But, although it would not be necessary, I can't seem to think about anything other than knocking Cyrus' teeth in.

He doesn't know Mikhail. If he'd seen him last night—his eyes sunken in, skin pale—perhaps he'd have a different opinion of him. All Cyrus remembers is the Levushka twin he drank and partied with. But that is not all Mikhail is.

"Sorry," Cyrus stammers, looking to Boris as though he expects some kind of backup from him. Boris lets out a low growl and Cyrus snaps his eyes back to me. He should be quiet. Now would be the time to stop talking and hope we will forgive his errors.

Instead, Cyrus doubles down. "But see? That is exactly what I mean. You are the serious one, Aleksandr. The one with boundaries. Standards. I've heard more than a few people suggest you should inherit the family after your father. It makes the most sense. Mikhail doesn't have what it takes to be a leader."

Boris takes a step closer to me so we are almost shoulder-to-shoulder and shakes his head. "The idiot isn't worth it."

I know he is right, but that doesn't stop me from rearing back and driving my fist into Cyrus' eye socket.

Punching him feels like a sigh of relief. A moment of reprieve after days—weeks?—spent clenched. As much as I hate to admit it, Cyrus was right about one thing at least: I am the one with boundaries. Mikhail would have had a knife to Cyrus' neck the moment he even breathed a word against me. But me? I held back. I waited until I couldn't contain it anymore. Honestly, I'm not sure which strategy is better.

"Fuck!" Cyrus cries as he drops to the floor. His knees crack against the concrete, and he winces. "What in the hell is wrong with—?"

"I wouldn't finish that sentence if I were you," Boris says, unmoved by my sudden outburst.

Heat radiates from my center, flooding through my arms and legs, and my vision is blurred around the edges. The only clear spot in my vision is Cyrus crumpled on the ground. I grab his sweat-stained gray sweatshirt by the collar and haul him to his feet. If it weren't for the wrinkles around his mouth and eyes, I'd think I was beating up a teenager. He is too scrawny to show up to meetings like this alone. I decide to teach him the lesson the hard way.

"...'Wrong with me'?" I ask, finishing his thought. "Is that what you were going to ask? What is wrong with me?"

He shakes his head, eyes wide. "No, that isn't what I—"

"*You* are what is wrong with me," I spit, pulling his face closer to mine until he has to tuck his chin in to keep us from touching. Until he has to lower his eyes and turn his head, avoiding my gaze the way he should have when I walked through the door. "Your obvious disrespect for the Levushka family and its members. That is what is wrong with me, Cyrus."

"I didn't mean any disrespect," he stammers, his legs flailing as he tries to find purchase on the floor so he can stand up. Most of his weight is hanging from my hand.

"Then what did you mean?" I ask. "Were you seeking to flatter me by insulting my brother? Did you think I would turn on my own family and gossip with you? Is that what you expected?"

"No, I just—"

"Or were you trying to sow discord in our ranks?" I tilt my head to the side, examining him. "Are you a mole seeking a weakness that can be used against us?"

He shakes his head vigorously, the thin hair on top of his head flap-ping from the force. "I'm not a mole. I've worked with your family for years. I would never double cross you."

I drop him down onto his knees. He curses as his kneecaps smack into the floor again, but the curse turns to a hiss when I pull the knife from my hip and press the flat part of the blade under his chin.

"Aleksandr." Boris sounds relaxed, but I hear the warning in his tone. Cyrus is an important connection for our family. Killing him because I'm a little pent-up wouldn't be the best look. But that doesn't mean I can't scare him a little.

"I've worked with enough traitors to know that everyone has a price." I slide the knife along his cheek, the sharpened blade leaving a thin cut in its wake. Blood blooms from the slice.

Cyrus looks past me, his eyes pleading with Boris, but I know he won't find mercy there. Boris isn't the forgiving type.

"I'm not a traitor," Cyrus pleads. "I swear."

I tighten my fist in the material of his sweatshirt and drag the knife back to his throat. "Maybe you aren't. But perhaps you could do with a little reminder of who is in charge."

"You are," he practically screams. "You are. I work for the Levushkas. I know that."

"Do you?" I glide the knife across his weak chest towards his stomach. "Or should I trim a little off the top to remind you?"

He whimpers, and I shush him. "Don't worry. No internal organs. Just a little skin. It will grow back."

"Please, Aleksandr. Please," he repeats, his hands folded together in a prayer. "I'm sorry. I'll apologize. To you. To Mikhail. To Vlad."

I stare into his pale brown eyes and consider him for a moment. I wasn't lying when I said I've worked with traitors before. It is a part of our world. I can sniff them out easily enough. Cyrus isn't one, but he could be. He is weak, frightened. Like a rat, he will run for higher ground as soon as the water starts to leak in. He'll turn his back on me and my family and abandon us all if he sees a better opportunity. So, I need to make sure he knows that any opportunity he takes, if it harms my family, will end with him being separated from his skin.

Without warning, I let go of his shirt and throw him backwards. He falls on his back, the air whooshing out of his chest in one burst, and then scrambles to his feet, backing away from me quickly.

"Not necessary," I bite. "But disrespect me or my family again, and you won't even have the opportunity to apologize. I'll slit your throat before the words are out of your mouth."

His hand moves subconsciously to his neck and he nods. "Of course. Yes."

Cyrus is still staring up at me, eyes wide and glassy when Boris claps his hands. The sound echoes around the room and the weapons importer snaps his attention to my uncle.

"Now that we're all clear on who is in charge," he says. "Can we talk business? I don't want to miss lunch."

Cyrus scurries to the back wall of the warehouse and shuffles back with a bag slung over his arm. It looks heavy enough to tip him over, but there should be three more of them at least.

"You were supposed to bring half of them today, right?" I ask, gesturing for him to open it.

He drops it on the floor, rolls a kink out of his neck and shoulder, and then unzips the bag. There are a smattering of handguns and a few semi-automatic rifles, but not near the amount we paid for.

"What the fuck is this?" I turn to Boris, but he is staring down at the bag, forehead wrinkled like he is trying to count them each individually.

"Half," Cyrus says. "This is half."

"Half of what?" I kick the bag, and Cyrus takes a step back, his hands folded behind his back. "Not half of what I paid for. Where is the rest?"

Cyrus looks to Boris for a quick second, his eyes flitting around the room nervously before they land on me. "Did no one tell you?"

Now, it is my turn to turn on Boris. "Tell me what?"

My uncle waves his hand dismissively. "It is nothing. Not really."

I gesture to the sad bag of weapons on the floor. "Yeah, I know. This is nothing. Where are the weapons we paid for?"

He shakes his head and runs a meaty hand down his face. "It is just a rival family. A small group of wannabes causing some trouble in St. Petersburg."

Cyrus had been expecting Mikhail to be at the meeting for a reason. He usually handled the St. Petersburg side of things. I spend most of my time in Moscow, so I don't expect to know everything going on, but I do expect to be informed if another family is cutting in on our territory.

"What kind of trouble?" I ask, turning back to Cyrus now. Boris had plenty of opportunity to tell me about this threat to our power, and he'd kept it to himself. I can't count on him to be honest about the scope.

"Vlad knows about it," Boris cuts in. "Mikhail told your father after his last trip here. He knows."

Everyone knew except for me. I do my best not to show my discomfort at that fact and keep my attention on Cyrus.

"What kind of trouble?" I repeat.

His face pales, and he shrugs. "They want my business. My loyalty." He holds up his hands to shield himself as though I'm lunging at him, even though I haven't moved. "But I would never. I work for your family, and I would never betray you. The problem is, I told them that, and there have been raids. My inventory isn't what it once was."

"That doesn't sound like wannabes causing trouble, Uncle. That sounds like a fucking problem I should have been informed about."

Boris cows. "Perhaps, but it isn't anything we can't deal with."

"You're right," I say, bending down to pick up the duffel and throw it over my shoulder. Cyrus really must be weak; it isn't nearly as heavy as he made it look. "Because we will deal with it. And soon."

4
ZOYA

The estate has been less busy than usual. Boris Levushka has never been one to throw wild parties or keep a lot of guests, but he hosts family. His brother and twin nephews visit St. Petersburg regularly for business, which always adds a long list of chores to my already overflowing workload. However, in the last few weeks, the house has been quiet.

Everything has seemed quieter since my father died. When my mother and I aren't screaming at one another, the cottage is silent. I no longer hear the sound of my father humming as he searches the cupboards for an evening snack or the creak of his footsteps across the wood floors. Now, it is just the forlorn and disappointed sighs of my mother coming from underneath her bedroom door.

Before the pregnancy, I could count on my mother coming up to the main house to visit me once a day or more, usually bringing with her a fresh cut bundle of flowers from our garden or from the more immaculately landscaped flower beds surrounding the estate. Occasionally, she would finish her duties early and take on mine to allow me time to devote to my drawings.

"You need to focus on what is important," she'd say as she practically pushed me out the door and across the lawn. "Cleaning is my specialty. Drawing is yours. Don't let it go to waste."

That is what my mother thinks I am doing: letting it go to waste. My life, my talent, my potential. All a waste, now that I'm pregnant.

The thought leaves a sour taste in my stomach, and I do my best to force it down. I've thrown up enough for a lifetime due to morning sickness, so I have no desire to do it again.

"If you're going to stand there lurking in the corner, the least you could do is chop some vegetables."

I look up to see Samara waving a carrot at me, her narrow face split wide in a smile. I roll my eyes and snatch the carrot from her, grabbing a vegetable peeler off the counter.

"Cooking is your job, remember?"

"And is standing around doing nothing yours?" she teases back. "I'd love to get paid to stand around and watch me cook. Want to trade?"

I throw one of the orange peelings towards her. It falls short, landing in the sink, and Samara sticks out her tongue at me.

"I can't help it that I'm an efficient worker," I say. "I finished all my work for this morning. The only thing left is to clean the kitchen once you finish."

"I've even been taking on that job recently," Samara sighs. "Boris has been eating dinner later than usual."

"You should leave the kitchen. I can get to it in the morning." Dishes and pans covered in stuck on food flash through my mind, and I fight back a wince, but say nothing.

Samara wrinkles her nose, having the same thought. "It's easier for me to take care of it right away than let it sit all night. What we need to do is get Mr. Levushka on a better schedule."

I've always had a closer relationship to Boris than the other employees, but I still glance around nervously to make sure no one overheard her. As innocent as our conversation is, it wouldn't be good if word of it made its way back to Boris.

"He is a busy man."

Samara shakes her head and leans forward, finally lowering her voice. "I'm not convinced what he is doing is for work. If it was, why would he need to stumble in after midnight?"

"He made you cook for him at midnight?" I ask, eyebrows raised in surprise.

"No, are you kidding? There is no way I'd get my ass out of bed to make him a full meal in the middle of the night," she says with a snort. If Boris asked her to, I know she would, but I don't say so. "But I heard him slamming cabinets in the kitchen from my room."

Samara doesn't live at the estate full-time the way my mother and I do, but she has a room in the servant quarters so she doesn't have to make the hour-long commute back to her apartment on the other side of the city.

"And he didn't sound entirely…sober," she whispers.

"You could tell that from the sound of him banging cabinets?" I ask.

"Yes, I could," she says, chest puffed up with indignation. She throws a handful of freshly-chopped vegetables into a preheated skillet and wipes her hands on the front of her apron. "He stumbled around and cursed under his breath. When I woke up in the morning, he'd knocked things over and there was blood in the sink."

"Blood?" I wrinkle my forehead. "People don't usually bleed when they are drunk. Maybe he was hurt."

"They do when they cut themselves on a knife while trying to cook… *drunk*," she says, driving home the point. Then, she waves a hand like none of it matters anyway. "Anyway, the point is that your work has been slowing down while mine has been picking up, and I know it would make me a good friend to be happy for you, but I'm too busy feeling sorry for myself."

"What's new?" I tease, walking around the counter and bumping her hip with mine while I add my chopped carrots to the pan.

"Hey, if you were a good friend, you'd feel sorry for me, too. My life is miserable." Samara turns her attention to a pot of simmering rice. When she lifts the lid, a cloud of steam rushes out, and she dodges it, blindly stirring the pot with a wooden spoon before replacing the lid. "More miserable than yours, anyway."

I smile and nod, trying my best to look like I'm in on the joke, but the words make my throat feel tight. I've never been much of a crier, but the pregnancy hormones have made me feel more emotional than usual.

"God, I'm sorry," Samara says, stepping close and laying a hand on my arm. "I'm an idiot. You know that, right?"

"No, you aren't." The words come out sounding choked, and I hate it. "You're fine."

She pulls on my arm until I'm facing her, and she squeezes my fingers. "No, I'm not. I suck."

"My life isn't miserable," I say, but my smile is weak, and I know Samara doesn't believe me. I certainly wouldn't.

"Of course, it isn't. But joking about whose life is worse after your father just died and…" she doesn't mention the pregnancy, but her eyes dart down to my still flat stomach. It isn't the baby that makes discussing it uncomfortable, but my mother's reaction. Samara has had a front row seat to our feud. She knows all of the details. She sighs and bites her lower lip. "It isn't nice."

I grab both of her elbows and shake her slightly, trying to plaster on a genuine smile. "It's fine. The pregnancy hormones have made me weepy. It isn't you."

Samara reluctantly accepts my explanation and goes back to work, and I start cutting out small circles of dough for the top of the *kurniks*.

"You could just tell her, you know," Samara says quietly, her voice the softest it has been all morning. "Or me. Or someone. It might make you feel better."

I look up, but she isn't looking at me. Her eyes are fixed on the pan of sautéing vegetables, so I decide not to say anything.

There is nothing to say.

My mother thinks I'm staying quiet on the identity of the father of my baby because I'm ashamed of him or because I want to protect him. Or, perhaps, because she thinks I want to raise my child alone and be a single mother. To her, I'm sabotaging my own future by insuring a lifetime of working my ass off to pay bills, feed a kid, and take care of myself. But my mom doesn't know the truth. No one does.

Samara's phone rings, interrupting my thoughts, and she wipes her hand on the towel hanging over her shoulder and pulls it out. She stares at the screen for a few seconds, weighing whether to answer it or not.

"Who is it?" I ask.

She wrinkles her nose. "I'm not sure. I don't recognize the number."

"Voicemail," I suggest. I never answer my phone to a number I don't know. Samara takes it anyway, looking up at the ceiling as she says hello.

Immediately, her face falls. She turns her gaze to me, staring at me as though she is trying to remind herself this isn't a dream. I reach across the island and grab her hand.

"Is she okay?" Samara asks, her voice wavering. She nods as the person on the other end of the line speaks. Then, she pulls the towel from her shoulder and drops it onto the counter. "Yes. I'll be there soon. Thank you."

She is in motion before the call has even ended, grabbing the pan of rice from the stove top and taking it over to the aluminum pie dishes.

"Who was that?"

Samara begins dumping a layer of rice into the bottom of each cup, measuring it out with a skilled hand. "The hospital."

"Shit. Is everything okay?"

Her hands are surprisingly steady as she tells me her mom was in a car accident. "A truck hit her in an intersection. She is in surgery."

She puts down the rice pan and reaches for the sautéing veggies, and I swat at her hand. "Stop cooking. You need to go to the hospital."

"But I have to—"

"Go to the hospital," I finish, grabbing her shoulders and pushing her away from the stove. "I can finish up here."

She shakes her head. "You aren't a cook, Zoya."

"I've watched you enough to pick up a few things," I say, giving her a sad smile. "Besides, I've eaten kurnik before. I know enough to figure it out from here. Go."

She looks nervously towards the food for a moment before whipping off her apron and grabbing her purse hanging from a hook next to the door. "The oven is preheated and the pies need to go in for thirty minutes or until the tops are—"

"Golden brown." I wave her on. "I know, I know. Go be with your mom."

The mention of her mom seems to bring the reality home, and she chokes back a sob, her eyes going misty. "Thanks, Zoya."

I nod. "And don't worry about dinner, either. Stay as long as you need to. I'll be here."

"I'll call you," she says over her shoulder as she heads out the door. "I love you."

As soon as she is gone, I worry I'm in over my head. Boris has never been a particularly picky eater. According to Samara, he eats whatever he is served without much complaint. But perhaps that is because he has always eaten Samara's food and it is delicious. He might have a complaint or two if he bites into a bit of raw dough or uncooked chicken. I push aside my doubts and finish the meal.

The rice is already cooked and Samara, ever the planner, has prepped the meal by making the chicken mixture the day before. So, really, all I have to do is layer the different ingredients and make sure to cook it all the way through.

She has already filled the cups with the rice, too, so I make my way around the tray with the chicken mixture, followed by the softened vegetables, and then repeat the entire process again. It is simple, and my mind begins to wander as I work.

I hope Samara's mother is okay. She mentioned surgery, but not what kind. For a broken leg? For a brain bleed? I had no way to gauge the severity, and I hoped she would call with an update when she knew more, though I vowed not to pester her while she was at the hospital. There would be enough people messaging her condolences and prodding her for information without me joining the ranks. Plus, Samara and her mother were really close. I should have driven her to the hospital. My mom went with me to my doctor appointment this morning just in case the doctor gave me bad news about the baby, and yet, Samara received bad news, and I just let her go. Hopefully, she makes it all right.

I wonder what I would do if something happened to my mom.

With Dad, he was sick. We knew he would die. So, when he did, it was almost a relief. Not because I was glad he was gone, but because I had been mourning him for months while he was still alive. Looking at him as he lost weight and seemed to shrink into himself was difficult and at a certain point, death seemed like the better option. The last time we spoke before he lost consciousness, he told me he was ready.

I can't imagine my mom sick, though. Her personality couldn't fit inside a frail body. Her stubbornness and fire and anger—mostly at me—needs room to breathe. Seeing her body emptied of those things would wreck me, I think. Because, despite what she thinks right now, I love her. Very much. And I know the things I'm not telling her are tearing her apart, but the ugly truth is that I couldn't tell my mom who got me pregnant even if I wanted to.

Because I don't know who he is.

I don't know his name or what he does for a living. I don't even know what he looks like.

∼

He wasn't wearing a mask or anything. At least, I don't think so. Truthfully, I don't remember much of anything.

Samara had been hounding me to go out on a date for months, and I'd finally agreed, dolling myself up in my best dress with my brown hair twisted back in a knot of braids and a full face of makeup on. But at the last minute, Samara couldn't make it. Something came up, and I was left with the prospect of wiping away an hour of hard work and staying home with my parents, or flying solo. So, I went out. The club was in a seedier part of St. Petersburg, but I didn't feel unsafe there. I went straight to the bar for a drink, hoping to dance, maybe meet a nice guy.

Everything after that goes fuzzy. If I was drugged, I have no clue who it would have been, but that feels like the only adequate explanation for the black spots in my memory. My thoughts around that night are like a picture on a dry erase board that has been partially scrubbed clean. There are faint lines here or there where the eraser missed, but it isn't enough to piece anything back together.

I remember a car and the feel of leather against the backs of my thighs, and I remember waking up in my bed the next day with the feeling that something was *wrong*. My body hurt in ways I'd never experienced before, and I desperately combed through the scant memories I had, trying to figure out if I'd chosen to lose my virginity to a stranger I met at a bar. I'm still not sure. Did I know him? Did he take advantage of me? Did I want it?

I lay the circles of dough over each of the pastry tins, brush them with an egg wash, and fold down the corners, crimping them with a fork. The work is repetitive and it helps me focus on something, anything, other than the swirl of panic in my stomach that rises up each time I think about that night.

I want to tell my mom the truth, but what will she think about me? And, even worse, what will she do when she learns the real story?

We are maids living and working for the estate of a well-known crime family. My father's position as the groundskeeper guaranteed we were useful to Boris, but now that he is gone, my mother is doing her best to cover the gaps. Boris doesn't seem to mind, but he would not take kindly to her running around the city trying to enact vigilante justice on whoever did this to me. Especially when her actions could reflect poorly on Boris. People would think he couldn't keep his employees in line. They would question his authority.

I don't know for certain that my mother would seek justice, but I can't imagine her sitting idly by, wondering with me whether I was victimized or not. She would want to find the answers, and I'm not sure if I want to know. If it was a powerful person in the city, someone with connections to the Levushkas or another crime family, I would rather let the matter drop. I have enough on my plate with bringing a child into the world that I don't need to add worrying about my mother's safety or our jobs at the estate to the list.

No, as angry as she is with me, I am doing what is best for her. For us.

Besides, I don't know anything for certain. Maybe I drank more than I remember and blacked out. Maybe I threw myself at an attractive man and wanted this.

I choke back another bout of nausea as I finish crimping the edges of the pies and slide them into the oven. Try as I might, I can't fight back the one thought that has raced through my head over and over again since I found out the true cost of that night:

Maybe this is all my fault.

5

ALEKSANDR

"Cyrus is a dumbass." Boris shakes his head, an amused smile on his face.

"I guess I don't find it as funny that we regularly worked with dumbasses," I say. "If he isn't competent, we should find someone else."

Boris lays a thick hand on my shoulder. "He is competent at importing weapons, which is all we need him for. Everything else will come with time. And fear." Boris laughs. "I thought he was going to piss himself when you threatened to dice him up."

With a little space, I can see that I maybe took my intimidation too far. I could have scared Cyrus shitless with words alone. Still, though the knife play might have been unnecessary, I won't feel bad for it. He should know better than to talk about a member of the Family that way. Especially to me. Now, I can be sure Cyrus wouldn't make the same mistake again.

"How much money do you think Mikhail has lost us by not paying attention?" I ask.

Boris glances over out of the corner of his eye and sighs. "I wish I knew. Probably more than you'd be comfortable with."

I hate that Mikhail's business failings are common knowledge and that no one thought to tell me about them. More than that, I hate that I didn't realize he was screwing up. As his brother—the 'responsible one,' as Cyrus called me—I should have recognized that Mikhail was too deep in whatever shit he was doing to do his job properly. I should have caught it before he made himself into a laughingstock. And I absolutely should have known about the rival family in St. Petersburg.

"What did Vlad say?" Boris asks, referring to the urgent message I'd sent him during our meeting with Cyrus. I should have known about our rivals before I stepped foot off the plane. The fact that I didn't needs to be addressed, and I need to know what my father wants me to do about it.

"He said he'd call me." I pull out my phone and click the screen on. No new messages. "I need to see him in person."

Boris snorts. "Good luck."

I try calling him, but the link clicks dead after a single ring. My father is the boss, but he only comes out when absolutely necessary. He has several houses all over Russia, and very few people know where he is at any given time. For all I know, he could be in St. Petersburg right now, just like me. He keeps his movements a secret. If I need to know where he is, I usually call Mikhail, but he isn't exactly available right now. I check my watch. He should be checked into his rehab program by now, which means they'll have his phone. I wonder if he told Dad about rehab. Should I bring it up?

Just as I'm about to slide my phone back in my pocket, it buzzes.

<V: *Can't talk now. Call you later.*>

"Shit." I drop my phone in my pocket and run a hand through my hair. I know I shouldn't dwell on it, but I can't help but think he would have taken the call if it had come from Mikhail. Regardless of everyone else's high opinion of me, my father always favored Mikhail. I don't know if it was because Mikhail was slated to take over the family or if he simply didn't like me as much. Regardless of the reason, I'd spent my life trying to be as important to my father as Mikhail, and it had earned me nothing but heartache.

"He cancel?" Boris holds open the warehouse door for me, and I step outside. Next to the car Boris and I arrived in, there is a second identical black car.

"Clearly he doesn't understand what 'emergency' means," I grumble. I nod towards the car. "I thought you were going home."

"I have another meeting," he says. "But you should get back to the house and settle in."

I shake my head. "I have another meeting, too. With a weapons dealer. Cyrus needs to know he isn't the only game in St. Petersburg. If he can't keep his shit from being raided, we'll find someone else."

"Your father know about that?" Boris asks, bushy eyebrow raised. "He and Cyrus have been tight almost as long as you've been alive."

"He would know if he picked up his phone."

Boris pauses for a moment, and I wonder if he is about to say something in defense of his brother, try to persuade me to talk with him before doing anything rash. But instead, he slaps a hand on my shoulder and then walks over to his car. He doesn't look back as he peels out of the gravel parking lot.

～

It takes me less than ten minutes to drive to the hotel where the dealer was staying. He has booked a private conference room off of the main lobby for us to meet. Hotel staff bring us espresso and a plate of biscotti that sit untouched.

"I know you and my brother began negotiations last month, so maybe you can catch me up on what you discussed." I pull my chair in closer to the table, hands folded in front of me. My tie feels too tight around my neck, but looking the part of a professional is important, even in the criminal world. I don't know Leonid, and as badly as I want to loosen the tie and unbutton the top few buttons of my shirt, I want to make it clear the Levushka family is a serious operation. We don't enter into contracts lightly, and we take our business dealings seriously.

"I'm glad we are meeting up," Leonid says, sliding a few papers to the center of the table and turning them sideways so we can both read them. "I've been trying to get in contact with Mikhail, but he hasn't returned any of my messages. The contracts he left for me don't make any sense."

I pull my brows together. "Don't make sense how?"

He folds the top page back and points to a paragraph in the middle. "I've highlighted all of the places where the names, drop of locations, and monetary amounts are incorrect or ridiculous."

Over half of the page was highlighted.

"I'm not sure if this contract was meant for someone else or not," he says. "My name is in here a few times and it does talk about importing weapons, but then there are other paragraphs that seem like they were copied and pasted in from another contract."

I grab the contract and begin to skim the document. In it, Mikhail referred to Leonid as "Leonard," "Lev," and "Nikolay." And there is no clear explanation of how frequently payments will occur, but the base amount listed is a laughable amount—barely half of what we pay Cyrus now for one of his shipments. The contract is nonsensical and it looks like it was written by a person with no grasp of business or reality. It's embarrassing.

"Mikhail gave you this?" I ask.

Leonid has the good sense to look embarrassed when he nods his head. "We had a great conversation, but then he left this for me. I tried to get in touch with him right away, but I haven't heard. I wanted to give you guys priority since the Levushkas have always been good to me, but I didn't have a choice. I have to make money, so I signed a contract with another family."

"Another family?" I ask. "Who?"

Leonid shakes his head. "Sorry, man. You know I can't say."

I know, but that doesn't quell my curiosity. Is he working with our rivals in St. Petersburg? If so, between the weapons they've taken from Cyrus during raids and what they are now going to get from Leonid, we will be embarrassingly overpowered if someone doesn't take care of this situation immediately. And I don't have to wonder who that 'someone' will be. It's me, of course. It's always me.

"I get it. Business is business," I say. "But what if I can get you a corrected contract back within the week?"

Leonid winces. "It will be tight. Most of my shit is spoken for. You know I want to help you out, but if I pull back on another contract, they will have my head."

"We'll take whatever you have left." I sound like I'm begging, which I basically am. "This contract can be a placeholder until you have more liquid inventory and we can renegotiate."

"Okay, yeah," Leonid says reluctantly. "Get me a contract within a week, and we'll see what we can do."

We shake hands and part ways. I take the contract with me, but I ball it up and throw it in the backseat as soon as I'm in the car. It is useless. Just another example of how bad I let things get. Of how far I let Mikhail fall off the wagon.

I push thoughts of Mikhail out of my head and head towards Boris' estate. I need to get out of my suit and make myself a stiff drink.

Boris' car isn't in the circle drive when I pull in, but I let myself in the side door with my key. If I go in the front, I'll be surrounded by his helpful household staff. Usually, I wouldn't mind, but I'm not in the mood today. I want to go to my regular room, take a shower, and figure out what I'm going to eat. I could have had one of the biscotti in my meeting with Leonid, but my father always emphasized the importance of not eating or drinking while conducting business. It is a common interrogation tactic—to wine and dine a person before plying them for information—and it can be just as damaging in business. If you allow someone to feed you, you give them power over you, however slight that power may be. So, I arrive to Boris' beyond hungry.

The side hallway is dim, only half of the hallway sconces turned on, but I've spent enough time in the house throughout my life to be able to make my way around in total darkness. Mikhail and I would play hide and go seek as kids while my father was in meetings. Once, Mikhail hid inside of a laundry chute, and I didn't find him until I heard a maid scream when she opened the hatch to drop in an arm load of bedding and found Mikhail crouched inside like a tiny troll.

The thought of my brother compels me, despite my hunger and exhaustion, to call him. If he is following the rules of the rehab, then he won't have his phone. But the last few times he went into the program, he charmed the charge nurses into letting him keep his phone in his bedside table. I know it would be better for him to disconnect from everything completely, but I still want to talk to him.

I want to yell at him for fucking everything up and screwing our family over. I want to ask him how he is feeling and whether getting clean is going to last this time. I want to tell him that I will take care of things until he gets back. But really, I just want to hear from him. My entire life is devoted to "the Family," but Mikhail is the only person who has been my actual family. Mother and Father have always been at odds with one another, going so far as to live in separate houses, and while Father and Mikhail are close, he and I never shared that same bond. Since I was a kid, it has just been me and Mikhail, and without him, I start to wonder why I devote so much of my time and energy to this family when they give so little back.

It rings twice before going to his automated message, and I know it is turned off.

Good, I think. *He is doing what he is supposed to.*

However, something pricks the back of my mind. A question. A doubt. Before I can stop myself, I stop in the hallway, dropping my luggage at my feet, and search for the number of the rehab facility. I find it and dial. It rings five times before a friendly female voice answers.

"Hello. I'm calling to make sure Mikhail Levushka has checked in. He was supposed to arrive this morning."

"Mikhail?" the woman asks, sounding like she recognizes the name. "No, I haven't seen him."

I pause, waiting for her to elaborate. She doesn't. "You haven't seen him or he isn't there?"

"If I haven't seen him, he isn't here," she says plainly. I hear a rustle of papers through the phone line. "It looks like we got a call that he would be checking in, but he never showed up. Maybe he is running late."

"Maybe," I agree, though I don't put my stock in my own words. If Mikhail isn't there, it is because he has chosen not to be. I ask the receptionist to call me when he arrives, and she says she will, but I'm not holding my breath. Mikhail will call me when he is ready. Probably with some half-assed apology about changing his mind and getting clean on his own. He'll be confident he can handle everything himself, and when he fails, I'll be the one to pick him up off the floor.

I grab my luggage and the bag feels heavier than it did a minute ago. Like someone snuck a bundle of rocks in there when my back was turned. I need a break. From work, Mikhail…everything.

But I will never ask for one. Not when so much is resting on my shoulders.

The suite at the end of the hallway has always been reserved from me. It is far from the main house, making it the quietest room in the estate, and it is close to the side exit, allowing me to come and go as I please. It was especially nice when I'd come into St. Petersburg with Mikhail and go out on the town. Rather than take a woman back to a motel, I could bring her to the Levushka estate. We'd slip in the side door without anyone knowing, and I'd send her on her way before morning. Boris wouldn't have minded that I used his house to get laid —he probably would have been proud in the way only an uncle can be happy to know his nephew is successful with the ladies—but it wasn't anyone's business. Unlike Mikhail, I've never liked to broadcast my personal life. I give enough of myself to the Family without letting them in on my sex life, too.

I push the door open, excited to drop my things and flop down on the bed, except, the mattress has been stripped bare.

I sit my bag next to the door and step into the dark room. The curtains haven't been opened, there are no towels or wash cloths in the on-suite bathroom, and the room smells musty, like it hasn't been aired out since the last time I came to St. Petersburg for a visit three months ago.

Fucking fantastic.

My fingers vibrate with pent-up frustration, and I would give anything to have Cyrus' face in front of me again. I'd give him a black eye to match his other one. My hands ball into fists at my side.

I know it is as simple as pulling back the curtains, opening the windows, and requesting fresh linens, but I shouldn't have to. I have enough on my plate without having to worry about doing Boris' maids' jobs, too. This should have been taken care of. Boris knew I was coming, which meant his staff knew I was coming. Someone should have had the room ready for me.

I turn and storm into the hallway. The carpet is plush enough I still move soundlessly through the house, but I can feel the floors vibrating with every step. Everyone else must be able to feel it, too, because as I walk into the circular entryway in the center of the house, a maid with tight black braids swirling around her head pops her head out of a closet, quickly bowing when she sees me.

"Welcome, Mr. Levushka."

"Who was responsible for preparing my room?" I snap.

The woman opens and closes her mouth several times, unsure how to respond to my obvious anger. I recognize her from previous visits, but I don't remember her name.

"That would have been Zoya," she says quietly. "If there is a problem, however, I'm happy to help."

"Not necessary." I remember Zoya. She is the petite brunette one that Mikhail always had an interest in. I only remember her name because of the repulsive way he would talk about her. Even Boris would join in on occasion, commenting on how she looked from behind while dusting a table. "Just tell me where Zoya is."

She glances at a clock in the hallway. "On lunch, I believe. In the kitchen."

By the time I get to the kitchen, my stomach is growling, and the frustration of everything having gone wrong all morning is settling in. This trip was supposed to be routine: meet with Cyrus, sign a contract, take a nap in the suite. Instead, Cyrus couldn't deliver the agreed-upon shipment because of a rival family no one bothered to mention to me, Mikhail fucked up another deal that could have covered the weapons Cyrus lacked, and then my beloved brother was a no show to rehab, which means he might truly and finally be cut out of the family business.

More frustrating than anything though, is that so much of this is my fault. If I'd kept a better eye on Mikhail, if I'd paid attention to the many ways he was falling apart, I could have stopped this. And the worst part is that I wasn't even the one who recognized Mikhail needed an ultimatum. That had been my father. If it had been left to me, Mikhail would have gone on fucking up the family business until we had no business partners left. So, Mikhail screwed up, but I was the one who let him do it. Everything is my fault.

The kitchen door bounces off the wall, and the woman sitting at the island hunched over her plate jumps back, her hand pressing against her stomach in surprise. When she sees that it is me, her shoulders relax slightly.

"Mr. Levushka." She tips her head. "Welcome back."

Her hair is pulled back into a thick ponytail that is flopping to one side, wisps sticking out around her face. She should look like a mess, but the halo of flyaways only serves to highlight her wide, blue eyes. They are slate blue—almost green—and I can't believe I never noticed them before. I have blue eyes. I see them in the mirror every morning. But mine don't look anything like Zoya's.

Her large eyes should overpower her slight frame and round face, but they are balanced by full pink lips. She chews on the corner of her lower one the longer I stare at her without saying anything. I don't remember her being this attractive, and right now, even that is annoying to me.

"No one prepared my room." She is eating a kurnik, steam billowing out of the golden crust. The sight of it makes my stomach turn. "The bed hasn't even been made."

"I'm sorry, but I was not informed you would be arriving—"

"My uncle knew well in advance." I cut her off. "There is no excuse."

Her lips press together into a line, and her nostrils flare. "I will take care of it as soon as I am finished—"

"Now."

"Excuse me?" It is clear she is not asking because she didn't hear me. It is a challenge. Of my authority and my position. A maid in my uncle's household is taking a stand against me. If I didn't feel so murderous, it would almost be funny.

"I've waited long enough as it is," I growl. "I'm tired from travel, and I expected my room to be ready when I arrived."

She crosses her arms over her chest. "Had I known of your arrival, I would have been sure to have that done for you. As it is, I need to finish my lunch break."

"You need to finish your fucking job!" I yell.

She shifts her weight to one leg, her opposite hip jutting out, highlighting the soft curve of her body from waist to thigh. It is distracting. Her blue eyes burn into me, leaving angry, scorching marks across my face. She raises a dark eyebrow. "And what if I don't?"

Heat pulses through my core, leaving me unsteady and uncomfortable. I stare back at her with every bit of rage I've gathered throughout the day, every bit of frustration and disappointment. The anger seeps out in my words like acid, burning across the space between us.

"You'll regret it."

Zoya meets my gaze and then throws her head back and laughs.

6

ZOYA

I must have a death wish.

I know I shouldn't laugh. If my mother was here, she'd slap me herself. She'd probably think I'd finally lost my mind. I am laughing in the face of Aleksandr Levushka. Third in line to the Levushka crime family. Maybe I have lost my mind.

After a long morning of chores and taking over Samara's lunch prep, I felt like I was starving. Before being pregnant, I could easily skip lunch with no issues. Sometimes, I would even forget to eat. Now, however, I'm hungry all the time. Hunger claws at my insides and turns my stomach. If I don't eat, I'll get sick.

So, I have to take regular breaks. Not long breaks. Just a pause long enough to shove a handful of walnuts in my mouth or drink a glass of milk. Plums have been a favorite. Samara noticed I was picking the plums out of the fruit bowl, so she started keeping extras in the kitchen pantry. My fingers have been stained purple from eating them every day.

But I've been busy enough today that I haven't even had time for a plum. When I finally sat down to eat something, I'd only managed one bite of the chicken pie when Aleksandr stormed through the kitchen door and began barking orders. No one could really blame me for being frustrated. I'm a pregnant woman. No one can possibly begrudge me five minutes to sit and put some food in my body.

No one… except for him.

His eyes are deadly. He'd turn me to ash on the spot if he could. I don't need to ask to know Aleksandr Levushka's presence doesn't usually elicit laughter. His own surprise is probably the only reason he hasn't run across the room and grabbed me by the neck. Before that can happen, I try to bite back the response.

"I'm sorry," I say, still smiling. I shake my head and try to bite back the grin. "I didn't mean to laugh."

He grinds his teeth together. "You'll have to forgive me," he says sarcastically. "I must have missed the joke."

I don't fully understand it myself. Suddenly, nothing seems funny. Nothing at all. I swallow past the knot in my throat. "Are you going to kill me?" I ask him quietly.

His eyes narrow. Did I guess right?

"Because otherwise, I'm not really sure how you could make my life worse." I choke back a giggle. I feel delirious now. Like I've been awake for days on end and my mind is fuzzy. "I was born and raised to be a maid in this house, and my lunch break is the highlight of my every day. The only thing I'd truly regret would be letting this kurnik get cold."

Aleksandr takes a step towards me, silencing my rambling. He is still on the other side of the island from me, but it feels like he could be standing an inch from my face. The urge to laugh dwindles and dies as he stares at me, his pale blue eyes slicing me open. "You think I can't make your life worse?"

A shiver races down my back, and I fight to keep my body still. I don't want him to know how much he frightens me, and I certainly don't want him to know that the chill down my back wasn't just out of fear. Aleksandr is handsome.

He and Mikhail have come to Boris' house regularly enough over the years that I've seen them both around. I knew they were handsome, but seeing Aleksandr up close makes me realize that he is…kind of, well, *beautiful*. His skin is pale and smooth over his cheekbones and jawline. He looks like he could have been sculpted from the purest marble. The men are twins, I know, but Mikhail never struck me as beautiful. His eyes are more sunken in, dark circles pressed beneath them, and where Aleksandr is full and strong, Mikhail seems hollow.

Part of the allure might be that Aleksandr never paid me any attention. Mikhail made his interest in me—and every other young maid on the estate—common knowledge. He would whistle as I walked by, let his pale hands wander up my thighs when we talked in the kitchen, and winked lasciviously every time I passed by.

Aleksandr, on the other hand, hardly paid me any mind. So now, the fullness of his attention on me has me feeling flushed. Like the difference between feeling the sun on your back and then turning to stare straight at it.

I sigh. This has gone too far. I'm hungry and exhausted and emotional. I just need to apologize. In addition to being my employer's nephew, Aleksandr has always been the nephew that the staff respects. I've heard plenty of the household staff complain about Mikhail and his bad habits, but no one has a negative word to say about Aleksandr. He can be intense – clearly – but if this argument gets out of hand, no one will take my side. Even Boris, regardless of his fondness for me, won't turn against his nephew.

It'd be me versus the world.

"Listen, Aleksandr, I'm sorry for—"

"Mr. Levushka."

I pull my brows together. "What?"

"Call me 'Mr. Levushka.'" He crosses his arms over his chest and looks down his straight nose at me.

I bite back one hundred different snarky replies. "I'm sorry, Mr. Levushka, for acting unprofessional just now. It has been a long day, and I allowed my emotions to—"

"It can't have been too long of a day," he interrupts. "Considering you didn't even do your job."

My hand tightens into a fist, and I realize I'm still holding my fork in my hand. How easy it would be to stab it through his thick bicep.

"I was not informed of your arrival," I say, each word strained and tense. "If I had been, I would have prepared the room. And if you can allow me ten minutes to finish my lunch, I will take care of everything for you, and I will do it gladly."

"I do not care if you do it gladly," he snaps. "I care that it is done. *Now.*"

"What is your problem?" I drop my fork so I won't be tempted to wield it like a weapon and walk around the island. "Aren't you supposed to be the reasonable Levushka? That's what everyone says, anyway. Why are you taking your problems out on me?"

"You are my problem," he says with more anger than one unprepared room should cause any person.

"I'm sorry, *Mr. Levushka.*" I snarl around his name, eyes narrowed. "I'm sorry that I was born without the ability to read minds and anticipate your every need before it can even be spoken to me. How horrible that must be for you."

A line forms between his brows. His handsome face is twisted in frustration, red creeping up his neck and into his cheeks. "I should talk to my uncle about you. If he knew the state his home was being kept in, surely he would hire better help."

I gesture around the room. "We are not living in squalor, *Mr. Levushka*. You know that because you come here to stay regularly. I have been the one to prepare your room many times before. The reason your room is unprepared is because the bedding was being washed, which happens regularly. So, the reason you are angry is because the room was being regularly maintained, which is what you just said you want. Do you see how confusing that is?"

"Do not condescend to me, girl. The room should always be ready. I am a member of the Levushka family; therefore my room should be treated the same as Boris' room."

"I clean Boris' room every day." I raise a defiant brow and cross my arms over my chest. Whatever Aleksandr's problem is, it isn't me. No one could be this irrational about something as silly as sheets being in the washer.

Aleksandr lifts his chin. "Exactly."

I snort. "You want the room you stay in for a few nights every three months to be dusted and cleaned every single day?"

He looks down his nose at me, his blue eyes seething, but he doesn't say anything. Because even he has to know he sounds ridiculous.

I roll my eyes and turn away from him. "That's what I thought," I mumble.

Before the words are even fully out of my mouth, Aleksandr wraps a hand around my forearm and spins me back to him. "What did you say?"

He is stronger than even he realizes because his eyes widen when my body slams against his chest. Aleksandr is tall like his brother, and he towers over me, forcing me to tip my head back to look up at him. He smells like wood and spices, and I can't help but breathe him in as I take a shuddering breath, trying to ground myself. I know I should be scared, but I'm just…overwhelmed.

"Mr. Levushka."

Aleksandr lets go of my arm and steps away as my mother walks into the kitchen. Her voice is tense, but her smile is wide and warm. She doesn't acknowledge the position we were in or even look at me. When it comes to being a friendly face, she has years of practice. Apparently, I need a few more.

"I heard you were at the estate and went into your room to find that nothing was ready." She clicks her tongue. "I'm so sorry for the inconvenience."

"Yes, it was inconvenient," Aleksandr growls in my direction.

"I told Mr. Levushka I would take care of it after my lunch," I said, glancing up at the clock. My stomach drops when I realize my lunch break is over. I spent the entire time arguing with Aleksandr rather than eating. As if in protest, my stomach growls.

My mother shakes her head. "This is an issue that should be resolved immediately. I will take care of it right now, Mr. Levushka."

"Thank you, Agatha," Aleksandr says. I'm surprised to realize he knows my mother's name. He rotates to stand next to my mother and crosses his muscled arms, facing me. "Perhaps, you should take a more active role in teaching your daughter how to conduct herself during business hours."

Blood fills my cheeks, and I look to my mother, expecting her to defend me—or, at the very least, remain quiet. Instead, she nods vigorously. "Absolutely, Mr. Levushka. She has not been feeling well, which I'm sure played a part in her behavior today, but I will be sure to train her to—"

"I am not a dog, mother."

Aleksandr scoffs and shakes his head in disbelief at my outburst. My mom's eyes are sharp and filled with betrayal. I've embarrassed her in front of our boss's family. If I thought she was mad at me before, it will only get worse now.

"Zoya, could you come with me now?" she asks, her voice trembling with frustration.

I'm not eager to incur my mother's wrath, but I would rather be with her than spend another second in Aleksandr's company. I usually manage only to encounter him once or twice during his visits to the estate, so it is unlikely I will see him again once I leave the room. I nod and begin walking towards my mother. Immediately, however, Aleksandr's arm is around my bicep.

"Actually, I'd like Zoya to stay with me." His grip on my arm tightens, and his hands are so large that his fingers overlap his thumb. "I would be happy to begin her education on etiquette myself."

My mother does not hesitate or show any concern for my safety, despite Aleksandr putting his hands on me. She simply nods, casts me one final warning glance, and then hurries from the room. Off to serve this man who disrespected her parenting.

She may be ashamed of me, but I'm equally ashamed of her. Being a maid doesn't mean she can't stand up for herself.

As soon as my mother turns into the hallway, I yank my arm out of his grip. "What will be my first lesson, *Mr. Levushka*?"

"Using the proper address for me means nothing if you continue to say it like you just smelled dog shit."

I wrinkle my nose. "Now that you mention it, something in here does stink."

"What you smell is probably your lunch," he says, tipping his head towards my barely touched kurnik.

Samara prepared all of the components for the kurniks, but I don't bother telling Aleksandr that. Rather than change his mind about the food, it would probably just make him unfairly dislike Samara, as well.

"So, I assume you won't be wanting one for your own lunch?" I ask.

Aleksandr shakes his head once quickly like a man who is used to getting exactly what he wants without apology. He does not need to make an excuse or politely decline. He can just shake his head and wave his hand and things are either presented to or taken away from him.

"Make me something else."

My experience in the kitchen is severely lacking. Growing up in the cottage with my parents, my mother did all of the cooking. She taught me a few things, and I've learned a bit from Samara, but not enough to please Aleksandr, I'm sure.

"I am not the chef," I say.

"Then what skills do you possess?" he asks, tilting his head to the side. His blonde hair falls over his forehead, and his blue eyes narrow to study me. It is truly unfair that someone so awful can be so handsome. "If you cannot cook *or* clean properly, I fail to see why you are employed here at all."

The desire to defend myself writhes inside of me like a cat caught in a bag, but I resist. It will only make things worse. Instead, I jut my chin out and grab the apron hanging from a hook on the side of the island. "The regular chef had to leave today to deal with a family emergency, so I'm happy to do what I can."

I open the fridge and find a stock pot of borscht Samara had prepared the day before. I offer it to Aleksandr, and though he doesn't say anything, I take his silence as a passive agreement. So, I pull out the stock pot and put it on a low burner to heat it through. Samara is a great chef, but her soups are regularly under-seasoned. It is one of Boris' only complaints about her cooking. So, I throw in a dash of kosher salt and freshly ground black pepper to the batch. Then, while the soup is warming, I wash and peel a beet and then grab a handful of dill weed from the pantry.

Aleksandr sits silently while I move around the kitchen, and I feel his eyes on me every second. I do my best not to let it bother me, but it is the most significant amount of time we have ever spent together, and it is not going the way I imagined.

Though, to be fair, I only imagined it once.

Mikhail and Aleksandr came up to the estate five years before when they were eighteen. They had recently been given more legitimate positions in the family, and their father wanted them to learn about the St. Petersburg side of the business. I was fifteen at the time, barely old enough for Mikhail to notice me, so I know Aleksandr didn't pay me any mind. But I paid him mind. One day towards the end of the week they spent at their uncle's house, I saw Aleksandr coming in from a jog. His white shirt clung to his body. He was not as broad as he is now, still just a boy, but I didn't know any better.

To fifteen-year-old me, Aleksandr was perfect.

I was hiding behind a large bush at the corner of the house, and as Aleksandr walked up the steps to the estate, he reached behind his back and pulled his shirt over his head. I caught a quick glimpse of the muscles of his back and the indentations above his hip bones, and I wondered what it would be like to touch them myself. It was just a flash of a daydream, imagining Aleksandr catching me watching him and then coming over. In my mind, he pushed me against the stone side of the house and pressed his hips into mine.

Back in the here and now, I feel my face heating through with the long-forgotten dream and do my best to push it aside. Aleksandr did not notice me that day or any day thereafter. Until today, of course. And if he felt any passion when looking at me, it was passionate anger and frustration.

"How long does it take to warm something up?" he barks, pulling me out of my thoughts and confirming my belief that he did not care for me in the least.

"As long as it takes," I say with a shrug. "I can't make fire burn any hotter."

His stool screeches as he pushes away from the island and walks around to stand over my shoulder. "It looks warm enough to me."

The soup is barely simmering. It is cool enough that I could stick my finger into it without being burned. "If your preference is cold soup, then yes, it is ready."

He makes a growling sound, his breath hitting the back of my neck and sending goosebumps across my skin. "Make me a bowl."

I am tired of arguing. Tired of trying to please a man who clearly will not be pleased. So, I do as I am told.

The borscht is thick and congealed as I scoop it out, clearly not warm enough, but I do it anyway. With Aleksandr less than a foot away, I move the bowl to the cutting board and grate the freshly peeled beet over top. Then, I scoop a dollop of cream into the center and sprinkle freshly minced dill weed over that. It looks delicious. Even better than when I ate it the day before. Except, it is cold.

I slide the bowl across the island to where Aleksandr had been sitting and then turn to look at him, a fake smile spread on my face. "Lunch is served."

His top lip pulls up at one corner, disdain obvious in every line of his face, before he spins around and walks to reclaim his seat. I hand him a napkin, which he roughly pulls out of my hand and lays in his lap. Then, without any show of gratitude, he plunges his spoon into the soup and takes a heaping bite.

For a second, I hold my breath and think he might actually enjoy it. He swirls the soup around in his mouth, face neutral. Then, he spits it back into the bowl.

"It's fucking cold."

I pound a hand onto the countertop. "Obviously. I told you that."

He pushes the bowl away and stands up. Even from across the island, his height is intimidating. "Do you do everything at your own pace? Heating up soup should not take ten minutes."

"How would you know?" I scream. "It's not as though you have ever done anything for yourself before. Maybe if you had, you'd realize that cleaning and cooking and keeping a house running takes actual work."

"Do you think I don't know anything about hard work?" he asks, leaning across the counter. Even twisted in anger, his face is handsome. Sharp jawline, straight nose. In fact, his eyes seem brighter and more alive when he is upset, and I can't seem to look away.

"I know you don't," I say. "You have been served your entire life, and you believe you can treat me like I'm beneath you. I'm a maid, not your servant."

There is a beat of silence between us. His chest is rising and falling wildly, his nostrils flared. Then, he stands up, straightens the lapels of his jacket, and looks away from me, his gaze cast on the wall.

"You're fired. Get the fuck out."

7

ALEKSANDR

Part of me wanted her to beg.

But Zoya didn't crumble when I fired her. She didn't weep or beg for her job or express anything beyond a strong dislike of me. Plenty of people haven't liked me throughout my life, but no one had been bold enough to make this clear to my face. Zoya was the first person to ever stand up to me.

"The only person who can fire me is Boris." She lifted her pointed chin and pressed her full lips together. "You do not have the authority."

Just as I warned Zoya he would, Boris took my recommendation seriously. I called him the moment she stormed out of the room, and though he seemed disappointed to have to let Zoya go, he agreed that the level of disrespect she showed me was unprofessional. He called her to deliver the news as soon as we hung up.

It felt good for an hour or two. The idea that Zoya got what she deserved. She disrespected me and my role in the family. She showed no concern for the quality to which she performed her job and even her mother admitted she was acting inappropriately. Is it not a servant's role to serve?

Then, a sticky feeling began to creep into my chest. As I sat on the bed Zoya's mother had made up for me and called every person I could think of to try and track down Mikhail's whereabouts, I wondered whether I hadn't overreacted. Whether my fight with Zoya had been about more than just her duties. Guilt was not an emotion I was accustomed to, so I pushed it away, but as one day turned into the next, Zoya refused to leave my mind.

During my previous visits, I rarely saw her around the estate, but now I looked for her everywhere. Boris told me he had given the woman three days to move off of the property, so I glanced towards her cottage every time I walked outside to get in my car. I took note of my surroundings as I moved through the house, expecting to catch a glimpse of her.

I didn't even know why I looked for her. I didn't want to see her. Every second I'd spent with her had made me furious. More than any other woman I'd ever met, she had set me on edge. The gaze of her too-large blue eyes felt like feathers brushing over my skin, like an itch I couldn't scratch. She unsettled me in a way I was not accustomed to and did not enjoy. Once she was gone, I would rest easier.

And I needed the rest. Mikhail had screwed up more contracts than just the weapons deals. Several of our business connections were in a state of disarray due to his carelessness. Debts had gone unpaid and deals had fallen through because no one could get in touch with Mikhail. Not unless he wanted them to. I spent half of my day in meetings trying to mend fences and the other half calling all of our friends and family in search of my brother. I knew it wasn't a good look to admit that I didn't know where my own brother was, the heir to the Levushka crime family, but as more and more time passed since I'd last heard from him, I cared less about what others would think and more about finding my twin.

It was this sense of desperation that drove me to visit my mother.

∽

She didn't know I was coming, but somehow, she greets me at the door, arms open wide.

"Aleksandr." She wraps her thin arms around me and pulled me against her chest. I dwarf her now, but she still insists on trying to wrap me up in a hug as though I am a child. "It has been too long."

"We talked on the phone last week." I pat her back and pull away. "But it is good to see you."

She steps aside and ushers me into her house. It is a townhome, wedged between two identical homes in the center of the city. The noise of cars rushing past and people walking down the street filters inside in a whirr of noise and movement. As soon as she closes the door, however, it all seems to fade away.

"I always love having a visitor," she says, handing me a glass of water when we get into the kitchen. "I don't have many of them. Your brother neglected to come see me the last time he was in town. I saw him in passing, but..." Her voice trails off and she bites the corner of her lip nervously. "How is he doing?"

I knew I'd have to tell her about Mikhail, but I hadn't expected to get into it so soon after walking through the door. Though, I don't know why I'm surprised. My mother has always had a knack for getting to the heart of an issue. In my opinion, it is why she and my dad couldn't stand to live in the same house together. She saw through all of his bullshit and called him on it. He couldn't handle it day in and day out.

"You haven't talked to him recently?" I ask, already knowing the answer. Mikhail has always been closer to my father, and I've always been closer to my mother. The only reason she knows anything about Mikhail's life is because of me.

She shakes her head and brushes a graying strand of hair behind her ear. "Your father mentioned last time we spoke that he wasn't doing well."

"You've talked to Dad?" This surprises me more than anything else. Though they are still married, my parents rarely see one another. Somewhere along the way, they decided that staying married but living separate lives was easier for both of them. It is a strange arrangement, but one they don't seem to have any interest in changing.

"We do keep one another informed on our comings and goings," she says a little defensively. "We are not strangers."

"I never said you were." Though, I'd thought it many times. "Well, honestly, Mikhail is part of the reason I came to see you."

She sets her glass on the dining room table and folds her hands in front of her, brows pinching together. "Is he okay?"

"I'm not sure," I admit. "Dad forced him into rehab, but when I last called the facility, he hadn't arrived."

"Rehab," she whispers to herself. "And Mikhail agreed?"

"He seemed to. I saw him the night before he left, and he seemed ready to go and make a change. But now I haven't heard from him in three days."

She stands up and paces across the floor. Though she had been home alone with no obvious plans to leave, she had on a shiny black pair of flats with gray trouser pants. It is strange to see my mother outside of business wear. Even when we all lived in the same house, I couldn't remember ever seeing her in pajamas. My mother looked presentable from the moment she walked out of her bedroom every morning. She was the one who taught me the importance of dressing for success.

"Have you talked with Boris' staff?" she asks. "Maybe some of them have seen or heard from Mikhail."

I shake my head. "I've been staying there the last three days, and I haven't seen him."

"What about Zoya?"

I'm so surprised to hear the maid's name come out of my mother's mouth that I freeze for a second. Long enough for her to clarify her meaning.

"The pretty brunette maid. The groundskeeper's daughter," she says. "Maybe she would know where Mikhail is."

"I know who she is. The important question is why you know who she is."

"She has lived in the cottage on the estate since birth," she says. "I've seen her before."

"But never with Mikhail." As far as I knew, Mikhail's interest in Zoya was recreational. He enjoyed taunting the maids and making them uncomfortable. Even if he did ever decide to fuck one of them, he wouldn't be sticking around to pillow chat afterwards. Zoya won't know anything about where Mikhail is.

She nods slowly. "I've seen them together a few times."

I'm not sure why but something like jealousy rises up in me. "Well, you won't see her around anymore. She was fired a few days ago."

My mother's attention snaps back to me, her eyes wide. "Fired? Boris fired her?"

"He did. On my recommendation." I cross my arms on the table in front of me and lean forward onto my elbows. I try to remain relaxed, but my mother doesn't move or speak or turn her attention from me. I feel her eyes boring into me, and when I finally look up to meet her gaze, horror is written on her face.

"Did you have a particular liking for the maid?" I ask.

She clears her expression and then narrows her eyes at me in warning. "I hardly knew the girl, but every interaction I ever had with her was pleasant. I can't see why you would recommend she be fired. Did Mikhail put you up to it?"

The suggestion that Mikhail would put me up to anything was insulting. He could hardly take care of himself, so why would my mother think he spent any time considering my actions? "And I can't see why you are insistent upon tying Mikhail and the maid together. They didn't know one another. Not well enough for him to care about her or vice versa."

My mother looks down at the floor, the toe of her shoe pressing into the tiles, and twists her lips to one side. She looks nervous.

I stand up. I have too much energy to sit. The last few days have been constant activity and movement and this is the longest I've gone without being productive. Clearly, it allows for too many unwanted thoughts to flood in. That is why I can't stop picturing the defiant set of Zoya's mouth and the way her angry fist pressed into the curve of her hip.

"What are you not telling me?" My voice is not kind or gentle. In the past three days, I've learned too many secrets. About the rival family in St. Petersburg and Mikhail's unorganized dealings. I'm not going to allow myself to be left out of another one.

"Does Zoya have another job?" she asks without answering me. "Will she be allowed to live in the cottage?"

"Boris gave her until today to leave the property." I sigh and run a hand down the back of my neck. "But that does not answer my question. Why do you care about this maid?"

Her eyes go glassy, filling with tears. "She is pregnant."

I shake my head. "I just saw her. She isn't—"

"She is too early to be showing," she says. "But she is pregnant. I know."

"How?" I growl, tired of walking around the secret. "You said you hardly know this girl. How do you know she is pregnant?"

"Boris told me."

My brow furrows. Boris hadn't mentioned anything about Zoya being pregnant when I'd called him to rage about her. If he knew then, he clearly didn't care. Enough so that he had no problem firing her and kicking her out of her house. Everyone knows Boris can be ruthless, but even I have to admit dismissing a pregnant woman on one mistake feels harsh.

"That still doesn't explain why you care so much," I say. "Or why you seem to care more about this maid than your own son. He is missing, you know. I've called every one of his friends and dealers I can think of, but no one has seen him. I might have been the last person to see him. I know you and Mikhail aren't exactly close, but he is still your son and—"

"The baby is Mikhail's."

The words die in my mouth. A tear slips down her cheek, and she quickly wipes it away.

"Mikhail is the father," she says again in case I didn't understand the first time.

"Did Boris tell you that, too?" I ask. If he did, I don't care that he is my uncle; I'll knock him on his ass. I am third in line to being the boss, and I shouldn't be kept in the dark on important family matters.

She shakes her head. "I just know."

I wring my hands at my side. "That isn't something you can just know, Mother. Someone had to have told you. Mikhail or Zoya, maybe?"

"I haven't talked to the girl. I was considering it, actually," she says.

"Does Mikhail know?"

"I don't know what Mikhail knows. He doesn't tell me anything."

"You aren't making any sense." I drop back down into the kitchen chair and roll my head on my shoulders, trying to ease the tension in my muscles. "If you haven't talked to Zoya or Mikhail, and Boris didn't tell you, then I don't understand how you can be sure about anything."

"Because I am."

I throw my hands up and push away from the table. "I'm done. I came here to see if you knew where Mikhail was and clearly you don't, so I'm leaving."

"You don't have to go," she says quickly, stepping forward and reaching out for my arm.

I move out of her reach. "I do. You aren't telling me anything, and I don't have time to waste talking about nothing. I have to find Mikhail."

Before she can say anything, I walk out of the kitchen and down the hallway towards the door. I know it will likely prove fruitless, but I pull out my phone to call the rehab facility again. Maybe Mikhail went on one final bender before checking into rehab. It wouldn't be the first time. Maybe he has finally checked into the facility and all of my worry has been for nothing.

I'm halfway through dialing the number for the facility, which I've memorized by this point, when my phone begins to ring. It is a number I don't recognize, but I answer it immediately.

"Aleksandr, wait," my mother says, following me into the entryway.

I wave for her to be quiet. "Hello, Aleksandr Levushka speaking."

"Mr. Levushka." The voice on the other end of the line is soft and female. "I am Detective Petrov with the Moscow Police."

I feel the blood draining from my face as she continues speaking. It takes all of my energy to remain standing, but as soon as I hang up the phone, I sag against the wall.

8

ZOYA

Boris actually fired me.

The son of a bitch fired me just because his asshole nephew asked him to. Years of good service and loyalty tossed aside in one decision. I wouldn't be quite as angry if I hadn't expected more of Boris. My mother had warned me to be more professional, but I'd assumed my relationship with Boris was stronger than that of any regular employer and employee. I'd grown up on his estate and worked for him for four years. Apparently, I'd been wrong.

And now, it had cost me everything.

"You should never have yelled at Mr. Levushka," my mother says, wringing her hands in her apron while she stands in our small kitchen. Pots are steaming behind her on the stove. It is the first meal she has cooked for me since she found out I was pregnant. It is unfortunate that it took me getting fired for her to talk to me.

"There are so many 'Mr. Levushkas' that I can't keep them straight," I sigh, leaning forward to rest my head on my folded hands. "You're talking about Aleksandr."

"Yes, obviously!" she snaps. "I could hear the two of you arguing halfway down the hallway. It was unprofessional. You should have just done what he asked."

"I'm not his servant," I say, repeating the same argument I made to Aleksandr. "I am a maid, and I have rights. It was my lunch break. I shouldn't have to jump up and take care of him while my food gets cold."

"Well, now you won't even have food to get cold," she says, shaking her head. Her hair is graying at the temples, wiry wisps of it sticking out in every direction. I don't remember her having gray hair before Father died. "You don't have food or a house or a job. And you are pregnant."

"I'm well aware, but thank you for reminding me."

My mother spoons me out a bowl of soup, slides it across the table, and drops a spoon against the ceramic edge. "Eat," she commands, walking across the small kitchen to her bedroom door in the back corner. Just before she disappears inside, she calls over her shoulder. "And enjoy it while you can."

∼

Since I no longer had to spend my days working, I had two entire days to tour as many apartments in St. Petersburg as possible. The trouble is that, since I no longer have a job, I can't afford anything on the nice side of town. And even in the shadier areas of the city, a studio apartment runs for half of what I make per month as a maid.

A dark-skinned woman with tight curly hair and heavy mascara stands in the corner of the studio apartment I am touring with her arms crossed tightly over her chest, looking as though she is doing her best not to touch anything. I can't blame her. The yellowing tile floors are sticky with an unknown substance, the carpet has misshapen stains around the corners of the room that look like water damage or blood, and when I open the single cabinet in the bathroom, I find a roach belly-up inside. It shows how desperate I am that the fact that it is dead gives me great solace. Maybe it means they've recently sprayed for pests. I highly doubt that, though, so I don't ask the woman. I'd rather remain in denial.

"And it is a month-to-month lease?" I ask.

She nods. "Yes. Our leasing program is very flexible."

It has to be flexible. The only tenants a place like this would have are people so desperate and down on their luck that they'd live here rather than on the streets. Then, as soon as they are back on their feet, they get the hell out. That's my plan, anyway. I have enough savings from my maid position to get me through two months—maybe three if I really skimp—and as soon as I find a decent-paying job, I'll cancel my lease and find a place where I could actually imagine caring for a baby.

A baby. The thought sends a bolt of panic through me.

When my mother wasn't speaking to me, I still knew I had a place to turn if I needed it. I knew that she would soften towards me and the child once she saw it. We would live in the cottage with my mom until I felt ready to get a place of my own. I would take my time and make sure I was financially secure. Now, however, that was all out the window. I was jobless and homeless and desperate.

And pregnant, I imagine my mother saying, making sure I didn't forget for a moment how bad my situation was.

As much as I didn't want to stand in this studio apartment let alone live in it, I didn't have a choice. It was the only place I could afford to stay for two months without a paycheck coming in. So, if it did take me awhile to find a job, I'd at least have a roof over my head. For two months.

"I'll take it."

Almost as soon as the words were out of my mouth, the woman from the building's front desk led me back down to the leasing office to sign paperwork, letting out a sign of relief once she stepped into the hallway.

～

My mother is too busy working to help me pack, so I do most of it by myself. Though, Samara stops by during her lunch break one day to say goodbye.

"This is so unfair," she says, folding the comforter from my bed into a tight rectangle and then rolling it like a sleeping bag. "You are one of the best maids Boris has. Why would he fire you?"

"Because of cold soup." I shrug and roll my eyes.

"I can't believe Aleksandr would get mad about something like that." She shoves the rolled-up comforter into the corner of a box that holds a pillow folded in half and three of my old sketchbooks from my nightstand. "He was always the reasonable one. Not nice, exactly, but he didn't order us around like the other men in the family."

"There was more to it," I admit. "His room wasn't ready, and I didn't jump at the chance to take care of it the moment he asked."

Samara pinches her lips together nervously. "Yeah, I may have overheard some of the other staff talking about the argument. You all had a captive audience, apparently."

My face flushes. "I didn't realize anyone was listening."

"Nadia said she walked into the kitchen during the fight and saw you two standing pretty close," Samara says, her voice soft even though it is just the two of us in the cottage. "She thought you were going to start making out until you started fighting."

The memory of Aleksandr's hand wrapped around my bicep and his flat stomach and chest pressed against my body makes me feel warm from the inside out. I shake my head. "We definitely were not going to make out. He hates me."

Samara sits on the corner of my bare mattress and sighs. "That doesn't make any sense. Especially since Mikhail always seemed to like you so much."

"Just because they are twins doesn't mean they have the same taste in women."

"I know that," she says. "But you'd think Aleksandr would take his brother's feelings into consideration when trying to get you fired." Then, she gasps. "What if he did take his brother's feelings into account?"

I raise an eyebrow and look over my shoulder at her. "You aren't making any sense. Mikhail and I weren't going steady or something. We barely ever spoke."

"And what if Aleksandr wanted to keep it that way?" she asks. "What if Mikhail really liked you, but the family didn't think him dating a maid would be a good look? What if he got you fired because of that?"

The insinuation that I am not good enough for one of the Levushka brothers stings more than I expect, but I brush the hurt away quickly. "Trust me, that is not the reason. It is definitely because I called him a spoiled brat and refused to follow his orders."

"You called him a spoiled brat?" Samara asks, eyes wide.

"Not in so many words, but yes." I bite back a smile. The insult likely cost me my job, but I'm still a little glad I stood up for myself.

"Wow." Samara stands up and begins throwing shoes from my closet into a duffel bag. "I just feel bad because none of it would have happened if I'd been there."

I spin around before she can even finish the sentence. "Your mom was in the hospital, Samara. This is not your fault."

"She broke her wrist," she says, rolling her eyes. "I should have known my mother was being dramatic about the entire thing. If I'd asked more questions, I would have stayed at work and been there to make the kurniks, which means you would have had your lunch at the normal time, so when Aleksandr came in looking for help with his room, you would have been available."

"Even if that is all true, I probably still would have called him a spoiled brat. Because he was being a spoiled brat."

Samara laughs and shakes her head. "God, I'm going to miss you."

"I'm moving away, not dying."

"I know, but it won't be the same."

I nod and do my best to fight back the wave of tears threatening to overcome me. I've been avoiding crying for days because if I cry, I'm not sure when I'll stop. So, it is better to keep it all inside.

"Do you have a job yet?" she asks.

"Not yet. The only experience I have is cleaning up after people, but I'm not sure I want to get another maid job. I interviewed at a diner this morning, but they said I won't hear back until tomorrow."

Samara grabs a bundle of my clothes and throws them, hangers and all, on the bed. "Do you really have the time to be picky? You'll start showing soon, and then nowhere will want to hire you."

I know she is right, but settling for a shitty job and a shitty apartment is way too much shit to bear at once. "I have a little bit of time. I'm only nine weeks pregnant, so I have plenty of time on that front, and living with my parents has allowed me to put away a bit of money for rent."

Even though I'm not showing, the nausea and exhaustion has been a killer. Just the thought of being on my feet all day, as a maid or a waitress, makes me want to lay down and take a nap. But those are the jobs I'm most likely to get, so I'll just have to push through. If I can prove myself to be a valuable employee, then hopefully my employer won't be upset when I need to take time off for doctor's appointments and maternity leave—if I even get maternity leave.

"I'm glad it helped you out somehow," Samara says. "No offense, but living with your parents sucks in just about every other way."

I look around at the room I'd grown up in. Half of the stuff was packed away, but I'd decided to leave the pictures on the wall. I would let my mother decide what to do with them. My dabbling in graphic design seemed to mean more to her than it did to me, anyway. "It wasn't so bad."

Samara puts her hands on her hips and turns to me, eyebrows raised. "How many men have you been with in the last year?"

I hesitate like I'm thinking, but I don't even need to. I know the answer immediately. "One."

My answer must be worse than Samara thought because her eyes go wide and her shoulders slump. "One guy? You slept with one guy all year and got pregnant?"

I bite my lip and shrug. "I guess so."

"That fucking sucks."

"Tell me how you really feel," I joke, kicking her softly in the ankle.

"Sorry," she says. "But that is depressing. I hope he was a good lay, at least."

I turn away before she can read my expression. If she knew I'd only slept with one guy all year, and I can't even remember it, she would probably think I was the most pitiful thing she'd ever seen. And my life is pitiable enough without throwing the unknown baby daddy into the mix.

"You have some shit luck, girl. Pregnant, homeless, and jobless."

I groan. "I wish everyone would stop listing off all of my troubles like that. I know my situation. Also, I have a home, so you can scratch that one off the list"

"Damn Aleksandr," Samara says suddenly, stomping her foot on the ground. "This is all his fault. Fuck him."

"I wanted to at one point," I joke.

Samara turns to me, eyes wide. "Are you serious?"

"God, no. It was a joke." Not entirely, though, and I suspect Samara knows that. Any woman with eyes knows the Levushka boys are attractive, and between the two of them, Aleksandr always seemed the most centered. Rumors went around about Mikhail's recreational drug use and drunkenness and sleeping around, but there weren't ever any stories about Aleksandr. A man like him certainly has his fair share of sexual partners, but he didn't advertise it the way his twin did. He seemed more in control of himself. And from the outside, without knowing much about him, I'd imagined him as a gentle, caring man.

I realize now how ridiculous that thinking was. A man born and raised learning how to import weapons, build a drug empire, and operate under the arm of the law isn't a man who will bring his girlfriend flowers and rub her feet at the end of the day. He is going to be demanding and controlling, just like he was in the kitchen a few days ago. So, I don't know why I feel such a sense of betrayal.

Aleksandr didn't betray me. He just didn't live up to the unrealistic expectations I'd set for him. And that isn't his fault. It's mine.

9

ALEKSANDR

Mikhail is dead.

My mother tries to grab the phone, and I push her away. Hard enough that her back hits the other wall of the hallway. I am too disoriented to apologize or care.

Mikhail is dead. That is what the detective told me. Officers found his body in a crack house early that morning.

"You can't know it was an overdose until you do an autopsy," I say. "It could be foul play."

She is kind but firm. "He still had the needle in his arm."

Telling my mother is easier than I expect, which is good because I wouldn't have been able to handle it if she'd broken down. I am barely keeping myself together as it is.

"I knew this would happen one day," she says, squeezing her eyes closed. "The longer he went without getting clean, the more I prepared myself for it."

I'm not prepared. Not at all. I pull out my phone and call Mikhail's personal bodyguard. I talked to him a few days before, but Mikhail hadn't been returning any of his calls or messages, either.

"Is it true?" I ask as soon as he answers the phone.

He sighs, the sound coming through like static. "Yeah, it's true."

"Shit." I rear back and hurl my fist at the wall. The drywall dents beneath my knuckles, and I hear my mother release a sob behind me.

"The police called me first because I was the last name in his phone," he says. "He told me he was just going out for one last hit."

"He told you?" I growl. "He told you he was going out to get high, and you didn't mention anything to me when I called you three days ago?"

"He told me not to." His deep voice sounds raw with emotion. "And considering I couldn't even find him, it wouldn't have mattered if I had told you. He was gone either way, man."

"Don't call my dad. And fuck you." I hang up the phone and shove it deep in my pocket before I give in to the impulse to chuck it at the wall. I've caused enough damage in my mother's house as it is.

"This isn't your fault," my mother says, moving closer to me slowly like she is approaching a wild animal. "He made his own choices."

"I didn't say it was my fault."

"I know," she says softly. "But you're thinking it. You have always tried to take care of Mikhail, but he is a grown man. Was a grown man. He was always going to make his own decisions and there was nothing anyone could say or do to change his mind. You tried your best but his sobriety was always going to be his decision."

I clench my teeth and turn away. "I have to go. I have a lot to do."

"Aleksandr." Her small hand wraps around my wrist and tries to hold me back. I could yank away from her grip with almost no effort, but I let her comfort me for a minute. In a lot of ways, I think it means more to her than to me. "You don't have to leave. You can stay here."

I shake my head. "I have to tell Dad. Before someone else does."

Her hand falls from my arm and she nods. Tears are silently streaming down her face, but neither of us acknowledge them. "He'll want to hear it from you."

I truly doubt that, but I appreciate her saying it anyway. She pulls me into another hug, this one tighter and longer than the first. She stands in the doorway as I walk down the steps and across the street to where my car is parked. When I pull away, she is still standing there.

∼

Dad doesn't notice anything is wrong right away. A member of his staff lets me inside, and I find him in his den in the back, sitting in his leather recliner with a cigar and a book open in his lap. He is too relaxed, so I know no one has told him the news. He doesn't look up as I enter.

"Father."

He blinks and then turns away from his book. I haven't seen him in months, but he doesn't smile or show much enthusiasm at the sight of me. Instead, he looks back down at his book and puffs on his cigar. "I see you made it to St. Petersburg fine."

"I did." My palms are sweating, and I wipe them on my pants.

"And your meetings have gone well?"

I still need to talk to him about the rival family in the city and the contracts Mikhail screwed up, but it hardly seems like the right time. So, I lie. "Everything has been fine."

He nods, his lips twisted around the fat cigar. "Good, good."

"Listen, I need to talk to you." I move into the room and take a seat in the leather chair across from my father's. I've only been in his St.

Petersburg house a few times, and it was honestly a complete guess that he would be here at all. If he had been in Moscow, I would have had to deliver the news of Mikhail's death over the phone. Which, honestly, might have been preferable.

He sighs. "I'm trying to relax. If it is about an issue you can handle, I'd prefer for you to handle it without clueing me in."

"It's need-to-know information," I insist. "It's important."

My father doesn't look like he believes me, but he rests his cigar in an ash tray on a side table, kicks the footrest of his recliner down, and sits forward, elbows on his knees. "What is it? Don't make me wait."

I take a deep breath, not sure where to start. "Okay. Well, Mikhail showed me the letter you sent him."

He smiles at the memory, his mouth pulling up on one side. "Did he? Is he worried?"

"He was," I say, wondering if my father will catch the past tense. My stomach twists. "He told me he wanted to get clean and do better, so he agreed to go to rehab."

My father nods, but I noticed his smile slipping, his brows pinching together. "Why are you here, Aleksandr?"

"He left for rehab three days ago, but when I called the facility, they said he wasn't there."

"Is it a private facility?" he asks, growing angry. "Those public ones are shit, and everyone will know he is in there. How does it look for the boss' son to be in rehab? Not great."

"It's private. The one you picked out before," I say quickly. "But that doesn't matter because he never fucking showed up."

"Okay, so where is he?" My father's phone rings on the end table, and he reaches for it.

I jump up and grab it before he can. "Don't answer that."

His usually tan face has gone pale. "What is wrong with you? Why are you acting this way?"

"I got a call from a detective an hour ago," I say softly. "I confirmed it with Mikhail's bodyguard."

He shakes his head, his softening jaw looking chiseled from the way he is clenching his teeth together. "No."

"He is dead." I say it quickly because there is no better way to say. No easier way to deliver the news. "Mikhail died of an overdose early this morning."

"No," he repeats, standing up and pacing towards his wall of bookshelves. "No."

"I'm sorry." I hang my head when I hear him start to cry. My mother said she was prepared for this to happen, but clearly my father wasn't. Even though he'd sent Mikhail the threatening letter, he always expected his favorite son to turn things around. To find the straight and narrow—or, at least, whatever 'straight and narrow' looked like for the heir to a crime family. Now, he never would. It was over.

"You should be."

I snap my attention up, mouth hanging open, assuming I've misunderstood him. "What?"

"You should be fucking sorry," my father says, wiping his eyes with the back of his wrist. "You were supposed to look after him."

I run my tongue over my teeth and take a deep breath. My father is hurting. He is grieving, and he doesn't mean what he is saying. He'll regret these words later. Even if he'll probably never apologize to me for them, he'll regret them.

He paces back towards me and runs a hand through his hair. "You should have taken him to rehab. You should have made sure he checked himself in."

"What about you?!" I scream, unable to sit there and stay quiet.

"What *about* me?" he growls, eyes narrowed.

"You sent him that fucking letter. It freaked him out, and he thought he needed another bender. If you hadn't sent him that, he wouldn't have gone out for that hit. He would probably still be alive."

My father's eyes widen like I've slapped him, and he crosses the distance between us in two steps. "Are you blaming me for the death of my son?"

"Are you blaming me for the death of my brother?" I ask, staring right back at him.

His breathing is heavy, his shoulders rising and falling, nostrils flaring. "Get out."

His expression is rage, and I know he would have banished me from his house and the family if he could have. If he didn't depend on me to hold everything together, he would have had me thrown from the ranks and forgotten about me as soon as I left his sight. But he *does* need me. As much as my father never wanted to admit it, I am the son who takes care of things. The son who kept the family running while his other son got high and, apparently, got house servants pregnant. The thought of Zoya makes me clench my fist, and I quickly push the thought away. I can't deal with that right now.

I take a step back and hold up my hands. "I just thought the news should come from family."

"You should have let Ivan tell me," he says, referring to Mikhail's bodyguard. He drops back down into his chair, picks up his cigar, and waves me away. "Leave."

Without saying a word, I walk out of his house.

There isn't time to mourn. Like always, I'm too busy picking up the pieces Mikhail left behind.

Because Moscow police found his body, word of his death is spreading faster than any of us would have liked. Rumblings of it are already beginning to make their way through local news channels and within a day or two, everyone will know. *Vlad Levushka's Son Dead of Overdose.* Mikhail's death will be used to write opinion pieces on the state of crime in the city and my father's connections to all of it. Though they have no solid proof to connect any of the dots, they will say that our family got what we deserved. That a life of crime doesn't pay. It will bring the police closer to our operation than we want them, though we've been there before. We can handle it.

I just wish I didn't have to.

I'm halfway back to Boris' estate when my phone rings. It's Boris. Part of me doesn't want to answer it, if only because I don't want to hear any more bad news. Not for a few hours, at least. But my sense of duty overrides everything, and I pick up.

"Mikhail really fucked us up," Boris says in way of a greeting.

I pause, trying to decide if Boris knows my brother is dead or not. "You heard the news, right?"

"Of course I did," he snaps. "That is the problem. Mikhail went off and killed himself and now every thug he ever did business with is going to try to slip away without paying up."

"Shit."

"Shit is right," Boris says. "Your brother wasn't exactly organized, so I am trying to get Ivan to ship us his cell phone so we can dig through his texts and calls."

"I have the password for his email," I offer. "I doubt he did much official business over email, but it might give us a place to start."

"You do that, and I'll handle the cell phone. As soon as I know anything else, I'll give you a call."

"Won't I see you at the house?" I ask.

"Not today. Or tomorrow, either. I have a lot of meetings to schedule, so I'm going to work from a hotel in the city center." I hear a voice somewhere in the background, and Boris pulls the phone away from his ear to talk to them. Then, a second later, he is back. "I have to go, but let me know what you find. And if you are too broken up to handle shit, just tell me. I can take on more."

"I'm fine," I say quickly. "I'll talk to you soon."

~

And over the next few days, I am fine. If "fine" means exhausted and overextended and overwhelmed. If that is the case, I am beyond fine.

Somehow, even Mikhail's email is disorganized. None of his contacts have names, but are instead listed under descriptors like "red SPAR." After an hour of digging through back and forth correspondence, I learn the name referenced a deal Mikhail had done with a man driving a red convertible in St. Petersburg involving a shipment of Assault Rifles. According to Mikhail's last email to the guy, he hadn't paid up yet, so I add his name to the growing list of shit I have to take care of.

If Mikhail had died a month sooner, I may not have worried about any of it. I may have just wiped the debts clean, emptied his email inbox, and washed my hands of all of it. However, now that I know about the rival family in town, we can't afford to be seen as weak.

Word of Mikhail's death is getting around, and if we don't nut up and collect what is ours, it will be just another foothold our enemies can use to propel themselves higher up the ranks. Several of our biggest partners have already contacted me to say they've been approached by men and told to cut their ties with us.

We have enough trust built between us and our oldest partners that it would take a lot more than intimidation to scare them away, but still, the threat is there. If the Levushka family stumbles, there is someone there waiting to pick up the pieces. And I won't let that happen.

Because I'm next in line.

The reality of that doesn't fully settle in until two days after Mikhail's death. I'm going to be the boss of the Levushka family. Assuming my father doesn't have me banished, that is. I've texted him about the rival family moving onto our turf, but he hasn't responded. I can see that he is reading my messages, but I have no way to know if he is doing anything about it. If Boris is telling the truth—and I have no reason to believe he isn't—my father is a mess. Uncontrollable weeping followed by rage. He is working his way through the stages of grief and until he finds his way to acceptance, it is best for me to steer clear. So, I do.

By the end of day two, I feel like a mad man frantically patching holes in a dam on the verge of bursting. Just as soon as I plug one hole, another one appears. On top of that, I haven't eaten anything more than a plum from the kitchen all day and my body is jittery from all of the coffee I've had. So, I head down to the kitchen.

Even though I know Zoya is gone, I still look for her as I enter. I can imagine her sitting behind the island like she was the first day I walked in with her lopsided ponytail and full, pouty lips. Then, for the first time in two days, I allow myself to think about what my mother told me:

Zoya is pregnant. With Mikhail's child.

My mother wouldn't explain why she thought so, but she has never been a woman prone to engage in unfounded gossip. If she told me the baby is Mikhail's, she had a good reason. I just wish I knew what it was.

Dinner was hours ago, so I don't expect anyone to be in the kitchen. Despite what Zoya said the day we argued, I'm not as spoiled as I seem. I can open a refrigerator and make myself a sandwich. But when I pay someone to do it for me, I expect it to be done right. There is a difference. The problem is that, as I get more and more distance from my argument with Zoya, I can't help but feel like I instigated everything. As a paid employee of my uncle, she should have held her tongue, but I also shouldn't have insulted her.

Guilt—or hunger, I'm not sure which—gnaws at my stomach, and I try to ignore it. None of it matters anymore. Zoya is gone.

Just then, the pantry door opens and a middle-aged woman comes walking out backwards, a mop and broom in her hands. When she gets through the door, she turns around and sees me, jumping in surprise. It is Agatha, Zoya's mother.

"Mr. Levushka," she says, smiling up at me as though I wasn't the reason her daughter was fired. "Can I help you with anything?"

I consider asking her to make me some food. Agatha isn't the usual cook, but I've had enough meals cooked by her over the years to know she easily could be. However, the words that come out of my mouth are unplanned and unexpected.

"Where is Zoya?"

Agatha's eyes widen in surprise, and then she lowers her head, her feet shuffling nervously on the tile floor. "She isn't here."

"I know that," I say impatiently. "But where is she?"

I don't know why it is important to me, but I need to know Zoya isn't living on the streets somewhere. Perhaps, it is because she might be carrying my brother's child. Or maybe it is more of that unfamiliar guilt. I can't say for sure.

"She found an apartment," Agatha says with a shrug. "A studio space just across from the Obvodny Canal. Near a railway station."

"She is living in the Gray Belt?"

Agatha nods, and I can't believe how relaxed she is. Her daughter has moved out from under her roof for the first time and is now living in the crumbling industrial district of St. Petersburg. The area is the main source of smog and air pollution in the city, not to mention riddled with crime. After living so many years on an estate owned by a crime family, I expect Zoya knows enough to keep herself out of trouble, but that doesn't mean trouble won't find her. She is a beautiful, pregnant woman living alone.

Because of me.

"Do you have her address?" The words come out clenched and frustrated. I don't even know why I'm saying this. I have enough going on right now to stay busy for weeks, so why am I making this maid my problem? I don't know what I'm planning to do. I don't even know if I'll try to talk to her, but for reasons I can't explain, I need to see where she is staying. I need to see for myself what kind of life she and my possible niece or nephew might have.

Agatha doesn't ask any questions—either because she doesn't care or is too afraid to question me—and grabs a notepad and pen from next to the refrigerator and scribbles down the address.

I stuff it in my pocket with every intention of saving it for the next morning, but as I walk down the hallway towards my room, I feel my pocket for my car keys, and then pass my door and keep on walking. Before I can really think about it, I walk out the side door into the night and get behind the wheel of my car, headed towards the address Agatha wrote down for me.

I'm going to find Zoya.

10

ZOYA

I'm exhausted.

The job at the diner is just as much work as being a maid, if not more. I'm on my feet for eight hours straight with a fifteen-minute break in the middle to eat. My first day wouldn't have been so bad if I'd packed something to eat. Since I was working at a diner, I assumed there would be plenty of food around, but the boss is a lot stingier than he seemed during my interview. I get one free drink per shift, but the food is full-price, and since I didn't have any money on me, I just went without.

I knew if I'd mentioned that I was pregnant, the boss probably would have taken pity on me and given me some food, but I couldn't drop that bombshell on Day One. Not yet. If Mr. Savin realized I'd accepted the job without disclosing my pregnancy, he'd be upset, and I didn't know enough about him yet to know what he'd do when he was upset.

Though, I thought I knew Boris Levushka, but clearly, I'd been wrong. He had fired me for my first-ever offense without even talking to me about it face to face. If someone I'd known my entire life could do that, then I had no idea what Mr. Savin would do.

Just to be safe, I always called him Mr. Savin. He told me I could call him Robert like the rest of the employees, but since my mother had been right about my lack of professionalism with Boris, I decided not to make the same mistake again.

My apartment is a train ride and a few blocks walk from the diner, so by the time I get home, it is nearly three in the morning and my feet are killing me. Because I'm the newest waitress on the schedule, I'm stuck picking up whatever shifts were available, which means I have to be at the diner again in seven hours. Just the thought of it makes me want to collapse on the cement.

When I left the estate, Samara mentioned coming over sometime during my first week to help me decorate, but I knew that wasn't going to happen. Not only because I didn't want her to see the exact level of squalor I was living in, but also because there wouldn't be time. Every minute I wasn't sleeping, I would be working.

The Gray Belt isn't as bad as I thought it would be. The area is industrial and, just as the name suggests, rather gray, but it isn't dangerous. My apartment building is disgusting, but some of the other buildings look okay. I've seen parents playing outside with children during the day and young people walking their dogs. It isn't as nice as the city center, to be sure, but it isn't the worst area.

At least, not during the day.

Walking down the sidewalk at three in the morning, however, highlights a few safety issues. Every other streetlight seems to be burnt out and alleys open up between buildings like black, yawning caves. I rush past these openings, feeling each time like hands are going to reach out and pull me in.

None of this is helped by the fact I haven't eaten all day. My legs feel wobbly beneath me and my vision is swimming with every step. The worst part is that I know the only food I have inside is a bag of pretzels and some gummy candy I got from a vending machine when a pregnancy craving hit me. Otherwise, I haven't been to the store yet.

I glance around as I walk from the railway station, hoping to see a convenience store open, but the area is all industrial buildings. During the day, smoke spews from the stacks, clouding out the sun, and at night, it goes eerily quiet. I should have bought something before getting on the train, but Mr. Savin let me off a little later than expected, and I had to run as it was to make the train on time.

Running is probably part of the reason I'm feeling so unsteady. I can't remember the last time I ran anywhere.

By the time I round the corner and see my apartment building rising from the ground like a broken tooth, the gummy candy sounds like a delicacy. My stomach growls at the thought of it. I pick up the pace, hoping to make it inside before I lose the ability to walk, but when I'm halfway down the block, I notice a black car in front of the building.

I wouldn't have paid the car any mind except the engine is on. I can hear the low rumble of it in the air.

Even that wouldn't be too noteworthy, except the headlights are off.

I try to casually peek through the windows to see who is inside, but the windows are too darkly tinted to see anything. I grab my apartment key from my purse and hold it between my fingers. I don't know how I'll stab an attacker in the eyes with it when simply walking feels like a chore, but I'll cross that bridge when I come to it.

As every step carries me closer, I hate that one thought keeps rising to the forefront of my mind: *Aleksandr Levushka.*

The car is a similar make to the one I saw him driving earlier in the week. And the tinted windows are standard policy amongst the Levushkas, so it isn't impossible.

Except, it is.

Aleksandr would not come to see me.

The one time we had a real conversation, we screamed at one another, and I ended up getting fired. Not exactly the basis for a lasting friendship. Clearly, he didn't care for me, and I'd made it apparent what I thought of him. So, why then am I hoping he is the person waiting inside the car outside my apartment?

When the door opens, a man ducks out, and for one second I mistake his blonde head for another's. But then, the man stands tall, and I realize he is too short. It's not Aleksandr.

Then, the man looks up at me, and my disappointment quickly fades to fear.

I could try to run, but if the man isn't here to see me, I will look crazy. Even if he is here to see me, he parked strategically so he could cut me off on my way to the front door. I won't make it in time. Not on my already shaky legs. So, weighing those options, I decide to stop walking altogether.

The man moves around to the front of his car and steps onto the sidewalk, and as he does, the passenger door opens.

A dark-haired man with a leather jacket and thick-soled boots gets out of the car. I can tell he is meant to be the muscle. I can practically feel the earth vibrate as he walks down the sidewalk towards me.

I still haven't moved, and I'm not sure how to anymore. What do these men want with me? I've never seen them around Boris' estate, so I don't think they are Levushkas. Even if they are, what would any Levushkas want with me? I was a maid. I didn't have any secrets. Nothing worth getting out of bed at three in the morning for, anyway.

"Are you Zoya?" the short blonde man asks.

I nod and grip my key tighter between my fingers. It is becoming apparent that it will do little to protect me against two full grown men, but it brings me a small amount of comfort.

"Can we talk?" The two men are getting closer, crowding me. I want to step away, but there is an alley just behind me and the thought of what could be lurking in there is worse than the reality ahead of me.

The devil you know, I guess.

"I'd rather go inside and go to sleep," I admit. "But I doubt I have much of a choice."

The blonde man smiles, a silver crown sparkling in the back of his mouth. "I'm afraid not."

"What is this about?"

The dark-haired man growls at my tone like a dog who has just spotted a squirrel. "We ask the questions."

The blonde man holds out a hand to his partner, easing him back. "We know you work for the Levushkas."

I shake my head. "I actually don't."

"We know you *know* the Levushkas," he amends. "We have a message for Aleksandr."

My heart kicks up at the mention of Aleksandr's name, though I don't know why. "I'm not friends with Aleksandr. If you have something to say to him, may I recommend a voicemail?"

The dark-haired man steps forward again to intimidate me, but before he can even plant his large Frankenstein boot on the pavement, the blonde man raises his voice. "Quiet."

As if the command was meant for him, the dark-haired man once again steps back in line. I stand tall, hoping I look more confident than I feel.

"You are testing my patience, bitch." The blonde man smiles, and it is difficult to connect his tone with his body language. Everything about the man is at ease, relaxed. Yet, the fury in his voice sends goosebumps racing up my arms. "We are not here to be cute. We are here to warn you."

"Warn me about what?" I ask. "I don't have anything to do with the Levushkas. I work at a diner in the city."

"Don't tell me you cut all of your ties with the Levushkas twins in one week," the blonde man says. He runs a hand across his smooth round chin. "Surely, you can still contact them even if you've just been fired."

I don't want to know how these men know I was fired or when it happened. I don't want to imagine them tailing me for the last week without me even realizing it.

"I just need you to tell Aleksandr to back off," he continues.

"Back off from what?"

"From our turf," he says. "The unopposed reign of the Levushkas is over, and the sooner Aleksandr realizes that, the better."

So that is why I didn't recognize these men. They aren't Levushkas.

Samara told me she'd heard whispers about another crime family in the area. They were causing disruptions for the Levushkas and the city had seen a spike in criminal activity since their arrival. Beyond that, though, I hadn't heard much about them.

"I can try to get your message to him, but I'm not sure he'll listen to me," I say. "As you know, I was fired. They probably won't see me as the most trustworthy source of information."

The blonde man smiles at me and then turns to his friends. "Can you think of a way to make the Levushkas listen to her?"

The dark-haired man lifts an eyebrow and looks down at me. His fists clench at his side. "I can think of something that might catch their eye."

Now, dark alley be damned, I take a stumbling step backwards. My heart is pounding in my chest, each thud threatening to knock me off my feet.

"It's nothing personal, sweetheart," the blonde man says as his muscled friend approaches me. "When Aleksandr asks you why this happened, make sure to tell him it was because of him sticking his nose where it doesn't belong."

I take another step back and find myself pressed against the grimy brick wall. I could scream for help, but I'm afraid it will only make the man angrier. Perhaps, it would be better to stay quiet and just wait for it to be over with. For my baby's sake, I have to do whatever will cause the least amount of harm.

I squeeze my eyes shut and can practically feel the man's body heat radiating into me when I suddenly hear the rumble of an engine and the crunch of tires down the street. I open my eyes, and the dark-haired man has also turned around to see who is driving up on the scene.

It is a dark car—almost identical to the one driven by the two rival thugs—and my heart sinks. Reinforcements. More men to watch or, even worse, take part in my beating. Before I can stop it, a sob bursts out of me.

"Who the fuck—?" the blonde man starts to ask.

Then, a car door opens. "Zoya?"

I don't know how, but I recognize his voice. The moment he says my name, I know it is Aleksandr.

The man in front of me takes another step back, waiting for orders from his partner on how to proceed, and I can see Aleksandr standing in the gutter. His hand is resting on his hip—on a gun, I realize.

"Is there a problem here?" he asks coolly, eyes shifting between the two men like a lion sizing up their prey.

I'm too surprised to be relieved.

What is Aleksandr doing here? Is he working with these men? Did he know they were coming to harass me?

"No problem," the blonde man says, crossing his arms over his soft chest. "We were just talking to the lady."

Aleksandr looks at me for a minute. His eyes shift away so quickly that I can't read his expression. "It doesn't look like the lady wants to talk to you."

The man widens his stance and clenches his jaw. "The sidewalk is public property."

Before I can even blink, Aleksandr has pulled the gun from his holster and has it aimed directly at the man's blonde head. "And this gun is my personal property. Would you like to be more intimately acquainted with it?"

The dark-haired man jolts into action, but Aleksandr spins the gun on him in an instant, stopping him in his tracks. He takes a step back, but it isn't in retreat, it is strategy. Now, he can easily shift aim between the two men, keeping them both under control.

"We don't want any trouble," the blonde man says, his face split into a tight smile.

"Then leave," Aleksandr grits out.

"We just came to deliver a message—"

Aleksandr cocks the gun. The sound echoes off the buildings along the quiet street, and he tilts his head to the side. "Message received. Time to go."

Sweat has collected on the blonde man's head, and he nods quickly, his cheeks going red. With a quick nod of his head, he orders the dark-haired man back into the car. Without taking their eyes off of Aleksandr, they sidestep back to the car and get inside.

Aleksandr doesn't lower his weapon until the men have driven away and are out of sight. Then, he turns to me.

"Are you okay?"

All at once, the day crashes over me.

Exhaustion from carrying tray after tray of food from the kitchen to the dining room and refilling coffee cups and wiping down tables. Weakness from too many hours passed without food or water. The disappointment of the car outside my apartment not being Aleksandr and then the surprise when he did show up.

And fear.

So much fear.

Every emotion I've felt and kept buried for the last twenty-four hours overwhelms me all at once, and I feel my legs begin to give out.

Before I can hit the ground, I feel a strong arm around my waist.

"Zoya?" His voice is deep and concerned.

Aleksandr lowers me gently to the pavement, and I want to say something to ease his worry, but I can't summon the words. My mouth, much like the rest of my body, is useless. I let my tired eyes flutter closed and welcome the darkness.

11

ALEKSANDR

With Zoya in my arms, I pause for a moment on the sidewalk. I could carry her into her apartment—her key slipped from her hand when she passed out—and try to wake her, but one look up at her apartment building tells me all I need to know.

The façade has deep cracks running up the brick with haphazard patch jobs trying to hide the decay. Half of the windows are cracked and boarded over and trash overflows from the trashcans along the curb. It isn't a nice place, and Zoya shouldn't be there in her current condition. Or any condition.

Plus, it isn't safe for her here.

For whatever reason, our rivals are targeting her. Perhaps they know about her child with Mikhail? Maybe that is why she has a target on her back. Though, I don't know how anyone would know yet. I just found out a few days ago.

Either way, they know where she lives, and they won't stay away. I can't protect her here long-term. Zoya is lucky I showed up when I did. God knows what they would have done to her.

My arms tighten around her thin frame as I think about it. I don't know why I feel such a strong urge to protect her. I don't even know why I showed up at her apartment in the first place. I've never been the kind of guy to believe in fate, so I have to believe it is pure stupid luck.

And I have a feeling Zoya won't get this lucky again.

I need to get her to the hospital. She is pregnant and she just passed out on the sidewalk. She needs to be seen by a doctor. She and the baby both need to be examined.

I scoop Zoya up easily and adjust her weight in my arms. Her head lulls to the side, her cheek pressing against my chest. Her full lips are parted, and her breathing comes out slow and even.

She really is beautiful.

This realization does nothing to ease my confusion, so I push it aside as I open the passenger door and settle her in the seat. I strap the seatbelt across her chest, noticing how flat her stomach still is. If everyone is right and she is pregnant, it is still early.

Which means she and Mikhail would have been together within the last couple months.

The thought feels like ice water pouring down my neck, and I roll my shoulders to ease the tension. I don't know why I should care. I've never cared who Mikhail decided to fuck. That was his business.

So, why is Zoya different?

I close the passenger door and walk around to the driver's side.

She isn't. My feelings have nothing to do with her. I'm only feeling this way because Mikhail just died and I'm stressed out, and for reasons I will never understand, I feel guilty about getting Zoya fired and put in this position in the first place. Those two men never would have had access to her if she was still living in her family's cottage on the estate.

It is just a strange mixture of circumstances and emotions that are making me feel off. Once I get Zoya to the hospital and taken care of, the dust will settle, and I'll be back to normal.

I duck down into the car and start the engine. As I pull away from the curb, Zoya falls forward, and before I can even think about it, my arm shoots out and forms a bar across her chest, keeping her from head-butting the glove compartment. I shake my head and ease her back into the seat. I just need to get her to the hospital and everything will go back to normal.

For the rest of the drive, I slowly accelerate and transition gently to the brakes, keeping my arm on the console just in case she falls forward again.

~

The waiting room is empty this late in the night, and I can't pace anymore.

Zoya was still unconscious when we arrived, and I told the nurses helping her what little I knew, but it wasn't much. I don't know when she got pregnant or who the father is for certain. I don't know anything about her, and as far as I know, she is still unconscious, so I can't ask her for clarification.

She grew up on Boris' estate. I know that much.

Her parents have worked for our family since before she was born. I have vague memories of her running around in the grass around her family's cottage as a kid. I never paid her much attention, though. Even as she aged and filled out. Even as her flat lines and edges curved and her clothes could no longer hide her body. I noticed, obviously, but I didn't address it.

Not the way Mikhail did.

That is probably why she is carrying his child now. He made it apparent he was interested in her. I never did.

Because I wasn't interested in her. I'm not.

I run a hand down my face. I know the words are bullshit even as I try to convince myself they aren't. Of course, I care about her. I showed up at her shitty apartment in the middle of the night, for Christ's sake. I have to care about her on some level to do that.

The important question is, *why* I care about her?

Is it guilt because I got her fired?

Ever since our argument in the kitchen that day, I've had a gut-twisting feeling, but I don't think it is guilt. I'm not very familiar with the emotion, to be sure, but I don't feel bad for what I did. As an employee of my uncle, she should have done her best to make sure I was comfortable. She should have jumped up and done her job without complaint. So, getting her fired seemed like an appropriate response.

Or, more likely, do I care because she is carrying my brother's baby?

Now that Mikhail is gone, his child will be all that is left of him. Aside from me, of course. I've never cared about kids before, but my own niece or nephew might be different. Maybe the desire I feel to take care of Zoya is really an innate desire to protect my family, to defend my tribe.

I stand up and pace down the narrow aisle between the fabric-covered chairs. My eyes burn from exhaustion and my arms and legs feel heavy. I should be at Boris's house asleep, preparing for another day of meetings and intimidation to ensure my family gets what we are owed. Mikhail left a shitstorm in his wake, and I'm the one left cleaning up the pieces.

Zoya, included.

Except, thinking of Zoya as Mikhail's gives me that gut-twisting feeling again. It isn't guilt or a desire to protect her…it is jealousy.

The fact that Mikhail fucked Zoya makes me feel sick. My hackles rise at the thought of it. And the fact that he fucked her and then got her pregnant and died, leaving her to deal with it all on her own, pisses me off, too. He couldn't just fuck up his own life; he had to take everyone else down with him. Classic Mikhail.

No, my feelings for Zoya have nothing to do with her carrying Mikhail's child. In fact, I care about her in spite of that.

I pace back towards my chair, and I can see the night receptionist behind the desk watching me nervously. I look like a hungry tiger pacing his cage, and I'm making her nervous. So, I sit down and before I can fully think it through, I pull out my phone.

When my mom answers, her voice is raspy. "Hello?"

"Shit," I say, looking up at the clock on the wall. "It is so late. I shouldn't have called."

I hear shuffling on the other end of the line as she sits up. "Ridiculous. You can always call me. I'm your mom."

"I'm not even calling about anything," I admit.

"That is even better. We can just talk," she says. "I wasn't sleeping anyway. I haven't been able to sleep for the past few days."

My mother and Mikhail weren't close for the last few years, but I know that doesn't make his death any easier for her. She expected it, but she was still his mother. Still the woman who carried and gave birth to us both. I don't think that is a bond that can ever be washed away.

"Are you doing okay?"

"Okay," she says simply. Then, she sighs. "I knew he was killing himself slowly, but on some level, I didn't really think it would ever happen."

"Me neither." It is true. Even when I knew Mikhail was really bad, I imagined him overdosing, being rushed to the hospital, and then having an epiphany. He would get clean, take over the family for our father, and find purpose in running it. Even after Mikhail would stumble to my apartment drunk and high and half-crazy, I always thought it would be his last bender before he cleaned himself up. Now, there wouldn't be another chance. It was over.

"The funeral will be sometime next week. There isn't a date set yet, but they are doing an autopsy to determine cause of death and then he will be transported back to St. Petersburg."

"Cause of death?" I ask. "It's a drug overdose."

"I know, but they still have to determine it wasn't foul play. Which isn't so unlikely given what you both do for a living."

"Will it be a church funeral?" I ask.

She hums a yes. "I called the pastor of a church I used to go to. He'll preside over the funeral."

"Mikhail will love that," I say sarcastically. "Remember how much he hated going to church as a kid?"

She groans, though I can tell she is smiling. "I had to drag him through the doors by his collar and threaten him within an inch of his life to get him to stand up during the hymns."

"He always took two cups of juice during communion."

"And he'd steal yours half of the time, too." She laughs, and when the sound fades away, we sit in the silence for a minute. "I've thought about it, and I don't think forcing him into more church as a teenager would have helped."

"No," I agree. "Mikhail was stubborn. He would always have done exactly what he wanted. The only way his life would have turned out differently is if he wanted it to."

There is another long pause, and when my mom finally speaks, her voice is soft. "You don't think finding out he was going to be a father would have helped?"

I grit my teeth. "No. I don't."

She hums, but I can't tell whether it is in agreement or just thought. "I think maybe it would have."

I don't want to ask her about Mikhail and Zoya again. Partly because I don't want to know, and partly because I'm angry at her for not telling me the truth. I don't want to ask again if she is just going to refuse to tell me what happened. But I'm exhausted and alone in the waiting room, and if I'm going to sit here and wait on Zoya, I deserve to know at least one goddamn thing about her life.

"How do you know Mikhail is the father?" I ask suddenly.

"It doesn't matter how I know," she answers immediately. "I just do."

"Fuck," I growl. The gaunt woman behind the desk looks up at me, eyes wide, and I turn away from her. "Why are you protecting him?"

"How do you know I'm not protecting *her*?" she asks.

I don't know what that means, but I latch onto it. "I'm the one protecting her," I say. "From rival family members who showed up at her apartment tonight and wanted to beat the shit out of her."

She gasps. "Why would they do that?"

"I don't know. Maybe because they know about her connection to Mikhail? I don't know enough about anything to say for sure, but I do know that I'm the one sitting here waiting for her at the hospital doing my best to protect her. Not you. Maybe you should just tell me what is going on."

There is silence on the other end of the line, and just as my mother inhales—perhaps to finally tell me the truth—a nurse walks through the swinging doors and into the waiting room. She has curly black hair held back with a headband and a hand on her hip that lets me know she isn't planning to wait around for me.

"The doctor will talk to you now," she says, gesturing for me to follow her. She turns and moves back towards the doors, and as much as I want to finish talk to my mother, I can't.

"I have to go," I say, standing up and jogging after the nurse. "Talk later."

I hang up before she can reply and push through the double doors.

Hospitals exist outside of day and night. It is almost four in the morning, definitely still pitch-black outside, yet the hallway is full power, bright white light. I squint against it as I follow the nurse down one hallway and then another.

I glance in dark rooms as I pass. There are sleeping lumps under rough hospital blankets and machines beeping and dispensing and monitoring.

The nurse walks down a third hallway and then turns to the right where the hallway opens into a large circular desk where nurses in scrubs work behind computers and push trays of fresh blankets from room to room. She looks over her shoulder at me and points to a woman in a white coat standing at the counter with a chart in one hand and a steaming cup of coffee in the other. Her blonde hair is smoothed back into a flat ponytail and aside from a winged eyeliner and pink lipstick, she is bare-faced. She looks up as I approach.

"You are here for Zoya Orlov?" she asks.

I nod.

"Your relation?"

I hesitate for only a second. "Boyfriend."

"And father of the baby?"

I nod again, my stomaching turning, and I realize in that moment how much I wish it was true. Not that I want children right now, but I would rather be the father than Mikhail.

She narrows her eyes. "You told the nurses you didn't know how far along she was in her pregnancy."

"Was?" I ask, picking up on the past tense. "Is she not pregnant anymore?"

The doctor looks at me, assessing me, trying to determine how much she should tell me. But then she sighs and flips a page in the chart. "The baby's heartbeat is strong and Zoya is okay, too. She was dehydrated, and based on her weight, a bit undernourished."

Relief washes over me. "Okay. So, fluids and food. Does she need anything else?"

"A prenatal vitamin," she says, flopping Zoya's chart closed. "And you should have her add you as an emergency contact. Right now, there is no mention of you anywhere in her information. I probably shouldn't have even told you as much as I did."

"Thank you," I say genuinely. "When can I see her?"

"Right now. She hasn't woken up yet, but you can wait with her." She points to the room right behind me, and I nod my head in gratitude before rushing into the room.

Zoya looks even smaller in the hospital bed than she really is. Under the dim fluorescents, her eyes look sunken in and her cheeks look hollow. It doesn't seem like it should be possible, but she looks thinner than she did a week ago. She certainly doesn't look pregnant.

Her brown hair is spilling out around her shoulders, and her chest is rising and falling in deep, even motions. I sit in the chair next to the bed so I won't wake her. However, when the vinyl fabric squeals under my weight, her breath catches and she opens her eyes.

"Sorry," I say softly, standing up and moving to the edge of the bed.

Her eyes widen when she sees me. I half-expect the heart monitor next to her bed to start beeping like crazy, but it remains steady. "What are you doing here?"

"I brought you here," I say. "I found you outside of your apartment."

"Those men attacked me," she says, her delicate brow furrowed.

"They were going to."

She looks up at me and nods, her eyes glassy and distant as she remembers the events of a few hours ago. Then, she shakes her head. "Why were you at my apartment?"

That question is more difficult to answer. I haven't uncovered the answer myself yet, so I move around it. "You aren't safe there. Those men were going to hurt you."

"Because of you," she says almost as if she is uncovering the information as she speaks. She frowns and looks down at her hands in her lap. "They said you needed to back off. They wanted me to tell you to back off."

I take another step towards the bed, and Zoya's eyes flash up to me. The strong, defiant woman I argued with in the kitchen a week ago is nowhere to be seen. She looks scared. Of me? I'm not sure, but I hope not. She shouldn't be.

"Back off of what?" I ask.

She shrugs. "I don't know. They thought, for some reason, that you and I were…close. They thought I would be able to convince you."

The way she says it, as though the idea of us being close is absurd, makes me bristle.

"Well, whatever the reason, you aren't safe," I say. "You can't go back to your apartment."

Suddenly, her blue-green eyes are on me, narrowed, and I see a flash of the strong woman I recognize. "I don't have anywhere else to go. I can't go home."

Home. She means Boris's estate. That has been her home her entire life, and I made sure she couldn't go back to it.

"You can do whatever I allow," I say. "And you can go back to Boris's."

"It's too far from my job," she argues. "I won't be able to make it to work."

"Quit."

She sighs. "I have to make money. If I don't, then I won't—"

"Your connection to me got you into this mess, and I'll make sure to get you out of it."

She closes her mouth, but I can see she is far from in agreement. "I don't need your help."

"Don't you?" I ask with a dark chuckle. "It sure looked like you needed my help."

"I don't need it anymore," she snaps. "I can take care of myself."

I lean forward, my hands on the plastic rail running along the side of her bed, until my face is level with hers and we are only six inches apart. Zoya pushes her head back into her pillow until it looks like she is trying to sink into it.

"And what if you can't?" I ask. "What if I let you go back to your new job and your shitty apartment, and then you can't take care of yourself? What if you die?"

"What does it matter to you?" she snaps, eyes blazing green flames.

I bite my lower lip in frustration and push myself to standing. "The cottage isn't safe, either. It is too close to the gate, and your mother can't protect you. You will stay in my suite."

Her face pales and she sits up straighter, the blankets falling around her waist. "No, I won't."

"It will only be until the threat is dealt with."

"And how long will that take?" she asks, pushing back the blankets and swinging her legs over the side of the bed. Her hospital gown is pushed up to the tops of her thighs, and I can see every inch of her shapely legs. I swallow back a spark of desire as she stands up and grabs the back of her gown to make sure it stays closed.

"I'm not sure. I kind of have a lot going on right now."

"More maids to fire?" she asks, head tilted to the side in a challenge.

"And a funeral to attend," I say flatly.

She rights her head, and the anger in her face flattens. "Whose?"

She doesn't know. Mikhail might be the father of her child, and she doesn't know he is dead. I clench my hands into fists to keep them from nervously fidgeting and say it as straight as I can. "Mikhail's."

Her eyes widen, but rather than being flooded with grief, her face fills with pity. Her brows arch and everything about her softens. Her hands lifts like she is going to reach out and touch me, and my body tenses in anticipation. Then, at the last minute, her arm falls back to her side. "God, Aleksandr. I'm so sorry."

I nod, wondering whether I should apologize to her, as well. Or whether I should ask outright. I know I *should*, but the idea of having Zoya confirm it, of hearing her say that she slept with Mikhail and the baby is his, makes me feel unsteady. It is too late—or too early—to have that kind of discussion. We are both tired.

I nod in thanks and then point to her clothes folded on the small table next to the chair. "You should get dressed so we can leave."

She stares at me for another few seconds, and her lips move like she wants to say a hundred different things but can't decide on one. Then, she turns and grabs her jeans.

I look towards the wall as she slips her jeans on underneath her hospital gown, but when she turns away from me and pulls the strings on the hospital gown to let it fall open, I can't help but look. Her back narrows into a tiny waist and then flares out again towards her hips. There are two small indentations above her hip bones that I desperately want to dig my fingers into. I imagine my hands memorizing the curve of her body, my tongue licking across her ribbons, and I feel my pants become a little tighter.

Her bra is black and lacy, and I envision snapping the delicate straps with my teeth and grinding my body into her backside. How did I go years without paying Zoya any attention? How did I let her walk past me in Boris' house without falling at her feet with my tongue dragging on the ground?

She is gorgeous.

When she pulls her t-shirt over her head, I take a shuddering breath, realizing for the first time how entranced I'd been. Thankfully, I gather my wits in time to look away before she turns back around.

"So, I can leave?" she asks.

I nod. "The doctor said you need food, rest, and vitamins, but otherwise you can go home."

"Home," she says wistfully. "I suppose in this case, 'home' means your room?"

I'd suggested the idea only a few minutes ago, but somehow, I hadn't considered what that would really mean. Now that I'd seen Zoya half-naked, though, the reality washed over me like a wave. She would be in my room. In my bed.

I nod because it is the only thing I feel capable of doing.

Zoya bites her lip. "Fine. Let's go."

I follow her out of the hospital room, watching the sway of her hips as she walks. What have I gotten myself into?

12

ZOYA

There is a hidden door on the right side of Aleksandr's room that connects his to the room next door. The staff has never had need to open it, so I'd almost forgotten about it entirely, but when Aleksandr walked me down the hallway and into his room, I remembered it at once. It was almost an act of self-preservation.

Because sleeping in that bed with him would have killed me.

"These rooms connect," I say the moment the door closes. I walk over to the wall and find the small gap in the wallpaper and push. The door sticks for a second before opening.

"Oh, yeah," Aleksandr says, walking over and peeking through the door. "Mikhail and I used to use that door when we were kids. I almost forgot about it."

My stomach flips at the mention of his brother. I can't believe I didn't know he'd died. It had all happened right after I'd left, and though Samara had been calling me, I'd been avoiding her. I didn't want to talk to her until my life was a bit more put together. But if I'd answered the phone, I probably wouldn't have put my foot in my mouth with Aleksandr.

"Do you want to stay in there?" he asks, his square jaw working like he is thinking about it.

"It's better than sharing a bed, right?" I can't look at him as I speak. Aleksandr and I have hardly had a conversation without yelling at one another, so why am I thinking about what he wears to bed and how his sheets smell?

"There's no bathroom in there," he says, tipping his head to the room. "You can share mine."

"That's fair," I nod.

"And I'll lock your bedroom door from the outside."

I am halfway into the room, and I slam to a stop and spin around. "Excuse me?"

"I can't monitor that door from in here," he says.

"You mean you can't monitor *me*." I got a lot of fluids at the hospital and Aleksandr stopped and got me a ground meat and cheese blini from a twenty-four-hour corner store to eat on the way home, but I still feel unsteady. I widen my stance and plant my hands on my hips to gain some control.

He shrugs. "However you want to say it, I think it is safer for you if there is only one entrance and exit into our suite."

I want to argue his point, but I know if I protest too much, he'll consider me a flight risk. I didn't exactly enthusiastically agree to this arrangement in the first place. If I argue too much, he might force me back into his room all night. So, I roll my eyes and wander into the room, trying not to let Aleksandr see my hands trembling.

It hasn't been prepped, probably because no one has slept in it in months. I want to complain to Aleksandr about the room not being ready for me just to prove a point, but again, I'm trying to coexist with him until I'm no longer being hunted by rival gang members.

"Sorry the room isn't ready," he says from the door. "I can call someone to come take care of it."

"No, it's fine," I say quickly, shivering at just the idea of standing along the edge of the room while one of the maids I've worked with for years prepped a room for me. Rumors of what I'm doing in Aleksandr's room will start to spread soon enough without me adding fuel to the fire. I grab the folded blankets from the end of the bed and shake them out until they drape over the bed. "I can do it myself."

"Should you really be—" Aleksandr starts, moving towards me before he stops and fidgets with his shirt sleeve. His button-down shirt is rolled halfway up his forearms, revealing pale skin stretched over corded muscles. I have to tear my eyes away from him. "I mean, in your condition," he starts again.

"I'm pregnant, not paralyzed," I say flatly. I tuck the sheet around the corners of the mattress, feeling his eyes on me as I move. "How did you find out?"

"My mother," he says softly, sounding almost ashamed. Though, when I look up at him, his face is neutral.

"How did your mother know?"

I can't remember the last time I saw Natalia Levushka. She and Vlad never travel together, and since Boris is Vlad's brother, Natalia has little reason to come visit him. The few times she did was to see one of her sons when they were staying at the estate, and even then, she never spoke to me.

"Boris told her."

It is possible Boris and Natalia are closer than I ever knew, but I still can't understand why the pregnancy status of a maid would be of any importance to Natalia. Or why she would feel compelled to mention it to Aleksandr. Had he asked her about me?

The thought sends my heart racing, and I focus on making the bed so he won't notice the redness in my cheeks.

Suddenly, Aleksandr is standing over my shoulder, his hip pressed against my back. My breath catches.

"Are you sure you don't want me to get some help?" he asks.

I slide away from the brush of his body and nod. "I'm fine."

"You were just in the hospital," he argues. "I don't think you are fine."

"I can take care of myself," I say, repeating what I told him in the hospital.

"But you shouldn't have to." The words come out in a near-shout, and Aleksandr lets out a harsh sigh and shakes his head. "Someone should be here to help you."

I straighten the top edge of the comforter and fold back the corner like I've done every day for years making Boris' bed. When I'm finished, I turn to Aleksandr, who is only a few steps away and far too close for comfort. At this distance, I can see the pale gold streaks in his light blue eyes and the blonde stubble growing in along his jaw. I can see a white scar near his hairline from a long-ago cut and the indention in his lower lip from where his teeth dig in when he is frustrated. As I study him, his teeth find that familiar groove, and I have to look away so he won't see the smile that is threatening to break free.

"I'm done now, anyway," I say, pointing to the bed.

He follows my finger and then slowly drags his eyes back up to my face. A line forms between his brows, pinching together in thought. "That isn't what I meant."

I know I should tell him goodnight and go to sleep. I'm sleep-deprived and exhausted and not thinking clearly. But instead, I take a step towards him and lay my hand on his elbow.

Aleksandr flinches from the contact and looks down at where my hand rests on his arm. I can feel his body heat leaching into my fingers, and I want to absorb and save it for the next time I get cold.

"Thank you," I say softly. It takes a lot to get the two words out, but once they are, the rest seems to follow quickly. "I don't know what would have happened if you hadn't shown up when you did. I don't know why you came to see me, but I know that you saved me, and I'm grateful."

"Zoya," he says, holding up a hand and shaking his head.

"No, it is important," I say firmly. "Whatever differences we may have, I want you to know that I understand what you did for me and what you are doing for me right now, and even if you never hear me say it again: thank you."

Aleksandr blinks and something like a smile pulls up the corners of his mouth. For one second, I see what he could look like if he was unburdened. If his life was light and normal and less riddled with crime and violence and commands.

But just as quickly as it comes, it disappears.

Aleksandr pulls his features back into a scowl, nods to me once, and then backs out of my reach and goes to the door.

"Goodnight." He doesn't look over his shoulder as he pulls the door shut between us.

~

I don't see Aleksandr at all the next day.

I sleep late, waking up when the afternoon sun is streaming through the sheer curtains, and stay in bed until my bladder won't let me anymore. When I knock on the door that separates our rooms, Aleksandr doesn't answer. I knock again and wait. And then again. Finally, I walk inside before I pee my pants.

His room is empty.

I rush to the bathroom and decide to take a shower while I am in there. It would be better to be showered by the time he got back to the room to avoid any awkwardness. But when I get out, he still isn't back yet.

I wander back to my room and wait for a while. When I test the doorknob, it is locked from the outside just like Aleksandr said it would be. So, then I try the door in his room. And it opens.

I'd practically grown up on the estate, yet walking the hallways feels strange and forbidden.

I am not supposed to be here.

I don't know if anyone besides Aleksandr knows I am here at all.

What should I say if I ran into my mom? Or Samara?

"Zoya!"

I freeze, unsure how much of my situation I am supposed to explain. Can I tell people I am being targeted by a rival family? Can I tell them that Aleksandr saved me? We haven't talked through any of the details, so I have no idea how to explain anything.

As it turns out, I don't have to.

A round-faced woman with dark black hair and freckles across her nose walks towards me. I've never seen her before.

"Hi," she says, lifting her hand in a wave. "I'm Alena. Aleksandr asked me to be there when you woke up, but it looks like I missed my cue."

"Hi," I say nervously.

"There are only a few rules," she says, holding up a hand to count them off one by one. "First, you are not supposed to leave the estate without Aleksandr. Second, you are not to do anything physical or laborious. And finally, you are not allowed to skip a meal."

She nods her head once, twice, and a third time as she makes sure she recited all of the rules correctly and then smiles at me. "Are you ready for breakfast?"

"I'm sorry," I say, almost in a whisper. "I don't know who you are."

"I just started." She puffs out her chest slightly. "This is only my third day."

For a moment, I'm surprised because I didn't know Boris was looking to hire anyone. Then, reality sinks in.

This woman is my replacement.

"Oh, okay. Well I know this estate better than almost anyone. I don't need an escort." I smile, hoping I won't offend her too greatly, but I also want to get my point across. *Back off.*

"I'm sure you do," she says genuinely. "But Aleksandr has asked me to stay close to you, and I would be failing in my duties if I disobeyed."

I suck in my cheeks, annoyed but unable to argue. Then, I walk past her towards the kitchen. I stop a few steps later, however, and Alena nearly runs into my back. I raise an eyebrow. "And just a warning, you should really call him Mr. Levushka."

Alena nods, but the sweet smile is gone, replaced by wide-eyed confusion.

After our almost confrontation in the hallway, Alena is more reserved around me—hardly talking except when necessary—but she does exactly as Aleksandr instructed her to. She makes sure I am well-fed and my glass is never empty.

When I get up to use the restroom, she sticks close to my side, waiting in the hallway, and when I go for a walk around the estate, she follows behind.

My fears about my mother and Samara are unfounded, because apparently, everyone knows I am here.

My run-in with the rival family became hot gossip the moment Aleksandr brought me home with him from the hospital and everyone has been talking about it ever since.

"Seriously, why was he at your apartment, anyway?" Samara whispers to me when I stop in the kitchen for lunch.

I tell her I don't know, but I'm sure she doesn't believe me. I wouldn't believe me either if I was her.

Samara is in the process of begging me for more information when the kitchen door is flung open and Boris walks in. She bolts back into the pantry like there is some kind of vegetable emergency she must tend to immediately, leaving me alone at the island.

Boris sets his sights on me and stomps over, every pound of his meaty frame driving into his heels and shaking the floor.

"What are you doing here?"

The measly excuse I'd come up with in my head should this situation arise—*talk to Aleksandr. He'll explain everything to you*—washes away like the tide, and instead, I stammer. "Um. Uh..."

"What?" Boris asks, even though he knows I didn't really say anything.

The man I thought I knew—the man who, only a short week ago, I believed had a special fondness for me, is standing in front of me with a red face and clenched fists, and I can't come up with a single word to say.

"I fired you," Boris repeats. "I ordered you removed from the premises. Why are you here?"

I open my mouth to try and say something, anything, but words fail me, and I want to shrivel up on the floor and roll under the countertop. This is humiliating.

"Aleksandr—" Alena starts, only to look at me and then back at Boris, clearly torn. She clears her throat and continues. "Mr. Levushka brought her here. As his guest."

Boris turns to the maid and raises an eyebrow. "*I* am Mr. Levushka. Not my nephew."

Now that Mikhail is dead, Aleksandr is next in line to the Levushka crime family, which means soon enough, he will be Boris's boss. He wouldn't take kindly to Boris making it seem as though he is the top dog.

Alena nods, and her mouth tightens into an annoyed line at my faulty information. "Yes, sir."

Once he is satisfied the maid has been properly cowed, he shifts his beady eyes back to me. "You are with Aleksandr now?"

He says it as if there was someone else I was with recently, despite the fact I haven't ever had a boyfriend before.

"I'm here as his guest," I clarify.

Samara confirmed that everyone in the house knew I'd been attacked by a rival family, but I don't want to say as much to Boris. If he has questions, he should take them up with Aleksandr.

"So your fight the other day," he says, waving his hand in the air like he's trying to conjure up the words. "Was it some kind of lover's spat? Have you two made up?"

"You should ask Aleksandr," I say. "He'll explain everything."

Boris narrows his eyes and then leans forward, his voice low. "Or, did you leave your mother's cottage and realize you had no skills beyond your good looks. Did you whore your way back into my house?"

My face reddens immediately, and I hear Alena intake a sharp breath, but before I can say anything, Boris stands up and smiles. "A guest of my nephew's is a guest of mine, I suppose."

After he leaves, Alena still follows after me the way Aleksandr asked her to, but she keeps her distance. Especially when Boris is nearby.

I don't blame her.

∽

After three days of nothing more than brief glimpses as I'm getting out of the shower and a quick goodnight before he closes the door between our rooms, I'm tired of not knowing what is going on. Of being kept in the dark about my own safety. So, I push open the door between our rooms without knocking and walk inside.

Aleksandr told me goodnight almost an hour before, so I expect to find his light out, but instead he is sitting at the desk pushed up against the windows with his laptop open in front of him. He turns around as I walk in.

"Did you forget something?" he asks. I can see the tendons in his neck as he turns, and the bulge of his bicep is even more obvious now that he has stripped out of his button down and is in a short-sleeved t-shirt.

I planned to burst into his room and demand answers, but suddenly, I'm much more civil.

"No, I didn't forget anything," I say. "I just. Well, I wanted to…ask. The rival gang. About me." He wrinkles his forehead, and I sigh, running my hand through my hair. "I want to know how long I'm going to be staying here."

"Ah." He tips his head back and pushes away from the desk, shifting around so he is straddling the chair rather than sitting in it normally. I hate that my first thought is to imagine myself between his legs instead of the chair. "Are you not happy here?"

"Would you be?" I ask, moving forward to stand by the corner of his bed. It is a four-poster with thick oak posts that are intricately carved. I run my fingers down the finished wood. "Alena hovers around me like a nervous shadow all day, and I think I caught her weighing my dinner plate earlier to make sure I'd eaten enough."

"Maybe I could tell her to give you some space," he says.

"Thank you." I sit on the corner of his bed. "But I want more than that. I want a life."

Aleksandr wraps his arms around the back of his chair. "This isn't forever. Just until I know you are safe."

"See?" I jump up and point at his chest. "What does that mean? Why do you care?"

"Care about what?"

"Don't play dumb," I demand. "Based on the way Boris treated me my first day here, you are the only person who cares at all about my safety."

Aleksandr frowns and stands up, moving the chair out of his way. In only a few steps, he is standing directly in front of me, forcing me to look up at him. "What did Boris do?"

"Nothing."

Did you whore your way back into my house?

My face heats at the memory. How many people on the estate think I am sleeping with Aleksandr? What does my mother think?

I've seen her since being back on Boris' property, but she has done her best to avoid me. And considering Boris's clear anger towards me, I haven't wanted to risk her position in his house by letting him see us together. He knows we are mother and daughter, but he also knows we haven't been on the best of terms. For now, it seems better to let him keep thinking that.

Aleksandr lays his hand on my shoulder, and his touch is so gentle and unexpected that I just turn and look at his fingers draped over my shoulder. He is warm, like a personal space heater, and I want to press my face into his palm like a cat and purr.

"What did he do?" he asks more seriously this time.

"It isn't important." I pull away from his touch and shake my head, trying to clear my muddled thoughts. "He just made it known that I'm not wanted here."

"That isn't true," he says. "I want you here."

"But why?" I practically scream at him, and as soon as the words are out of my mouth, I realize how aggressive they sound. I look down at the floor and repeat them, softer. "But why?"

The silence between us stretches and grows uncomfortable. When I look up, Aleksandr is staring at me as though he is trying to peer straight through my skull and read my thoughts. He blinks when he realizes we are making eye contact and runs a hand along his jaw. He shrugs. "Because this is all my fault, anyway."

"How? Because you got me fired?" I ask. "Because honestly, I think I was kind of asking for it."

Aleksandr opens his mouth to say something, and then he pulls back and raises one eyebrow. "Excuse me? Did you just admit that our argument was kind of your fault?"

"What? No!"

The corners of his mouth are turned up in a smile he is trying to bite back, but he can't hide the light dancing in his eyes. Aleksandr is emitting pure amusement. "Because I think that is what you just admitted."

"I admitted that I was having a bad day, and I may have taken it out on you."

Aleksandr takes a step back and claps, bowing his head to me. "That takes real courage to admit."

"But," I add, stepping forward and jabbing him in the chest with my finger. "You were being a huge asshole. *Call me Mr. Levushka.*"

My deep mocking voice and shrugged shoulders push Aleksandr over the edge, and he tips his head back and laughs.

The sound is like thunder during a summer storm. It is deep and completely earth-shaking.

As soon as he lets loose, allowing me to see this softer side of him, my foundations are rocked. Suddenly, I'm the teenage girl watching him come in from a run. I'm standing at the edge of the house, daydreaming about what it would be like to hold his attention, to be near him, to touch him.

The emotions come flooding back too quickly, and I stumble away from him. He is still laughing too hard to notice, so I recover by sitting on the edge of his bed and tucking my hands in my lap lest they decide to go rogue and stroke the sharp cut of his cheekbone.

Finally, he looks at me, and his smile is breathtaking. All pearly white and straight. He presses his hands onto his hips, looking handsome and rugged. "Fine. Maybe I was having a bad day, too."

"We were both having bad days," I say. "That's it."

"That's it," he agrees, nodding his head. As he does, his smile begins to fade. "One bad day, and I ruined your life."

He looks truly broken up about it, so I chuckle. "Hardly."

When he sits next to me on the bed, the mattress dips under his weight and gravity forces me closer to him. I have to actively fight to keep my shoulder from brushing his. He folds his hands in his lap, his thumbs circling around one another like boxers in the ring. "Your life was already ruined?"

I shrug. "Not ruined, I guess. But not great."

"Why?"

I bite my lip and then point at my stomach. "Pregnant and single, for starters. And on top of that, my mom isn't exactly thrilled about the news, so she hasn't been talking to me for the last few weeks."

"You just found out a few weeks ago?" he asks, looking down at my stomach. I can tell he is trying to decide how far along I am.

"I'm not showing yet. I'm only nine weeks." I stop, brow furrowed as I count back. "Or, I guess, ten weeks now."

Aleksandr's shoulders stiffen, and he stands up, pacing away from the bed. He glances over towards the desk, and I follow his gaze. His laptop is still open, though the screen has gone dark.

"I'm sorry." The words are out before I'm entirely certain what I'm sorry for. Then, I remember Mikhail. I'm complaining about my life when his brother just died days ago.

"For what?" he asks.

I want to tell him I'm sorry. I want to talk to him about what happened, how Mikhail died and how he is feeling, but it feels too heavy. So, I nod towards the desk. "For distracting you. It looked like you were working when I came in."

He shrugs. "I'm always working."

"Shouldn't you have people below you to take care of that?"

"You'd think." He smirks and it hits me like a pure ray of sunshine. "But everyone else seems to pile everything on my desk for some reason."

"Hmmph."

Aleksandr pushes a strand of blonde hair off of his forehead. "What does that mean?"

"I don't know," I say, a smile bubbling up on my face, too. "I just never took you to be the kind of guy who would let other people tell him what he was supposed to do."

"I'm not," he says quickly.

"Sounds like you are," I say, pointing to the desk.

He looks over his shoulder at his desk, and then in the next instant, he stalks across the room and slams the laptop closed. For a moment, I think he is angry, but when he turns around, his face is split in a smile. "I do what I like. See?"

"So, you like working, then?"

He sits next to me on the bed again, his thigh brushing against mine. Suddenly, I feel self-conscious in the t-shirt and short cloth pajama shorts I'm wearing. Aleksandr had new clothes ordered for me to wear, and all of them are a little more on the sexy side than my normal clothes.

"Is this a conversation or a therapy session?" he teases.

I don't answer, but instead just hold his gaze until he sighs.

"I guess, I've always enjoyed the work. Having something to do and some way to contribute to the family feels good. Being busy gives life meaning."

I frown. "That is depressing."

"Having a purpose isn't depressing."

"Yeah, but having no fun is," I say. "Work is what you do so you can have enough money to have fun."

"I already have enough money."

I roll my eyes. "Exactly. Which is why it is even more sad that you think work for the sake of work gives life meaning."

"Not for the sake of work," he says. "It isn't like I'm digging a hole in the ground just to stay busy. My work is meaningful."

"Fine," I say, holding up my hands in surrender. "Your work is meaningful and it gives you a purpose. But when you aren't fulfilling your purpose, how do you relax at the end of the day?"

"I sleep."

"Try again."

"What do you mean 'try again'? You want me to change my answer?"

I nod. "Absolutely."

He groans. "I go out. Have drinks. Meet people."

The thought of Aleksandr sitting at a bar with a drink in his hands revs something in me that I'd like to explore. "Where do you go out?"

"The Mendeleev."

"There we go. That isn't lame. I've been there," I say. "But I've never seen you before."

He looks at me out of the corner of his eyes, and I feel him assessing me. I wonder if he is imagining what it would be like to run into me in public. If he is thinking about what it would be like to see me outside of my capacity as his uncle's maid.

"I don't go often." He chews on his thumbnail for a second and then crosses his arms, his muscles bulging even more than normal. I have to look away so I won't make a fool of myself and reach out to touch him. "And when I do, I don't stay long."

I'm about to tell him he is lame again, but then I see the smug smile on his face, and I understand.

"Ew."

"What?" He feigns shock.

"You're telling me that you have sex for fun?"

He leans down, his excited whisper hot on my neck. "Well, isn't it?"

Goosebumps run down my arms and legs and heat builds between my legs.

I wouldn't know.

Though, I can't tell Aleksandr that. That I don't know who the father of my baby is. I can't tell him that I'm pregnant without ever having had an orgasm before. It is too humiliating.

Aleksandr chuckles to himself and then nudges me in the arm. "What about you? What do you do for fun?"

"Sex," I blurt out. "Lots of sex. Just like you."

He snorts in surprise. "What?"

I don't need a mirror to know my face is as red as a tomato. "I was joking."

He raises his eyebrows and tilts his head back, looking down his straight nose at me. "So, you don't have sex?"

"Well, I mean, yes," I say, the heat from my face moving down my neck and chest. "But not in the way it sounded. The way you said it. Not with you—or, not in the same way."

Aleksandr's face is pinched into a mask of restraint as he tries to keep from laughing in my face, but I can see how much he is enjoying my nervousness. "In what way *are* you having sex, then? If it isn't the way I'm having it?"

I stand up and shake my head, refusing to engage. "Have you had dinner yet? I didn't see you at dinner, and if you are going to insist I eat every meal, then I won't let you skip, either."

"Zoya," he says warmly. "You are avoiding the subject."

"No, I am just concerned about your welfare."

"Are you?" he asks, eyebrow raised. "Since when?"

"Since you started caring about mine, apparently," I shout, flinging my arms at him.

His amusement turns more solemn, and Aleksandr stands up. "You want to know why?"

"Why what?" I ask before I can think about what he is asking.

He takes a step towards me. "Why I care about you?"

No. Definitely not. I don't care. "Yes."

Aleksandr takes another step towards me until he is crowding me, until I want to back away, but I also want to loop my arms around his neck and pull myself closer.

"I care about you because—" he looks down at me and then lower, and I think he is going to mention my baby, though I don't know why. His hand moves to my hip, his other curving around my waist, and I feel like putty in his hands.

"Because," he repeats, his eyes tracing my face and landing on my lips.

I wonder how many women he has done this with. How many women he has held this way and looked at like this.

I feel special. With his eyes on me, his hands massaging circles into my skin, I feel like the only woman in the world. How many women has he made feel this way?

I expect to be jealous, and I am, but not because he has been with and seen other women. I am jealous because other women have been with him. Since I stood in the yard of the estate and daydreamed about Aleksandr, other women have touched him and felt him, and I wish I'd had the experience, too.

In the end, it might even be nice to find the other women he has been with. Start a support group or something.

Because Aleksandr has simply laid his hands on me, and I'm not sure how I'll ever fully recover. My heart is pounding against my chest, and my legs are weak. The only thing holding me up seems to be the magnetic pull I feel towards his mouth. I stretch up on my toes out of necessity, desperate to be closer to him.

His lips move around another word, but I don't care about the explanation anymore. I don't care why he cares. Or if he really does. I just want to know what it would be like to be with him.

To be with someone.

So, I curl my fingers around his neck and pull. I don't have to pull hard because at the same time, Aleksandr bends forward and our lips meet.

And just like that, I'm kissing Mr. Levushka.

13

ZOYA

It is the kind of kiss that drains you and fills you up all at the same time.

The moment our lips meet, I feel like I'm floating, like the only thing tethering me to the ground is Aleksandr and his hands on my body.

But then there is a heavy feeling between my legs, like a weight is pushing down on me from the inside.

Aleksandr is softer than I thought he would be. Even with the stubble around his mouth scratching my cheeks, he is tender and warm. His hands slope up my back and then press down my spine, dragging across the soft material of my shirt. I arch my back and press myself closer to him, hungry for more of his touch.

I'm trying not to think about where this will lead.

Not because I don't want it to lead *there*, but because I'm not sure what that is going to mean.

Aleksandr doesn't know this is my first time since – well, since ever, really. I don't count the night that gave me the baby in my belly. I don't even remember it, after all. I certainly didn't participate actively. Meaning, I have no idea what I'm doing now. What if he just thinks I'm bad at sex? What if I do something wrong?

His fingers drag across my neck and then cup my chin. He pulls away from me and frowns down. We've only been kissing for a few minutes. Or, at least, I think it has only been a few minutes. But already his lips are red and his eyes are puffy like he has been sleeping.

"Stop thinking," he says, squeezing my jaw.

I feel drunk. "What?"

He shakes my face back and forth. "You think too much. Stop it."

"How do you know—"

He circles his hips against me, letting me feel his hardness against my thigh, and my mouth falls open, a surprised sigh slipping from my lips.

"How do you know I was thinking about anything?" I ask, my voice higher than normal.

Aleksandr lets go of my jaw and glides his hand over my collarbone and down my chest, his finger drawing a line directly over my breast. Because I was already in my pajamas, I don't have a bra on, so his finger flicks at my pebbled nipple, and I gasp.

"You got tense." He runs his other hand up my thigh, his thumb tickling the strip of skin between the top of my shorts and the bottom of my shirt. His paw of a hand cups my waist and then shifts higher until I can feel his heat pressed against my ribs and the side of my breast. "I just want you to relax."

How am I supposed to relax when I feel like I'm on fire?

He laughs, and I realize I've said it out loud. My brain really is fuzzy.

Leaning forward, he kisses my shoulder and then my neck. I shiver when his warm breath washes over my skin. And when his stubble scrapes against my jaw, I lose my mind.

"Take this off." My fingers are jittery like I've had too much coffee as I grab the hem of his t-shirt and pull it up. Before I can even get it over his head, I pause, admiring the hard lines of his body. I reach out and let my fingers explore the dips and raises of his body.

Aleksandr pulls his shirt off the rest of the way, letting me map out his topography with both hands.

He is even more beautiful than I imagined.

All hard lines and smooth skin, he looks like an advertisement in a catalog rather than a real person. I can't help but lean forward and taste him. When my lips press against his chest, he sighs and wraps his arms around me. Then, I move lower, crouching down as I offer attention to each of his abs and the dip beneath his belly button.

When I reach the waistband of his underwear, I freeze.

I know what I should do—what would be the sexy thing to do.

I should unhook the button of his pants with a flick of my fingers, pull the material down his legs, and give some attention to the proud member I see outlined against his thigh.

Except, I've never done that before. To anyone. And the thought of doing it now for the first time with Aleksandr is too much, too fast.

I feel like I'm frozen there for hours but it can't have been more than a few seconds before he cups a hand behind my neck and pulls me to standing.

"Stop thinking," he whispers against my lips, taking a step forward and pressing his leg between my thighs. The hard muscle of his leg massages against my ache, and I groan.

He takes another step and another, pushing me closer to the bed while also driving me wild until I'm a vibrating bundle of nerves against his leg. I can't think about anything except getting more of him.

Aleksandr pushes me back on the bed, and before I can even prop myself up, his fingers hook under the waistband of my shorts. As soon as they are on the floor, he massages his palms up my legs, spreading my thighs wide for him to nestle between.

I haven't done this, either, but I can tell immediately there isn't much for me to do. Aleksandr is control. I'm supposed to lay here. And not think. A task that becomes infinitely easier when his finger draws a line across the center of my panties, and I lose all feeling or connection to any part of my body that isn't under his touch.

I press my hips up to get more, but he braces me with his forearm, forcing me back down onto the bed. Then, he slips his finger beneath the black lacy material and pushes it aside. When I feel the warmth of his breath between my legs, I whimper.

I need him to touch me, but if he does, I'll explode. It feels like a fitting end, though. A good way to go, if you have to.

His tongue laps at my center, and my entire body convulses. The only thing keeping me on the bed is Aleksandr's forearm, pressing into me hard enough I'm sure there will be bruises. I don't care.

He licks me again, and my thighs clamp around his ears.

Steadily, he builds up a rhythm until I'm writhing beneath him, helpless and inflamed with no desire to be rescued. I need more.

This doesn't feel the way it did alone in my bedroom. With my own hand between my thighs. This feels nothing like that. It is deeper, more animalistic. Aleksandr is lapping at me and sucking my bundle of nerves in a way that is more reverent than I ever touched myself.

Just when I think I can't handle any more, he brings the hand behind my thigh to my front and begins massaging small circles with his thumb just above where his tongue is destroying me.

It is the most I've ever felt at once.

The sensation is overwhelming and all-consuming, and I have to bite down on my own palm to keep from screaming out. The fire builds and builds, being stoked by the furious flicks of his tongue and thumb, until it breaks.

Wave after wave rolls through me. My entire body clenches and releases to a primal rhythm that only Aleksandr and I know.

I throw my arms over my head and turn my face into the comforter. I squeeze my eyes shut and ride the wave as he laps me up and then massages me back down. When I'm finished, I am limp and lazy, and I barely notice when Aleksandr pulls my panties down my legs.

He crawls over me, drawing his hands over my stomach, taking my shirt with him so he can pull it over my head.

His knees are planted on either side of my spent body, and he looks down at me, his eyes darker than I've ever seen them. And hungry.

"That was fucking hot," he growls.

I feel like I could roll over and go to sleep, but the deep baritone of his voices vibrates in my bones and wakes me up. Suddenly, I'm not scared or nervous. I reach down between us and unbutton his pants.

He lifts his knees to assist me in kicking his pants off, and then before I can lose my courage, I hook my fingers on either side of his boxer briefs and push them down.

I marvel at the size of him when he springs free between us.

I could feel when he was pressed against my leg that he wasn't small, but I didn't quite expect this.

Almost as if reading my thoughts, he smiles and bends down to nip at my lips. "Don't worry. I'll make it feel good."

"God, I know," I murmur, still feeling the gentle thrum of my first orgasm pulsing through my body.

A proud chuckle rumbles in his chest, but the sound is cut short when my hand wraps around his length. It transitions into a grunt as I pull down his length and slide back up.

Based on the small whimpering sounds coming from the back of his throat, I assume I'm doing it right.

Aleksandr falls forward onto one of his elbows, and I press a hand to his chest and roll him over onto his back. It is my turn to explore.

He flops over willingly, and I kneel next to him, amazed at the perfection of his body. The deep indentations that cut inward from his hips, directing me to the main attraction like flashing lights along an airstrip. The marble-cut edges of his pecs and the corded muscles in his arms flexing as he grabs a handful of the comforter.

"So good," he groans, as I slide my hand to his end and then back down. I feel like I should be more nervous, but admiring and appreciating his body is the easiest thing I've ever done. I simply let my hand explore where it wants to explore, and Aleksandr moans.

I'm just getting into a rhythm when he shakes his head, and then reaches out, grabs me by the hips, and pulls me over him. My legs settle on either side of his hips as he slides a condom on. When he is finished, I lean forward to kiss him, squeezing my eyes closed, trying to ignore the nervous thrumming of my heart.

What if it hurts? What if he is too big? Barring an immaculate conception, I know I'm not physically a virgin, but emotionally I still feel like I am. What is it going to be like to give that up?

Aleksandr tucks a strand of hair behind my ear and draws me in to a long kiss. He sucks on my lower lip and swirls his tongue against mine. It is intimate and close, and I melt down against his body.

Then, his hand moves from my neck to my waist and my hip. Then, he slides between us and positions himself at my opening. My breath catches.

"Stop thinking," he says softly against my cheek.

I turn my head and catch his lips with mine as he pushes up into me.

My lips part in a gasp. The movement is slow and gentle, but he is spreading me like I've never felt before. Each small thrust of his hips fills me more until I'm not sure I can take anymore.

Then, Aleksandr wraps his arms around my back and pulls me down. My legs spread further, and I can feel that we are as close together as humanly possible. I sink down onto his chest, reveling in the sensation.

Aleksandr purrs in my ear. "You are so tight."

I circle my hips over him, amazed that it could feel this good again so soon after my first orgasm. I lift my hips and drop down onto him. I rock and slide and experiment, and Aleksandr just digs his fingers into my hips and holds on for the ride.

Soon, I hit a rhythm that sends jolts of pleasure straight through my core. I lift myself up and lean back, balancing myself with my palms against his thighs. Aleksandr sits up slightly to watch me, his eyes drinking in the sight of my body working over his.

We make eye contact, and I relish the sense of control. Knowing that I have the ability to make a man as strong and commanding and handsome as Aleksandr Levushka bite his lip and groan. It feels good.

He presses himself up to sitting with one hand behind him, the other wrapped around my waist, and thrusts his hips into me as I circle him. The combination is too much, and I let my eyes fall closed and tip my head back.

Aleksandr moans and before I even know what is happening, he tips me backward and is crawling over me.

"You are too sexy," he says as if it is a bad thing. "You do it without even trying."

I reach down between us to find his length, desperate for more of him.

He chuckles. "You're greedy, too."

I stretch up and kiss his jaw and his neck. I lick a line up to his ear and suck the lobe into my mouth, nibbling at the soft skin there.

Aleksandr sighs and then presses a hand into my chest and pushes me back on the mattress. He dips over me, his lips coming so close to mine but never actually touching. His eyes are almost black, the pupils blown wide. He looks serious, and if I wasn't so desperate for his touch, I might be afraid.

"Roll over."

I do it without question, and when he grabs my hips and props me up on my knees, I arch my back to give him better access.

His hand smooths over my backside, and then without warning, he presses himself to my entrance and slides in to the hilt.

I fall forward onto my elbows and gasp.

Unlike the gentle touches and tender kisses at the start, his thrusts now are merciless. The sound of our bodies slapping together fills the room, and I have to grab the blankets to keep myself from sliding forward off the bed.

The backs of my thighs sting, but it is nothing compared to the friction between my legs. My entire body is humming with the onset of another release, grasping at him prematurely, desperate. And I can tell by the ragged sound of his breathing that Aleksandr is close, too.

He leans forward, his weight resting partially on my back, and wraps an arm around me. His finger finds my center easily, and with the first swipe over my sensitive clit, I'm a moaning mess.

I reach back and dig my fingers into his thigh, clawing at him to bring him closer, to beg him for more. Faster.

I don't realize I'm saying it out loud until Aleksandr groans behind me. "Tell me what you want."

"More," I sigh, pressing my face into the mattress and taking deep, greedy breaths. "Harder. More."

The slap of his thighs against me is brutal and punishing and yet still not enough. It won't be enough until he breaks me.

"Faster," I breath, gripping his thigh. "More."

His thrusts match with the thundering of my heart, and when he adds a second finger to my front, rubbing at me with abandon, I can't hold it back anymore. I arch my back, lift my head, and give in to the moment.

Pleasure rushes from my center to all of my extremities, and my legs are trembling from the release when I feel Aleksandr slow down. His thrusts become more purposeful, and I can feel him jerking inside of me.

He falls forward, his cheek pressed against my spine, his heart racing against my lower back.

When we are both finished and spent, he slides out of me and falls on the bed next to me, his chin resting on my shoulder. He kisses the back of my head and sighs.

"Still feel like you're on fire?" he whispers.

I can only laugh and whimper.

14

ALEKSANDR

I'm not the kind of guy who makes breakfast. Or lets a woman sleep in my bed.

But when I roll over and see Zoya sleeping behind me, her hair spread out across my pillow, one arm thrown over her head, I will do just about anything to keep her from leaving.

The sex was incredible.

Zoya took her time, and she took charge. Usually, I like to be the one in control. Most of the women I'm with end up with their hands pinned over the head just to keep them from pawing at me. But I didn't mind Zoya's touch. The feather-light touch of her fingers, almost nervous.

Watching her explore was almost as good as the actual sex. Almost.

Her eyelids flutter, and I almost turn away so she won't know I'm looking at her. But the temptation to watch her wake up is too strong.

Her tongue slides out to lick her lower lip and then she presses her full lips together and pinches her eyes closed as she stretches. It is so close to the O-face she made last night that I have to suppress a groan. When she finally rolls over and looks at me, I'm smiling.

"Good morning." She says it like she is surprised to see me next to her. "How did you sleep?"

"Well." Surprisingly well, actually. Considering I've only shared a bed with a woman a few times in my life. "How about you?"

"Good." She rolls over and nuzzles her face against my chest. Then, she wrinkles her nose.

"Do I stink?"

She looks up at me. "No. You smell amazing."

"Then why the face?" I tape her nose, and she wrinkles it again.

"Because it isn't fair that you look this good and still smell great first thing in the morning."

I laugh and lay a hand on her bare hip. She cleaned up after we had sex, but I insisted she keep her clothes off. Now, I'm grateful for that decision. I let my fingers trail down her leg, feeling the goosebumps rise across her skin. "You smell good, too."

She covers her mouth with her hand. "That's because you haven't smelled my breath."

I use my nose to try and push her hand away to get at her mouth, but she shakes her head and giggles, keeping her hand cemented over her lips. "No, it's bad."

My hand slips between her legs, and her giggles turn to sighs, muffled by her palm. I dip into her warmth, and she opens her legs wider. But still, when I lean forward, she widens her eyes and shakes her head.

I groan and roll away from her, taking my hand with me.

Her chest rises and falls rapidly. "God. It is too early to be this turned on."

"I would have taken you all the way, too," I tease, gesturing to her mouth. "But you were too self-conscious."

"No, I was worried I'd knock you out," she laughs, throwing back the covers and getting up.

Clearly, being self-conscious isn't an issue.

Zoya's naked body is silhouetted against the curtains. She throws her arms over her head, her body stretching long like a cat. Her ass is smooth and tight, and I can see a hint of the curve of her breast, and I'm tempted to drag her back to bed, morning breath be damned. Before I can, however, she spins away from me and moves towards the bathroom.

"I'm going to shower."

I start to get up immediately. "I'll come, too."

She laughs and shakes her head. "No thanks. I'll be out in ten."

I flop back on the bed and try to ignore the need between my legs. I can't remember ever feeling like this about a woman. Especially *after* I've already fucked them.

The water starts to run in the other room, and laying there thinking about Zoya's naked body dripping wet isn't helping my situation, so I pull on clothes and go down to the kitchen.

Boris has been in and out all week, so he has given his chef the last few mornings off, and based on the lack of breakfast in the kitchen, I assume she is off again. Which is actually fine with me. Breakfast is one of the few meals I can cook well, and it gives me something to do until Zoya is out of the shower.

I heat a skillet up, drizzle oil in the bottom, and crack five eggs in the bottom. I have to scrape eggshell out of the mixture, breaking a yolk in the process, but it is salvageable. While the eggs sizzle, I grab kolbasa from the fridge and slice off a few heart chunks, dropping them in with the eggs. Then, I grab tomatoes and bell peppers from the pantry.

Ask me to give a man a close shave with the edge of a sharp knife, and I can do it with my eyes closed. But chopping vegetables proves to be another skill entirely. By the time I finish with the tomatoes, they are a soupy mess of seeds and sludge, and I cut my finger twice trying to slice the bell pepper. By the time I get the vegetables to the pan, the edges are turning black and smoke is accumulating.

"Fuck." I turn and drop the vegetables back on the cutting board, wipe my hands on the towel hanging from the oven, and pull the pan from the burner. The handle is metal and burning hot, and I immediately feel the palm of my hand begin to welt. "Shit."

I grab a towel and use it to hold the handle while I try to scrape the eggs out of the skillet. The undersides are dark brown and crispy rather than golden brown and chewy. The smell of sausage has been replaced with the odor of ash.

"I usually like my eggs over easy, but extra crispy works, too."

I growl and look over my shoulder. Zoya is standing in the doorway in a long gray t-shirt dress that clings to every curve of her body, her hair hangs in a wet bundle over her shoulder, and her face is bare and pink from the heat of the shower. She looks good enough to spread out on the island and eat.

I continue scraping at the eggs for another second, hoping something of the meal might be saved, but Zoya lays a hand on my arm. "I think we have to call it, Alek."

I tense at the nickname.

Only Mikhail called me Alek. All at once, I realize he will never call me that again.

I almost correct Zoya and ask her to call me by my full name, but I don't. Because hearing the name on her lips didn't feel wrong.

It felt familiar. It felt intimate.

I drop the spatula and run a hand down my face. "I was going to make us breakfast."

"And you did," she says, wrapping her arms around my waist and pulling her body against mine. "It just isn't edible."

My frustration begins to ebb away when I see her playful smile aimed at me. "Maybe you were right about me. I'm better at being served than servicing."

"Oh, I don't know," she says with a shrug. "You did a pretty great job of servicing me last night."

She presses her hips more firmly against me, and I'm hungry for something other than food now. I lean down and nip at her exposed neck, breathing in the vanilla scent of her soap. She sighs, stretching out her neck, and then quickly pushes me away.

"Food first."

I sit down at the island while Zoya scrapes the burnt remnants of my breakfast attempt in the trash and cracks a few more eggs in the pan. She browns some of the kolbasa in a separate pan and throws in the vegetables I chopped near the end, hitting them with a dash of freshly ground pepper and salt. It smells heavenly.

"This was my dad's favorite breakfast," she says, smiling at me over her shoulder. "My mom or I made it every weekend."

"He was a good man," I say.

"You knew him?" She seems surprised.

I nod. "I spoke with him a few different times. He enjoyed his work here. Maintaining the grounds, being outside. He seemed really happy."

Zoya smiles. "He was."

Then she turns away from me, tending to the breakfast, but I see the slope of her shoulders change. Her head is hanging down. When she slides over and turns around, leaning back against the counter, she is biting the corner of her mouth. "My dad loved his job here, but he wanted more for me."

"Like what?" I ask.

My own father never seemed to want anything from me. In fact, the less he had to deal with me, the better. That is why I just did my best to do my work and not raise any alarms. Mikhail didn't live by the same principles, clearly. I'm fascinated by the idea of an actual father-child relationship.

"You asked me what I liked to do for fun last night," she says, crossing her arms over her chest. I do my best to ignore the way the movement presses her breasts higher and lifts the hem of the dress higher on her thighs. "Well, I've always liked graphic design."

She smiles as she says it, as though she is releasing some long-held secret.

"Really?"

"My dad saved up to buy me a computer so I could work on my designs. He wanted me to go to school for it and find a job in the city."

"Why didn't you?"

She shrugs, the smile fading again. "He got sick, and I wanted to be close by. I thought maybe when he got better, I would give it a try. But..."

"He didn't get better," I finish for her.

She nods and then looks down at her stomach. "And now..."

"You're pregnant," I finish again, clenching my teeth through the words. Even though he didn't mean to, Mikhail really did fuck up everything he touched.

Zoya takes a deep breath, filling her lungs and straightening her shoulders, and then lets it out. "Life happens. All we can do is roll with the punches."

I know she is talking about her father's death and the unexpected pregnancy, but I can't help but wonder if Mikhail's death was one of those punches.

Did she like him? Or was it just a fling?

And then, for the first time, I wonder whether sleeping with me wasn't some kind of rebound for her. A sick kind of closure.

Remembering the way she touched me, the way she felt on top of me, I can't believe she would really be thinking about Mikhail, but the thought tickles the edge of my mind as we eat breakfast and continue talking.

It is easy to be with Zoya. I don't think about work or what I need to do today. Instead, I just listen to her stories and share some of my own.

And for the first time since I got the call about Mikhail, I feel like I can finally breathe.

We clean our dishes together, and then she grabs my hand and leads me back to the room.

As soon as the door is closed, the rest of the world ceases to exist.

I strip off her dress, pull her bra off with my teeth, and press her against the wall, pinning her there with my hips.

We work off our breakfast all over the room, falling into a tangle of arms and legs on the bed between sessions while we gather energy for another round.

Being with Zoya is the closest I've ever been to being addicted. I want more of her. Even while I'm inside of her, I'm thinking about when we can do this again. How I can get my hands on her again.

It is hard to fathom she is the same woman I got fired ten days ago.

"How long are you staying in St. Petersburg?" she asks, drawing a circle on my chest with her finger.

"I'll be here until after the funeral, for sure," I say. It is the closest I've come to mentioning Mikhail since telling her he was dead in the hospital. I study her face for a reaction, but there is only pity.

"Right. Of course." She lays her head on my chest, and I like the weight of it. Usually, cuddling feels unnatural to me, but Zoya fits next to my body like a perfect puzzle piece.

"You could come with me." The words are out of my mouth before I can really think about them. It just seemed like the right thing to say. I'll have to go back to Moscow, and I don't want to be away from Zoya yet. Not until we know what this is between us. So, easy solution: she could come live with me.

She sits up and looks at me, eyebrows raised. "Are you serious?"

I tuck my arm behind my head and shrug. "Why not?"

"Because we hated each other before yesterday," she says.

"You hated me?" I ask with feigned offense.

She rolls her eyes. "You got me fired, so you can't pretend you liked me."

"The line between love and hate is dangerously thin." This time, I realize I've overstepped. *Love*. I reach out desperately to draw the words back in. "Not to say that this is…I mean—"

"I know what you meant," she says, patting my chest.

I let out a sigh of relief. Then, back to the issue at hand. "Well, what do you think?"

"About living with you?" she asks.

The more I think about it, the less crazy it sounds. "You wouldn't have to live *with* me if you didn't want to. We have apartments all over Moscow. I could put you up in one of those."

She chews on her bottom lip. "I don't want any charity."

"It's the least I can do." I drag my finger down her heart-shaped face, stopping at her chin. "Like you said, I got you fired. Giving you a place to crash doesn't seem so out of line."

She thinks about it for a minute, and then her eyes shift downward. "What about…the baby?"

The baby. Mikhail's baby.

I know now would be the perfect time to bring up Mikhail. To let her know that I know. To talk about what it means for us. But apparently, I'm a coward.

"Life happens, right? We can figure that out while we figure everything else out, too."

Zoya twists her pink lips to the side and tucks a strand of dark hair behind her ear. "Yeah, I suppose we can figure it out."

~

Over the next few days, the only thing we figure out is how many times two people can have sex before they physically can't take it anymore.

For the first time in years, I turn my phone off and cut myself off from the world. I don't want to think about work or our rivals or Mikhail. I just want to think about Zoya.

I want to focus on this beautiful person who, for the time being, is mine. When possible, I push every other thought from my head.

And this method works great, until I check my phone after Zoya and I get out of the shower and realize my mother sent over Mikhail's funeral arrangements.

"No one should look so sad after what we just did in there," Zoya says, wrapping her arms around me and kissing my back.

I can feel her bare breasts against my skin, her nipples pebbled from the chill in the room, and I put my phone down and turn to wrap her in my arms. "My brother's funeral is tomorrow morning."

She stiffens and then pulls away from me, her blue-green eyes cutting me open. "Do you want me to go?"

"Do you want to go?" I ask.

"If you want me to," she says. "If it would help you."

I want to ask if going would help her. If it would give her closure. But I don't. Instead, I just kiss her hair and tell her I want here there. Right now, Zoya is the only thing that feels right to me. The idea of being away from her makes me feel unmoored.

So, the next morning, I put on my best suit, and Zoya manages to make business formal look sexy by putting on a black pencil skirt with a dark-gray v-neck sweater. I bought her a few things to wear around the estate, but she had to borrow the funeral outfit from the chef, Samara.

I worry that having Zoya with me will feel like a betrayal to Mikhail. That bringing the woman carrying his child to his funeral is breaking some kind of unwritten brother code. But as soon as I see the casket at the end of the church aisle, I squeeze Zoya's hand and forget everything else.

The service is a blur. My mother watches Zoya and I carefully when we arrive, but by the end, she is weeping into a handkerchief. My father maintains his composure, but he arrives just before the preacher begins speaking, leaves the moment he is done, and doesn't look at me once. When he walks past our row, Zoya lays her hand on my knee, and I lean into her touch more than I ever have before.

By the time we walk out through the front doors of the church and into the day, I'm glad to be free of the church and the emotions inside.

I just want to forget about it.

Zoya checks up on me on the drive home and during lunch, making sure I'm okay, but I wish she would stop. When I pull her in for a kiss and tip her back, my hand curled around her neck, she pulls away.

"Are you sure?" she asks, face filled with concern.

I nod and pull her against me, crushing my lips on hers. In an instant, our funeral clothes are on the floor, and I'm channeling every emotion from the day into Zoya.

I bend her over the side of my bed and press into her with one quick thrust. She cries out and then stretches her arms out in front of her, arching her back into me for more.

She didn't cry at the funeral. Not that I saw, anyway. And I'm not sure what that means.

Did she love Mikhail? Was he just a fling?

Her concern has been for me all day, but I'm desperate to get inside her head and find out what she is thinking. How she is feeling.

Would she rather I be dead in his place?

The thought is morbid, and if Mikhail and I weren't identical twins, I probably wouldn't have even considered it. But since we are, I can't help but wonder who she is thinking of while she is fucking me. Is she imagining me or my brother?

When I come, I'm more frustrated than when I started.

Zoya flips over, a sated smile on her face, and lays a hand over her stomach. Over her baby.

It's almost easy to forget she is pregnant at times.

Her morning sickness comes and goes, though it mostly takes the form of nausea, especially when she is hungry. Otherwise, her symptoms are minimal. It's too early for any outward signs, so I have to remind myself she is carrying a child. My brother's child.

"What are you going to tell the baby about their father?" I ask, blurting out the question before I can second guess myself.

Zoya is still smiling when she looks at me, but as the question washes over her, the smile fades. She slides to the top of the bed and slips beneath the covers, pulling the sheet over her chest as though she is ashamed. It is the first time she has covered herself like that since I first peeled her clothes off.

"What do you mean?"

"I mean," I start, trying to figure out exactly what I do mean. "What are you going to say about him?"

She crosses her arms over her stomach and looks down at the mattress. "Nothing if I can help it."

The words hit me like an arrow in the chest. I'd felt bad for Zoya. For the hand life had dealt her. I felt bad that Mikhail would never be the supportive baby daddy he could have been and that she was left as a single mother. But now?

Now, I'm angry.

"Nothing?" I snap. I push off of the bed and grab my boxers from the floor. "You don't think the child deserves to know?"

Her cheeks are red and there are tears welling up in her eyes. "You don't understand."

"No, I do," I say bitterly, stepping into my pants and zipping them up.

"I understand perfectly. Now that he is dead, you can just forget about him entirely."

Zoya's attention snaps to me, her eyes narrowed, pointed jaw set. "What are you talking about?"

"What am I talking about?" I breath, buttoning my shirt with nervous fingers. As soon as I'm finished, I glare at her. "I'm talking about my brother, Zoya. The man whose funeral we just attended."

Her face goes as white as the sheets.

"He looks just like me. Maybe you remember him," I say sarcastically, throwing up a dismissive hand to wave her away.

"I don't understand what you are talking about." Her voice is shaking, near tears.

I'm tired of the dramatics. Clearly, Zoya was playing some kind of game. I showed up and saved her, and she thought she could turn my grace into a free ticket for her and her child. Fuck that.

"I know Mikhail is the father of your baby, so drop the act. My mother told me."

Her brows pull together, and she shakes her head. "Your mother?"

"She saw you two together about ten weeks ago. Timeline matches up."

Zoya looks like she is going to be sick. "Alek. Please. You don't understand. I—"

Before she can say anything else, the door to my room bursts open.

I turn to see Boris barreling into my room. "For fuck's sake. Knock."

"No time," he says, slightly out of breath. He turns and sees Zoya naked in my bed. She pulls the blankets higher around her shoulders and turns away, her cheeks red. Boris' eyebrow raises in either surprise or amusement—maybe both.

"Then what is it?" I demand, grabbing the door frame and threatening to close it in his face.

He puts his foot against the bottom of the door to stop me. "One of our warehouses was just attacked. It's rubble."

For the first time in several days, Zoya is out of my head and work takes over. It feels good to forget the drama for a minute. "Who?"

"Who do you think?" Boris says. The answer is obvious: it's our rivals. Clearly, they are not just some small-time gang we don't need to worry about. Otherwise, they wouldn't dare make a move this bold. "We have to go."

I look back at Zoya in the bed for an instant. She is still pale and shaky, her lower lip trembling. She opens her mouth to say something, but I hold up a hand to stop her. "We'll talk later."

As soon as I close the door on her, I want to turn back and hear her explanation. I want to be wrong about everything.

"Please tell me that girl is a fling," Boris groans.

The desire to protect Zoya is still firmly in place, and I turn on him. "What does it matter to you?"

"Me?" He asks, shrugging. "It doesn't. You should just know she is trouble."

"How so?" Before two weeks ago, I didn't know anything about Zoya. But in the short time we've spent together, I've learned that she is gentle and caring, though she also has a serious dose of snark. She is not afraid to share her opinion—unless, of course, it comes to the small detail of my dead brother being the father of her unborn baby. Zoya is tough when she needs to be, but she is also sweet enough to soften my rough edge, to make me feel things I've never felt before.

"Drama," Boris says with a disinterested wave of her hand. "She got herself pregnant, fired, and then in trouble with a rival gang. I mean, what more reason do you need? Though, the baby won't be a concern much longer, I suppose."

I snap my attention to him. "What does that mean?"

"Her mother said she is going to get an abortion." He shrugs. "Doesn't make any difference to me, of course, but it might to you."

Is that what Zoya was going to tell me? That she was going to get an abortion so it didn't matter who the baby's father was?

Except, it did matter.

Mikhail is dead and this child is all I will have left of him.

How could Zoya do this? To Mikhail? To me?

We'd talked about her coming to Moscow with me. She'd pointed to her stomach, insinuating the baby was part of her plans, and I'd told her we would figure it out. Why would she say any of that if she was planning to get an abortion?

Thoughts and questions swirl around my head as I get into Boris' car and we drive to the warehouse. Anger ebbs and flows, mingled with betrayal and shame. I let a woman distract me. I let her tear down my walls and step all over my heart.

But I won't let her distract me anymore.

If there is anything this experience has taught me, it is that I was right all along. There is nothing more important than the work. I just need to put my head down, get rid of this rival family, and become the boss of the Levushka family.

Fuck everything else.

Fuck my father and his disappointment in me.

And most of all… fuck Zoya.

15

ZOYA

It takes me thirty minutes to find the strength to crawl out of bed and put my clothes on after Aleksandr leaves.

His words ring in my head the entire time.

I know Mikhail is the father of your baby.

She saw you two together about ten weeks ago.

Timeline matches up.

In the moment, I wanted to shout that he was crazy. But then, reality hit me. I'd never been alone with Mikhail. And certainly never when his mother was around.

She saw you two together about ten weeks ago. Timeline matches up.

A wave of nausea washes over me as I walk towards the cottage where I grew up, where my mother still lives. Where I lived up until a little over a week ago.

I press my hand to my stomach and think the question as loudly as I can, desperate for an answer. *Who is your father?*

Mikhail had always been the Levushka twin most interested in me. But that was only because he was the Levushka twin most interested in everyone. He smiled easily, flirted often, and was always in search of the next good time. I talked to him a handful of times over the years, but there was always something shinier to distract him, and I actively avoided him when I could. So, the thought that he could have been my first time—Aleksandr's brother—makes me feel sick.

When my mom answers the door, her face is stern and unphased. She knows I've been staying in Aleksandr's rooms with him, but she hasn't come to see me. Even when Boris was away from the estate. I know she is still angry with me.

However, as soon as she sees me—really sees me—her eyes widen and she opens her arms. "What is it, Zoya?"

I fall into her embrace like a child and weep.

She has to drag me to the sofa in our small living room, my head on her shoulder the entire time. Her hand presses firm circles into my back, and she whispers words of comfort in my ear. I don't really hear them, but the soothing cadence of her voice is enough to calm me down after a while.

"Talk to me," she says, propping me up. "Is it about the baby?"

I wipe at my eyes and nod.

"Is everything okay? Is it healthy?"

"Yes," I say. "Or, I think so."

She seems relieved for a moment, but then she frowns. "Then what is the matter?"

I inhale and let out a shuddering breath. "You've wanted me to tell you who the father is since the first moment I said I was pregnant."

My mother leans forward and grips my hands, nodding, encouraging me to continue.

"And I've refused. I know it upset you, and I'm sorry for that, but I couldn't tell you the truth. It was too horrible."

Her lower lip trembles. "Who was it? Who could it be that you would keep it a secret?"

"That is the thing," I say. "I don't know who it is."

She pulls away slightly, her head tilting to the side. "A stranger?"

I shake my head. "Not like that. I mean, I don't remember getting pregnant. I don't remember sleeping with anyone."

Her expression is blank, unreadable, so I continue.

"I was a – well, I'd never been with anyone. At least, I didn't think so until I found out I was pregnant." I wipe residual tears from my eyes and sniffle, trying to compose myself. "I remember the night I went out. Going to the bar, buying a drink. But that is it. Everything else is a blur. I just woke up in my bed the next morning with no memory. But now, Aleksandr—"

She gasps. "Did Aleksandr--?"

"No!" I cut her off before she can finish the question. "No, not Aleksandr. But – but Mikhail…maybe."

Her top lip pulls back in a snarl. "How did you find out?"

"Aleksandr told me he spoke with his mother. She saw me with Mikhail that night, found out I was pregnant later, and did the math." It feels good to say it out loud. To explain the entire story to my mother the way I didn't have a chance to explain it to Aleksandr. I can only hope he'll listen to me. And if he does, that he won't hate me afterward.

"Have you talked to her?" she asks. "Have you made certain it was the same night? Because this is a serious accusation."

I shake my head. "I just found out."

Immediately, my mom gets up and grabs her phone. It is an old flip phone, barely from this century, but it stores her phone numbers and allows her to make phone calls, which is all she really needs. She scrolls for a minute and then hands it to me. "This is her number. Boris gave it to me years ago. I don't even know why I saved it."

"You want me to just call her?" I ask. "What if it is true? She doesn't want to know this kind of information about her son. Especially so soon after he died. Plus, it could cause trouble for you. With Boris."

"You aren't calling to make her feel better," my mother says, laying a hand on my shoulder. "Or for me. You are calling for *you*. For your peace of mind. And after everything you've been through, you deserve it."

Her lip begins to tremble again, tears welling in her eyes, and this time, they spill over. She covers her face with her hands and sobs.

I wrap my arms around her shoulders. "It's okay."

"It isn't," she sobs. "You needed me. You needed your mother, and I abandoned you. I turned my back on you because I was angry. Because I thought you were keeping something from me."

"You didn't know," I say.

"I should have." She pulls out of my hug and sets her shoulders and lifts her chin. "I should have known. Or, better yet, I shouldn't have cared. I shouldn't have cared that you were keeping things from me or that I didn't know every detail of your life. I should have been there for you, and I will never forgive myself."

"That isn't what I want," I insist, grabbing her hand and squeezing. "I understood why you were upset. Part of this is my fault for not coming forward and telling you what happened. I was just…so ashamed."

"Ashamed?" her brows pull together and her nostrils flare. "What would you have to be ashamed of?"

I look down at my feet. "Maybe I wanted it. Maybe I drank too much and hooked up with someone and just…forgot. Maybe—"

"Maybe nothing," she says. "If you drank too much, you'd remember more of the night. No, this wasn't alcohol, Zoya. And now you need to talk with Mikhail's mother and find out what she knows. You need to get answers and put aside your shame. Because the shame is not yours to carry."

∼

I call Natalia as soon as I leave my mother's cottage.

I'm still in the wide expanse of lawn between the cottage and the main house when she answers.

"This is Zoya," I say simply. Before, I would have offered more of an explanation, but I know she knows who I am.

There is a pause and then Natalia clears her throat. "Hi, Zoya."

"I'm sorry if I'm bothering you or if this is a bad time, but—"

"It's a fine time." She sounds like Aleksandr. Professional and composed. Even if I wasn't calling her about such a serious issue, I'd still be intimidated.

"Okay, great." I take a deep breath. My hand is shaking so much I'm afraid I'll drop the phone. "I'm calling because I talked with Aleksandr, and—"

"I saw you at the funeral with him," she says. "I didn't realize the two of you were together."

I'm not so certain we are together anymore – or if we ever were, really – so I just keep talking as though she hasn't spoken.

"Aleksandr told me something he heard from you. About me…and Mikhail."

Her tone is cold when she responds. "Yes?"

"Yes." I swallow. "He told me you saw us together a few weeks ago. Ten weeks ago, to be exact."

"If you are calling to ask whether I told Aleksandr that Mikhail is the father of your child, then yes, I did," she says. "I told him that, before I realized the two of you were together. It now makes sense why he was so upset about it. I had no clue you were dating both of my sons."

Aleksandr was upset about the news? When his mother told him, we hadn't slept together yet. I don't have time to really puzzle this thought out, though, because I'm too busy defending myself against her charges.

"I'm not dating both of your sons," I say. "I never dated Mikhail."

Silence. "I saw you."

"Did you?" I ask. "That is why I'm calling. I want to confirm that you saw us together because, if you did...I don't remember it."

"What do you mean?" There is a hint of panic in her voice, and I wonder how much she knows about her other son's personal life.

"I mean, I don't remember being with him. Ever," I say. "And certainly not in a way that would result in pregnancy. I saw him around Boris' house occasionally, but that is it."

The pause is so long I think Natalia might have hung up, but then she lets out a ragged breath. "I stopped by the estate to see Mikhail. Boris told me he was in town, and I needed to talk to him. But when I arrived, he was with you in the driveway. You were sitting in the passenger seat, and he had the door open for you."

A pit yawns open in my stomach. It is like Natalia is describing a dream she had. What she is saying can't have been real. Not if I don't remember it.

"He was short with me, and I could tell I was interrupting something." She stops, her voice hiccupping like she is fighting back tears. "It was late, and he was clearly on a date, so I left. I didn't even know it was you until I turned around and saw him leading you inside. I recognized you, but I was too far away to notice anything unusual."

"You couldn't tell that something was wrong with me?" I ask. It takes every ounce of willpower to keep the tremors out of my voice.

"No," she says firmly. "Zoya, no. If I had known...if I'd had any inclination that you were...not capable of making a decision like that, I would have stopped it. My son or not, I would have stopped it. You have to believe me."

"I do." My throat is tight and tears sting the back of my eyes.

"I found out you were pregnant from Boris, and I hoped Mikhail would do the right thing. But then, I heard you were fired and Mikhail...died." She lets out a choked sob. "I didn't realize this situation could get even worse."

That makes two of us, I think. I thought telling Aleksandr what happened to me would be the worst part. But now, telling him that his brother was responsible? How can I do that? How can this fragile thing we have survive news like that?

It would take a good man to raise another man's son. But to raise his own nephew as his own? That is too much.

"Thank you," I say quickly, realizing I won't be able to hold it together much longer. "For telling me what you know. For confirming things for me."

"I'm sorry if I misjudged you," she says. "I knew Mikhail had issues, but...this is beyond what I thought him capable of."

I end the conversation quickly, promising to talk with Natalia again, though I'm not sure I'll be following through on that. I can't imagine facing her. The woman who had a front row seat to my nightmare.

Understanding what happened to me is not easy. I had already assumed that something horrible had happened, but not knowing who had done it made it easier to push the thought away. It was like chasing after a ghost. But now, I know it was Mikhail. I can picture his face and the way he used to smile at me.

The thought makes me shiver.

Did he smile at me that night? Did he charm me? Or was it a surprise attack? I have no memory of the night, so I can't point back to horrible memories and relive the trauma. In some ways, it is better. In other ways, worse.

I don't know what Mikhail did or how I reacted. I don't know how aware I was or whether I was unconscious. I don't know anything, and now I never will. Mikhail is gone, and I'm pregnant with his child.

My hand falls to my stomach. Not his child. *My* child.

He does not get any claim on this child just because it has his DNA. The baby is mine. It belongs to me. I will raise it and care for it and love it.

With Aleksandr and Boris both gone dealing with the warehouse explosion, the household staff has disappeared. Everyone is treating it like an impromptu vacation, so the hallways are empty as I wander the house.

I can't go back to the cottage with my mother. She would be supportive, I know, but I need to be alone right alone. I need to think.

And I can't go back to the room I was sharing with Aleksandr. Laying in the bed where we first made love and not knowing whether I'll ever share it with him again is too big of a pill to swallow.

So, I walk aimlessly.

I try to map out what my future will hold. Whether Aleksandr will be in it or not.

And when that question becomes too much to bear, I think about my own dreams. My plans.

I told Aleksandr about my graphic design hobby, and he didn't seem to think it was a ridiculous idea. He'd never seen my designs, but the fact that one person aside from my parents thought pursuing graphic design might not be a crazy idea gave me the tiniest shred of hope that I could do it. That I could build a life for myself.

And I cling to that hope.

At the end of this, I might not have Aleksandr, but I'll still have myself and my baby. And working the night shift at a diner and living in a pest-infested apartment are not the future I want. I want to be independent, to be able to care for myself and provide for my little family.

I don't know if I'll go to school or look for a place that would hire me based on my portfolio, but I consider the options as I walk. I pass by rooms I've cleaned a thousand times—Boris' room, his library, the sitting room. And then I walk past his office, which no one has ever been allowed in.

Boris told us it was because there is top secret Levushka family information inside that he doesn't want exposed, but Samara has always joked that he probably keeps sex toys in there. I've never gone inside to know for sure.

I'm still deep in thought when I hear a creak in the hallway behind me.

But before I can turn around, there is a heavy blow to the back of my head.

And everything goes black.

16

ALEKSANDR

I see the smoke when we are still blocks away. The gray cloud mingles amongst the smog, darkening the sky.

"Shit," Boris says. "It's worse than I thought."

When we pull into the lot, we realize it is even worse than that.

Men, both dead and injured, are spread around the lot. Some of them are having wounds tended to. Blood soaks the ground and puddles amongst the gravel. It looks like a battlefield.

And in the middle of it is my father.

This is the first time I've seen him out in public in a year. He only comes out for serious family matters, so his presence reaffirms that this attack is a huge fucking deal.

"Where have you been?" he asks when he sees us approaching. I don't know if he is talking to me or his brother, or both of us, but I let Boris answer.

"I don't live in the city, Vlad. It takes me a minute to get here."

"This happened an hour ago," he says angrily. "You should have been here no more than thirty minutes after that."

Boris sighs in frustration and looks around. "What happened?"

"What do you think fucking happened?" my father asks, flinging an arm at the bloodshed around us. "We had our asses handed to us by a threat *you* said you were going to handle."

"And you," he says, turning to me, a finger pointed at my chest. "What have you been doing? I take a short break to mourn my son and suddenly the sky is falling down."

"A short break?" I snort. "You've been checked out for years. The only reason this family is still standing is because of me."

Boris takes one look at the two of us staring daggers at each other and walks away without saying a word.

As soon as he is gone, I turn back to my father. "I didn't even know about the rival family until I arrived in St. Petersburg. Care to explain that? Care to explain to me why I was kept in the dark about one of our biggest threats?"

"Boris told me they weren't a threat," my father growls. He runs a hand down his face, stretching his eyelid down, and I recognize the move as one I make often. "Plus, Mikhail was helping him deal with it."

I roll my eyes. "You wanted to believe Mikhail was helping Boris deal with it, but we all know he wasn't doing shit."

My father narrows his eyes. "Watch your mouth when you're talking about my son."

"I'm your son, too!" I scream, drawing the attention of a few of the injured men around us.

I clear my throat and fold my hands in front of me, trying to regain my composure. "I'm the son who has cleaned up mess after mess for

Mikhail. I'm the son who has always corrected Mikhail's mistakes and never once complained about the fact that you clearly preferred him. As much as you hate to admit it, I'm the son who has a head for this business, and as of now, I'm the only son you have left."

I expect my father to scream at me. To rage against my attacks on Mikhail. It would be no less than I deserve. I've never said any of this to him. Hell, I haven't been this honest with my father since the day I was born.

But to my surprise, his shoulders slump forward. "You're right."

I'm too stunned to comprehend what he is saying. "I am?"

He sighs. "Partially, yes."

"What part exactly?" I ask, still not letting my guard down. I've been blindsided by my father enough times to know I need to remain vigilant.

"I've always had a soft spot for Mikhail," he says. "He was the one who would take over after me, so I wanted to take him under my wing. From a young age, I could see the differences between you two. You were so much like your mother, logical and pragmatic, but Mikhail was like me. Like me when I was young, at least. I thought that, with time, he would mature. I thought he would become the kind of leader I grew into."

"You babied him. You made him soft."

"I know," he says, jaw clenching. "I thought a firm hand would crush his enthusiasm. I thought that if he lived wild and free for a while, he'd grow tired of it and clean himself up. Clearly, I thought wrong."

"We all did," I say, trying to comfort him. "I assumed he would grow up eventually."

He nods. "And I guess, in coddling him, I kicked you out of the nest too soon. But you always knew how to handle yourself and other people. You never seemed to need my help, so I stopped offering it. I thought it would be better to leave you on your own and allow you to do your work."

"A little appreciation would have been nice," I say. "It would still be nice."

My father looks down at the ground and then up at me, his face pained. "You do good work, Aleksandr."

I don't know what to say. Moments ago, we were screaming at one another. And now?

We haven't healed a lifetime of wounds, but we have made a start. And that is far more than I expected.

I give him a quick, tight smile and then turn towards the wrecked warehouse. The ceiling is still smoking and most of the windows are blown out. Heat rolls off of the building like a campfire.

"What are we going to do about our rivals?" I ask.

My father presses a hand to his forehead, observing the damage, and shrugs. "We have to strike back. Hard. We can't let this go unpunished."

"Do we know what they want?" I ask. "They sent me a message to 'back off' through a maid at Boris' estate last week, but what does that mean?"

"To back off of our territory?" he suggests.

"Maybe. Or maybe to back off of finding out who they are?" I offer. "Because we don't know who they are, right?"

"Right. Boris said he was close to figuring it out, but nothing has been confirmed yet."

I shake my head. "Something about all of this seems strange. We've made no moves to attack them, so why would they use such a show of force? Why would they start a war if we don't even know who they are?"

"Precisely because we don't know who they are," my father says. "We can't attack because we don't who they are or where they operate from. It would be like fighting a ghost."

He is right. Which means we are completely screwed. "So, what do we do?"

Before he can answer, my phone rings. The number is unknown, but given what just happened with the warehouse, I don't want to risk missing anything important. So, I answer.

"Hello, Aleksandr." The voice is low and clearly manipulated in some way, making it unrecognizable.

Immediately, I pull it away from my ear and put my phone on speaker phone. "Who is this?"

"That is not the right question."

My father and I make eye contact over the phone. We both know this is them.

The men who did this.

"What is the right question?" I ask.

The voice hums, the voice manipulation software turning the sound into a garble of staticky buzz. "How about 'where is she?' That's a good question to ask."

My heart stutters in my chest.

Zoya.

The rival family went after her before. For some reason, they thought she meant something to me then, so they tried to send me a message through her. Now, she means much more to me and they just blew up an entire warehouse. How much worse would they do to Zoya?

"Where is she?" I growl, squeezing the phone so tightly I'm surprised it doesn't shatter. "What did you do with her?"

"Who?" my father mouths. I know he is thinking about my mother. If it weren't for Zoya, that is where my mind would have gone, too.

"Where is Zoya?" I ask.

"She's alive," the voice says, clearly amused by my reaction. "She is with us, and unless you want her to die, you'll turn yourself over."

"Turn myself over to who?"

"Ah ah," the voice warns. "That is not the right question, either."

I growl, frustration bubbling up. "Enough with the fucking games. What do you want?"

"You. On your knees." There is a long pause. I hear what sounds like other voices in the background, but they are all too far away and garbled to make anything specific out. "Be ready to surrender in twenty-four hours. I'll send you the address."

"What if I don't?" I ask.

"If you don't show up, then I'll kill her and her baby." There is a low, sadistic chuckle. "See you tomorrow."

I stare at the phone even after the line goes dead, hoping for more information. Once I realize I'm not going to get it, I call Zoya. Her phone rings and rings and rings. We got in a fight this morning, but I have to assume she'd still answer my calls. If she isn't, it means something must be wrong. It means she really has been taken.

"Who is Zoya?" my father asks.

"The maid," I explain, telling him about the attack on her earlier in the week and that she has been staying with me. "They wanted to send me a message by hurting her, so I kept her at Boris' estate."

"Did she leave the property?" he asks. "Because she should have been safe there. No one should have been able to get to her."

"I don't know." I dial her number again, even though I know she won't answer. "I don't think she would leave."

But I don't know for sure. We fought just before I left. Nothing had been determined, but we hadn't left on good terms. Maybe she was going to bail and run away. Based on the apartment she had in St. Petersburg, she didn't have many options, but maybe she preferred that shitty place to being with me.

Or maybe she was leaving to come and find me. To explain things to me since I didn't listen the first time.

Either way, I have to help her.

Whether we are going to be together or not.

Whether the baby is Mikhail's or not.

None of it matters. I can't let her die.

My phone buzzes, and I look down, desperately hoping it will be a message from Zoya. It isn't. It's a text from a private number with an address. My father looks at my phone.

"I know that place. It's in the middle of nowhere. You can't go."

"What do you mean?" I ask. "What other choice do we have?"

He looks at me like I'm crazy. "We have the choice where you don't get slaughtered."

"They are going to kill her," I explain, wondering if he overheard the same conversation I did.

"Who cares?" he asks, throwing his arms out. "She is some random woman, and you are my heir."

I want to tell him that the title means nothing to me, but it seems like a good way to ruin our still very unsteady relationship. So, I try to appeal to his concerns.

"You heard them say she was pregnant?" I ask. He nods. "Well, the baby is Mikhail's."

My father stops, his face growing serious. "How do you know?"

"It doesn't matter how," I say. "She is carrying a Levushka. The next generation of Levushkas, and if we don't stop them, they'll kill her."

He shakes his head. "They could kill you. What about that?"

He doesn't get it, and I'm frustrated. Frustrated that I left Zoya this morning, that she got captured, and that any of this is happening in the first place. If they had threatened me with almost anything else, I wouldn't have cared. But Zoya? I can't let them hurt Zoya.

"I don't care," I admit. "I'll gladly go and die if it means saving her."

"Aleksandr," he pleads, grabbing my arm. "You aren't thinking."

"I am," I shout back. "For the first time, I'm thinking perfectly clearly."

Just then, Boris walks up, looking back and forth between us, his forehead wrinkled. "What is going on?"

My father turns to his brother. "Talk some sense into him, Boris. He is losing his head over a woman."

"Zoya?" Boris asks.

"You know who she is?" my father asks. "These rat motherfuckers have her, and they want to exchange her for Aleksandr."

Boris opens his mouth to say something, but he has made his feelings about Zoya perfectly clear when we left the estate. Plus, if Zoya is to be believed, he wasn't kind to her after she returned to the estate, either. His opinion means nothing to me.

"You aren't going to change my mind," I say. "I love her."

The reality of the words washes over me as I say them.

I do love Zoya.

I love her fire, the way she stands up to me and challenges me. But I also love the tender way she cares for the people she loves. She is loyal—to her family, her friends, her employers. Zoya possesses all of the qualities I most wish I could emulate myself, and the idea of losing her to such senseless violence is impossible to bear. I won't let it happen.

"I love her," I repeat. "And I'll do whatever I can to save her."

17

ZOYA

Waking up feels like fighting my way through a thick curtain. The material presses in on me, warm and suffocating, and no matter how hard I try, I can't see anything. My eyelids are practically glued together, and forcing them open starts a deep, painful ache at the back of my head.

I lift my hand to touch my skull and make sure it isn't split open, but my arm is rubber. Moving it feels like someone is lifting my arm by a puppet string, out of my control. I probe the back of my head with my fingers, running them slowly across my scalp. I don't feel anything damp or sticky, which means no blood, but there is a massive, tender bump.

That is when I remember the crack on the back of my head.

As if electrified, my eyes snap open, and I sit up.

Immediately, my head swims, but I plant my arms on the floor on either side of myself to stay propped up as I find my bearings.

The room around me is dark, but there is enough light leaking in from a window across the room that I can make out the fuzzy details.

It appears to be a log cabin. The walls are long horizontal planks of wood with no décor or anything that could help me distinguish whose cabin I'm in. There is a sofa and a chair near a fireplace to my right and a small kitchen with an island to the left. A set of stairs behind me leads to a second floor and a door to the left of the fireplace leads to what I expect is a bathroom.

A lack of sound from outside suggests a remote location, at least far from a road, though, based on the cabin, I suspect a wooded area.

I'm alone and untied.

But why?

My vision swirls as I try to stand, but I don't want to be caught laying down when whoever brought me here returns. They surprised me once in the hallway back at Boris' estate, but I won't let it happen again.

I pat my pocket for my phone but don't feel anything. I'm not surprised they've taken it, but I curse them for not being quite as dumb as I'd hoped.

The front door is in the kitchen. There is a fluttery yellow curtain hanging over the single pane of glass in the door, not allowing me any vantage point out unless I pull back the material. But since I'm untied, I have to assume I'm being monitored someway.

I spin in a circle, looking for a camera, but don't see anything. Then, I turn back to the door.

If I don't try to escape, I'll never forgive myself. Even if I get caught, it would be better than waiting for my captor to return. So, I reach for the curtain.

Just before grabbing it, however, I spin back into the kitchen and pull open a few drawers. There are no steak knives or butcher knives, but I find a butter knife and a fork, which will have to do. I hold both utensils in the same hand and move back towards the door.

Using the tip of the knife, I slide it beneath the curtain and pull it back gently, just a crack. Just enough to see out of.

I lean forward to see who or what might be on the other side, but as soon as the fabric moves an inch, the door handle turns and the door opens inward.

Rather than launching an attack, I stumble backwards, clutching the cutlery to my chest.

"You're awake!" The man in front of me is short, barely taller than I am, and thin. If he'd been in the room with me when I'd woken up, I may have thought he was being held captive, too. He looks gaunt. "Good."

I press my back flat against the wall. "Who are you?"

"Ah, introductions," he says with a smile. Deep lines form around his mouth and eyes. "My name is Cyrus."

I recognize the name but not the face. "Why am I here?"

He pulls a gun from a holster on his hip and points it at me, using it to gesture to the silverware in my hands. "Drop your...weapons."

I know the fork and knife would have done little to protect me, but it still makes me feel vulnerable to lay them down. As soon as I do, Cyrus kicks them away and then seems to relax, his shoulders easing down.

"You are here because of your connection with the Levushka family."

"I was a maid!" I shout, frustrated that no one seems to understand exactly how little of a role I had in the family. "And I was fired, so I'm not even that anymore."

"Right," he agrees. "You are much more than that now. Now, you are Aleksandr Levushka's girl."

I shake my head. "I'm not so sure about that."

Cyrus frowns and then looks at my belly. "Rumor is you are pregnant with a Levushka. Is that true?"

I don't want to be caught in a lie, but I also don't want to admit the truth. So, I say nothing.

He snorts. "I thought so. Well, *that* is why you are here."

"What are you going to do to me?" I slide down the wall, further away from him, but before I can move too far, Cyrus steps forward and cuts me off, slamming his hand against the wall next to my head.

"According to my boss, nothing," he says, his eyes tracing my face and sliding down my body. "But what he doesn't know won't hurt him."

My heart jolts in my chest. "Who is your boss?"

I need to remind him of his duty. Of what he stands to lose if he disobeys. That is the only chance I have of not being beaten or worse.

He shakes his head. "That is none of your business."

"Clearly, it isn't the Levushkas," I say, my voice shaking. "So, you must work for the rival family that has risen up in St. Petersburg."

He is silent, which I take as an admission.

"That's what I thought," I say. "They are ruthless. Violent."

He grins. "I'm flattered you've heard of us. Two weeks ago, Aleksandr didn't even know we existed. We've come a long way."

I furrow my brow. "You know Aleksandr?"

His smile widens. "For years now."

"Do you work for the Levushkas?" I cycle through my memories, trying to figure out where I've heard his name before. There was so much business talk happening all the time in Boris' house that I hardly paid any attention. The less I knew about the details of their work, the better. It meant I wouldn't be an asset to their enemies. Though, clearly, that plan had failed.

"I did," he says. "Aleksandr relished his power over me. He humiliated me for years. Even his fuck-up brother, Mikhail, spoke down to me. I smuggled weapons for their family for the better part of a decade, and they never had a kind word to say about me."

Cyrus. The weapons importer. I'd heard Samara mention Boris meeting with him in his office before. She had to make lunch for them. I never saw him face-to-face, though.

"So, when the opportunity arose for me to take my skills elsewhere, I didn't hesitate. It happened slowly over the course of almost a year, but finally, we are ready to take control of St. Petersburg."

"What does any of that have to do with me?" I ask. "I don't have any information if that is what you want. I don't know anything."

"You aren't here for information, sweetheart." Cyrus steps forward, his bony knee rubbing against the outside of my thigh. The touch sends chills straight to my core. He tilts his face to the side and lifts a hand, hovering just over my skin without touching me. "But with a pretty face like that, you will fetch a high price. Perhaps, even, the life of Vlad Levushka's only remaining son."

His words hit me like a physical blow, and I have to suck in a breath of air to keep from passing out. "You are going to kill Aleksandr?"

"That is the plan," he says, grinning. "He is going to surrender his life to save yours."

"No," I say, shaking my head. "No, he won't. He doesn't want me. We aren't together."

I say the words because I want them to be true, not because I'm convinced they are. Aleksandr might come for me. Even after our fight this morning, he might come for me simply because I am carrying his brother's child. He has sacrificed every part of himself to keep his family together, so why wouldn't he sacrifice his life?

The horrible truth is that he would.

Cyrus shrugs. "Even if he doesn't, we still have you. Aleksandr's treatment of me makes this situation all the better. To have his woman under my control. Even if he doesn't die, what sweeter justice could there be?"

My legs are shaking, knees knocking together, and it is a wonder I'm still standing.

Cyrus raises an eyebrow and appraises me, his gaze hungry. Then, he steps back. "I'll give you a few minutes to collect your thoughts."

He walks out the front door, and as soon as the door shuts behind him, I collapse to the floor.

~

Cyrus is gone for an hour, and I'm grateful he gave me the time alone to think.

I cried for a few minutes before I heard Aleksandr's voice in my head telling me to get up and do something useful. *Crying won't help, so find something to do that will.*

By the time Cyrus unlocks the door and steps inside, it is dusk, and I have a plan.

Crickets chirp loudly when he opens the door. I can still hear them when it is closed, but the sound is muffled, far away.

He drops a duffel bag by the door and then a plastic bag of basic groceries on the table—bread, cheese, and fruit—and tells me to eat if I want.

I lunge for the food and tear into it immediately, ripping hunks of bread from the loaf before I turn and smile at him. "Thank you for the food."

Cyrus stares at me a moment before his suspicion fades away. He lifts his chin and nods. "You're welcome."

The bread is stale and the fruit is soft, but I let small moans escape as I eat, writhing in the kitchen chair like I'm eating the best meal I've ever had.

"Is it good?" he asks, eyes trained on me from across the table.

I hum. "So good." I grab a strawberry and hold it out to him. "Do you want a bite?"

He leans forward slightly, looking tempted, but then shakes his head. "No. You eat it."

I smile, pressing my tongue to the back of my teeth, and then bring the strawberry to my mouth. As best as I can, I make love to the fruit. My lips wrap around the base of it, pouting out as I bite through it and juice runs over my lower lip. I could be imagining it, but I think I hear Cyrus groan.

I wipe my hand across my mouth and then giggle, juice dripping down my fingers. "Could I have a napkin?"

Cyrus looks annoyed, but doesn't hesitate to stand up and grab a dish towel from next to the sink. As he turns to toss it to me, I see the gun at his right hip. His shirt is tucked in behind the holster, so he can easily access the gun.

That means I can easily access it, as well.

I wipe my mouth and push away from the table. "Thank you, Cyrus. That was delicious."

He smiles, but his eyes pinch together quickly. I'm laying it on too thick. He is getting suspicious.

"Can I shower?" I ask, standing up and pointing towards the bathroom.

Cyrus starts to shake his head, but I grab the collar of my shirt and tug it away from my skin, revealing an "accidental" amount of cleavage. "I feel absolutely filthy. It would be incredible to rinse off."

I'm not lying. I feel sticky from the lack of air flow in the cabin, and it would be nice to rinse off the dust from laying on the floor so long.

He narrows his eyes. "You won't try anything funny?"

I shake my head innocently. "No."

He lets me shower, though insists he stand outside the door to keep watch.

"No peeking," I warn as I close the door. Though, I purposefully don't let the latch catch so the door pops open a tiny bit.

I pause in front of the sink and take stock of my appearance in the dusty mirror. Dark circles are pressed under my eyes and my hair is in long tangles, but otherwise, I look okay. My breasts have already started filling out because of the pregnancy hormones, which is only helping me in my attempt to seduce and distract Cyrus.

I've only been in the bathroom for a minute, and I can already see his shadow creeping into the crack of the door.

I stretch my arms up and tip my head back, stretching my spine. "How long have you been working for the rival family?"

As soon as I start speaking, he darts back from the doorway, which lets me know that no matter what Cyrus says, I am in charge. As my captor, he shouldn't be afraid of being caught by me.

"Like I said, almost a year," he says.

"Oh, right. And are you still just a weapons importer? That is what you did for the Levushkas, right?"

"It was an important job," he says, sounding defensive. "I supplied their army and gave them the ability to defend themselves. That is no small role."

"Absolutely not," I say. "They didn't appreciate you."

"Vlad and his two boys think their shit doesn't stink, but now I'll be able to show them what I am really made of. Now, I am a brigadier."

"Wow." I don't have to pretend to be surprised. The fact that anyone would look at Cyrus and consider him physically or mentally capable of being second to the boss is baffling to me.

I pull back the shower curtain, and then look over my shoulder. Cyrus darts away from the crack of the door quickly, not wanting me to see him watching.

Quickly, I step inside and pull the shower curtain closed. I slide out of my jeans and throw them over the shower rod. Then, I pull my shirt over my head and throw it over the top, letting it flutter to the floor.

"It is nice to finally be respected," Cyrus says, his voice clearer than it was only a minute before. He is in the bathroom with me now.

"I'm sure," I say, reluctantly peeling my bra and panties off and reaching around the curtain to drop them on the floor.

I hear a slight rustling on the other side of the curtain and know without looking that Cyrus has bent down to pick them up. He is growing bolder. More confident.

Good.

I turn the shower on and the water comes out freezing cold. I have to bite my lip to keep in a shriek.

"Maybe you'll come around and realize those Levushka men have been using you, as well," Cyrus says. His voice is just outside the curtain now. I can see his shadow creeping up the aging yellow vinyl.

"Maybe," I purr. "Crazier things have happened."

"That they have." I see his hand stretch for the edge of the curtain, and I know this is my one and only shot to get the hell out of this cabin.

Just as his fingers appear at the edge of the curtain, I spring forward with my arms and legs out like a ninja. Cyrus lets out a whoosh of air as the full force of me hits him square in the chest. The curtain is between us, keeping him from clawing at me or fighting as effectively as he normally would, so I use it to my advantage.

We stumble backward, Cyrus slamming into the bathroom wall, and I grab two handfuls of the vinyl material and wrap it around his round head.

Immediately, he opens his mouth to inhale and the curtain fills his mouth. Without air, he begins to panic, thrashing around, and I know I won't be able to hold on much longer. Not long enough to actually suffocate him, anyway. So, I drop my feet to the floor and use the extra leverage to shove him harder against the wall.

His arms wrap around me, squeezing tight enough that it is hard to inhale properly, but that is okay. Now, I know where his hands are. And they aren't anywhere near his waist.

My heart is hammering so hard in my chest I'm sure Cyrus can hear it, but my entire body is thrumming with adrenaline. I feel more in control of myself than I ever have before. My thoughts are clear, and I know what I have to do.

I count to three slowly in my head and on the final count, I pull the curtain away from his face and let it drop between us at the same time my knee connects with his groin.

Cyrus's face is red and purple and splotchy, and his mouth is open in a silent scream of agony. I'm completely naked and dripping wet, clinging to him like my life depends on it. Perhaps if my life didn't depend on it, I'd be able to laugh at how ridiculous we look.

He seems stunned by our predicament, as well. Once he can see me, his eyes widen, and he freezes for just a second. Just long enough for me to reach around his arm and grab blindly at the right side of his hip. Cyrus' face lights up with realization, but by the time he understands what I am doing, it is too late.

The gun is in my hand, and I push away from him with all of my strength, which is more than enough to overpower his hold on my waist. Naked and dripping wet, I aim the gun at his chest.

"Sit down."

Without hesitation, Cyrus drops to the floor with his hands held over his head. "Don't do anything you'll regret."

"Stop talking," I bark.

He pinches his lips together and nods his head quickly, looking more like he is vibrating than anything else.

I shake the gun in his face. "Move, and I will kill you."

He nods again, and I step backwards out of the bathroom and into the living room without ever taking my eyes off of him. I move around the sofa and into the kitchen where the duffel bag he came back with is laying on the floor. With my eyes still on Cyrus, I kick the bag through the house and to the bathroom door.

I unzip it and am relieved to see it is exactly what I hoped it was.

A hit bag.

Rope, zip ties, hand cuffs, a blindfold, and tape. Everything a person could want or need to hold someone hostage with.

I slide my finger over the trigger and nod to the bag. "Put the handcuffs on."

Cyrus grabs them and slips one of his wrists in. When he moves to put in the other, I shake my head. "Behind your back."

"Come on, Zoya," he says as he slides his hands around to his back. "You aren't a killer. Don't do this."

"Why do you think I'm handcuffing you?" I ask. "I'm not going to kill you. Not if you do exactly what I say."

All at once, he seems to relax, and I realize why Cyrus could so easily betray the Levushkas after so many years of working together. Because he only cares about surviving. Loyalty means nothing to him in the face of his own death.

As soon as his hands are bound behind his back, I order him to zip tie his ankles. Sure to keep the gun out of his reach, I lean down and tighten the zip ties until I'm certain he can't break free, but he also won't lose circulation.

"Turn around," I order, tired of his bloodshot eyes perusing my naked body. Even in dire straits, he can't help himself.

I check the handcuffs, tightening them each another notch, and then step back. For the first time since I walked into the bathroom, I take a deep breath.

While Cyrus tries to make himself comfortable on the floor, I get dressed one-handed, never putting the gun down. I decide against the bra simply because it would require both hands.

While I'm buttoning my jeans, Cyrus laughs. "Are you proud of yourself?"

I shrug. "A bit, yeah."

"Well, enjoy it," he says. "It won't last."

I grab a length of rope from the duffel bag and throw it over my shoulder and a handful of zip ties and shove them in my back pocket.

"Thanks for the tip." I salute him as I leave the bathroom.

"I'm serious," he calls. "Every road away from this cabin is being monitored. You'll probably be shot on sight if you try to leave."

I don't know if he is telling the truth, but I know one thing for certain: if I stay in this cabin, I'll be killed. Better a probable death than a certain one.

I slip through the door in the kitchen and into the dark of night, leaving the cabin and the traitor far, far behind.

18

ALEKSANDR

I spend all night and the next day plotting with my father on how to get Zoya back. Boris is in and out all day, helping the plans when he can, but mostly he deals with clean up from the warehouse explosion and organizes for additional men to be brought in from nearby towns to help. The more unfamiliar faces we can have in our operation, the better.

"I'm not sure you need to surrender yourself at all," my father says for what feels like the hundredth time. "It seems like an unnecessary risk."

"Doing anything to deviate from their demands is a risk," I argue. "At this point, we have no reason to believe they aren't going to do exactly what they say. And right now, they say they will hand over Zoya if I turn myself over."

"Bullshit," my father barks. "Absolute bullshit. They carried out an unprovoked attack on one of our warehouses. We are no longer operating within the bounds of good faith. We can't trust them."

"And we won't."

"Damn right we won't," Boris says, shoving his phone in his pocket and taking a seat at our round table. His estate has become our home base. Even my father left the usual comforts of his house to plan with us here. An attack like this on our family, especially on our own turf, is unprecedented. It has to be dealt with immediately.

Everyone in the house has been nervous since Zoya was taken. No one saw what happened to her, so there are too many questions left unanswered for anyone to relax. Samara has been baking nonstop all night, and Zoya's mother has paced the distance between her cottage and the main estate so many times I'm surprised there isn't a path worn in the grass.

Boris grabs a muffin from the batch Samara made for breakfast and eats it in two bites, crumbs spilling down the front of his shirt. "We are going to have men backing you up on every side, Aleksandr."

"You have reinforcements?" my father asks.

My uncle nods. "People are coming in from all over the place to help. We will have a small army here by lunch, and they'll be ready to move by this afternoon."

"I have to be at the address they gave me by mid-afternoon." I check my watch. Only four hours to go. "Will they be ready by then?"

"They'll be ready," he assures me. Then, he leans in, one eyebrow raised. "But are we sure this bitch is worth the trouble?"

My father gestures for my uncle to hold his tongue, but the low growl that rumbles from my chest is enough for Boris to raise his hands in surrender and back down.

"Fine. Fine. I'm just making sure," he says. "If we are going to lose good men today, I want to make sure it is for a good reason."

"We aren't going to lose anyone." I ripped a map of St. Petersburg from an atlas in the library and used it to mark our plans. I pull it towards me and point to the two biggest ports of entry for criminal goods into the city. "We are going to attack here and here. There are trustworthy sources saying that this is where some outspoken enemies have been making deals. If they are right, then we'll cut their numbers into thirds. They will be so busy dealing with the attacks that they won't be able to defend the home base."

"And if you're wrong?" Boris asks.

"Then I'll die," I say simply.

My father clenches his fist and pounds it on the table. "That can't be the only alternative."

"It has to be unless we want innocent men to die instead," I say.

"*You* are an innocent man," he argues, reaching out to grab my forearm. "There has to be a way to negotiate with them that doesn't put you in direct risk."

I pat my father's hand, surprised by his gentleness, and shake my head. "There isn't."

"He's right, Vlad." Boris pulls the map closer and studies it, his eyes memorizing the movements of our men. "The rivals want Aleksandr, and they won't talk unless he shows his face."

"And like Boris said, I won't be alone," I say. "It will look like I am, but there will be men ready and waiting in the trees all around the meeting location. As soon as Zoya is handed over, they'll attack, and I'll get her out of there."

I can still see the hesitation in my father's face. Even in the height of his leadership, he never involved himself much with the planning of missions. He had always seen himself as the figurehead, but Boris was the brains. So, as much as he wants to continue to protest, he knows any plan put together by Boris is the best option.

Just like Boris said, the reinforcements arrive shortly after lunch. They call Boris to confirm their placement near the meeting site and inform him they await his command. And thirty minutes before the scheduled meeting, Boris orders the men to take position and then slaps a hand on my back.

"Take care of yourself, nephew."

"You too, uncle." I clap a hand on his shoulder and pull him in for a hug. "Thank you for your help. We needed you today."

"Of course," he says. "You know it has always been my pleasure to work in the background."

When my father appears in the driveway, hands folded politely behind his back, Boris slips back into the house to give us a moment.

I don't have any plans of dying today, but for some strange reason, standing in front of my father feels like saying goodbye.

"I'll be back in a couple hours," I say lightly, shrugging off the dread that seems to be pressing down on me.

"I know you will," my father says. "You always come back when you say you will. You are dependable that way."

I smile, hearing all of the words he left unspoken. The years of feeling unseen and unappreciated. He is acknowledging them and trying to do better, and it is all I could ever ask of him.

When I make it to the end of the long driveway, I look in the rearview mirror, and he is still standing there in the gravel, watching me go.

～

The address I was sent is east of the city, deep in a pocket of trees that seem to crowd the narrow road more and more the further I drive. The sun should be just west of the highest point in the sky, but I can't see it through the heavy foliage. Only the car's headlights allow me to cut through the murky shadows and see the road.

Finally, there is a turn in the road and the trees begin to thin.

Dappled light covers the dirt road, and if I wasn't heading towards such a daunting meeting, it may have been pretty.

Instead, the beautiful day feels like a taunt.

I haven't heard a word from the people who have Zoya since the call yesterday morning, and I am desperate to see her. To see that she is okay and safe.

I study the trees as I pass, hoping to see a flash of movement that would signal the presence of the reinforcements Boris called, but I see nothing. I know that means they are staying hidden and doing their jobs, but it would make me feel better to know I'm not heading into this situation alone.

The tree line falls away all at once without warning, and I'm driving through the middle of a large circular opening, surrounded on all sides by forest. I'm exposed.

The plan was always to drive straight into the altercation with the rival family. To turn myself over and then fight my way out, but everything about the situation feels wrong now that I'm actually doing it. For the first time, I wonder whether my father wasn't right.

Then, I crest a small hill and see a cabin to the right.

It has to be where Zoya is being held. It is the only manmade structure I've seen in almost half an hour. So, I push aside my doubts, turn off of the road, and head towards the house.

I wait in the car, the engine rumbling, but there is no movement beyond the small windows of the cabin or in the surrounding trees. I slowly turn off the ignition and open the car door. All is quiet, and I wonder whether I've come to the wrong place.

Then, I hear a crunch of grass behind me, but before I can turn around, there is a cold press of metal to the back of my neck.

"Step away from the car."

The voice sounds familiar to me, but I am too stunned to place it. I move away from the car, my hands raised in surrender.

"I'm listening," I say. "I'm doing what you ask."

"Oh, I know you are." The loud crack of laughter is even more familiar than the voice, and a chill runs through me.

"Boris?"

~

My uncle walks a tight circle around me until we are face to face. He is smiling from ear to ear. "You fucking idiot."

My head is trying to make sense of what I'm seeing and hearing, but it is like trying to solve a crossword in another language. There are too many hurdles to jump through, too many questions to answer. So, instead, I just shake my head.

"You let me plan every part of this surrender," he says, still laughing. "You might as well have handed me your head on a silver platter."

Boris is the same square, meaty man I've always known, but he looks different now. Sinister.

His features are twisted in malice, his top lip curled back.

"Does my father know?" I ask, trying to understand how deep this conspiracy goes. If Boris has betrayed me, then there is no telling how many people have.

Zoya?

The thought crosses my mind. She was a major distraction for me in the last couple of weeks, but she never forced herself on me. I was the one who chased after her.

No, if Zoya is working for Boris, then she must have brainwashed me because I followed her willingly.

"Your father?" Boris asks licking his lips like a dog before a meal. He leans forward, teeth bared. "He knows."

I close my eyes, not wanting Boris to see how much this revelation hurts me.

My own father?

Over the last two days, we'd become closer than we ever had been. It felt like we were turning a corner together. And now, I realize it was all part of an act. A scheme. I feel sick.

"Well, he *knew*," Boris says, bobbing his head side to side. "He figured it out when I pressed a gun to his head."

I snap my eyes open and glare at him. "You killed him?"

He nods, lips pressed together in a smug smile. "Just after you left the estate. He didn't see it coming, either."

The information is coming at me too quickly, and I can't keep up. I know that is what Boris wants—to overwhelm me, weaken me until I'm compliant. I have to fight against the urge to shut down. Because somewhere, I hope, Zoya is still waiting for me.

"Where is Zoya?" I ask, putting all of my energy towards her. I have to channel it; otherwise, the series of losses I've suffered in the last two weeks will overwhelm me. First Mikhail, now my father. It's too much, and if I let it overwhelm me, I'll be dead, too. "Where is she?"

Boris rolls his eyes. "God. Can we forget about the bitch for one fucking second? I thought we were having a moment here. Uncle to nephew, you know?"

He steps forward and lays his meaty hand on my shoulder. I shrug away from his touch, and he shakes the gun in my face, reminding me who is in charge. When he puts his hand on my shoulder a second time, I don't shift away.

"Don't you want to know why I did it?" he whispers conspiratorially. "Aren't you interested in why I'd turn my back on you and kill my own brother?"

"Not especially," I say. Not now, at least. Now, I only care about getting away from him and finding Zoya.

"Well, I'm going to tell you, anyway," he sighs. "I've been waiting a long, *long* time to say what I really think, and I'm not quite ready for the moment to be over."

"You never did know when to shut up."

Before the words are even out of my mouth, the handle of the gun cracks across the side of my face. It feels like my cheek has exploded. Blood fills my mouth, and I lean forward, hands on my knees to keep from falling over.

Boris grabs the back of my shirt and lifts me up. "It is my turn to talk, nephew. *Listen.*"

He releases my shirt, letting me sag forward, but I do my best to stand tall. I've seen Boris torture men before. He feeds on weakness. Any sign of it will be like blood in the water. Regardless of his plans, he won't be able to keep himself from striking out again.

"Your father never appreciated me," he says, shaking his head, his eyes focused on some point in the distance. "He was older than me, which meant he would become the boss. I knew that growing up. I accepted it, even though I was the one better suited for the position. But then it happened, and he relied on me for everything. I was his second, but I made all of the decisions, while he received all of the glory. It was maddening."

I'd never considered the fact that my uncle and I shared the same position in the family. We were both second-born sons, more responsible and suited to leadership than our elder brothers. I'd grown up resenting my status in the family with no thought for how my uncle must feel.

But there is no pity in my heart for him.

"Then, he had sons," Boris says, glaring at me. "Two boys who ensured I would never see the top of our Family, even if I killed him. So, after years of living in the shadows, I decided to take what was rightfully mine. I decided to organize my own family, one in which I would be at the top, and overthrow my brother once and for all."

"He trusted you. We all did."

Boris shrugs. "That is no fault of mine. If a life of crime has not taught you to trust no one than yourself, then it only shows you were not suited for it."

"I should be able to trust family," I say.

He waves his arms. "I have a family."

I look around and realize men have stepped forward out of the trees. I couldn't see them as I pulled up to the cabin, but now that the truth was out in the open, they'd revealed themselves.

Boris's men walk in from the trees and gather behind him, forming a line between me and the cabin. Is Zoya inside? Can she see what was happening? Does she know I would come for her?

"You think you can trust them?" I ask. "You think you can trust them more than your own blood?"

"The blood of the covenant is thicker than the water of the womb," he says. "Did you know that is the true origin of that phrase? It means that the blood we shed in battle and the vows we make are more important than the families we are born into. It means," he says, leaning forward, his acrid breath washing over my face, "that these men are more my family than you ever were."

"Why do all of this?" I ask. "Why kidnap Zoya and bring me out to this cabin to surrender? Why not just murder us all in our beds? Clearly, we trusted you enough that it would have been an easy process for you. So, why the theatrics?"

His eyebrows flick up in excitement. "Good question, Alekasndr. You see, I knew killing you all would be the easiest way to get rid of you, but it wouldn't get me what I wanted."

"And what did you want?"

"Power," he says quickly. "I wanted to be powerful and for people to see that. So, I had to fool you all. I had to show my men that you would throw yourself down on the sword for a whoring maid and that your father would agree to it because he didn't know any better. I had to show everyone that I was capable of overthrowing the most powerful crime family in all of Russia by kidnapping one worthless slut. I needed people to see just how easily I could tear down your house of cards."

I can see it now, of course. All of the small signs I missed. All of the meetings Boris attended without my knowledge. The way he attempted to convince me the rival family in St. Petersburg was truly nothing to worry about.

Boris succeeded in proving to not only his men, but to me, as well, that the Levushka family was foolish and weak. Because we were. I was.

But if I make it out of this situation alive, I never will be again.

"Have you killed Zoya?" I ask. "If this was all just a show to prove that you are smarter than all of us, is she still alive?"

"Your desires are so singular," he groans. "At what point will you give up this puppy dog crush and fend for yourself?"

I don't answer him, so he sighs and waves a hand over his head.

Immediately, the men behind him part, allowing me to see the front door of the cabin. Two of them break away and march inside.

"She is still alive," he says.

Relief swells in my chest, threatening to lift me off of the ground. As long as Zoya is breathing, I have hope. I have a purpose.

"Don't get too excited." He leans closer, looking at me from beneath his bushy brows. "She won't be alive for long. And I'm sorry to say, her last moments aren't likely to be her best."

The momentary relief turns to a brick in my chest, crashing into my abdomen. "What are you going to do?"

"I'm going to find out why you and your brother were so infatuated with this woman," he says with a vulgar thrust of his hips. "She must be one hell of a fuck for you to turn yourself in for her. I want to know what I'm missing."

Rage turns my veins to ice and my vision is red. I step forward, and Boris lifts his gun and clicks his tongue. "Come on, Aleksandr. Calm down. You don't want to miss the show."

I don't care about the gun or what it will do to me. I just want to wrap my hands around Boris's neck. Even for a second. Even if I die in the process, it would be a good way to go. And I've nearly convinced myself to do it—anything to keep him from touching Zoya—when the men come out of the cabin with a person hanging like a sack of potatoes between them.

Except, that person isn't Zoya.

It's Cyrus.

Boris turns, excited to see his plan play out, but when he spots the weapon importer, his smile slips, and he curses under his breath.

"Where the fuck is she?"

The men shake their head, and I can't help but smile.

She got away.

19

ZOYA

Unfortunately, Cyrus had been telling the truth about the armed guards blocking every possible exit away from the cabin. In the woods, I was hidden, but any attempt to follow a road away from the cabin would have resulted in almost immediate capture, and possible death. So, I stayed hidden.

My childhood days of climbing trees proved useful as I chose a particularly thick tree just behind the cabin as my perch. Climbing it was more difficult than I remember it being when I was a kid, but I manage to find a branch thick enough to bear my weight and high enough to avoid being spotted by the patrols.

And there, I wait.

Evening turns to full dark, and I have to fight sleep. As the adrenaline from my escape wears off, fatigue like I've never known before takes over. My eyelids are heavy, drooping even as I actively try to hold them open. Eventually, I lean forward on the branch and wrap my arms around it, thinking it is better to prepare for the inevitable moment when I fall asleep and hope I don't fall to my death.

I fall asleep at some point, but I don't think it is for very long. When I startle awake, it is still pitch black, and I feel like I'm on a boat. The entire world seems to be swaying from side to side. My vision swirls and it takes me a moment to realize that it is all in my head and the world isn't actually moving underneath me.

My stomach produces a sick kind of whimper, and I realize the tiny bit of satisfaction from the bread and fruit Cyrus gave me has worn off. I'm hungry, and because of that, I'm incredibly nauseous.

Clinging to the branch, I lean over the side and throw up what little is left in my stomach. Over the next several hours, I drift into moments of restless sleep, only to awaken to the heaving of my stomach. There is nothing left to throw up, but that doesn't stop me from trying.

By the time the sun begins to creep into the sky, birds chirping in the branches around me, I'm exhausted and spent, drooping on the branch like a lifeless sloth. If Cyrus or whoever his boss is were to find me, I probably wouldn't even fight them.

From my spot in the tree, I can see the bathroom window of the cabin, and I check occasionally to see if there is any movement inside. If I did my job correctly, then Cyrus is immobilized, unable to escape. It also means he will be unable to alert anyone to my escape.

I climb down from the tree only once shortly after dawn. I go to the bathroom at the base of the tree and then climb immediately back up. I am thirsty and hungry, and I know there is still food sitting on the kitchen counter, but I don't want to risk going back into the cabin. If everything is going to go the way I think it will, Aleksandr will come for me. He will be here at some point today, and I will get out.

I just have to wait.

As the sun moves across the sky, I begin to wonder whether anyone is coming. Whether I'll be sitting in the tree for yet another night. And I'm not sure I can handle that. The thought is so upsetting that I almost break. I almost climb down and sneak into the cabin for just a nibble of cheese. Like a starving street dog, I'm desperate for even the smallest of scraps.

But just before my willpower fully gives out, I hear rustling on the ground below me.

Not even twenty paces from the base of my tree, there is a man.

He is dressed entirely in black with an assault rifle hanging from his shoulder.

I don't know if he works for the Levushka or the rival family. If he is there to search for me or to assist Aleksandr when he arrives—*if* he arrives. So, I stay quiet.

I cling to the branch and wait for the man to leave. Except, he doesn't.

He holds his position for what feels like hours, staring out on the open field in front of the cabin, not moving or saying anything. Then, finally, he shifts his feet and crouches down, lifting his weapon.

I follow the scope of his gun and see a large boxy vehicle appear on the horizon, and my heart goes wild in my chest.

Rescue.

Aleksandr.

Freedom.

The car – a Hummer, I see, as it gets closer – pulls around the cabin and then drives around to the back side. The engine turns off, and my eyes are laser focused on the driver's door, anxious to see who climbs out. If it is Aleksandr, I'm not sure I'll be able to contain myself. I'm so tired and thirsty and desperate for rescue that I might just roll from the tree and pray they he'll catch me.

Except, it isn't Aleksandr.

The man climbing out of the Hummer is Boris.

Cyrus told me specifically that Aleksandr was coming for me. That he was the person they wanted to exchange me for, so why would Boris come? Is it part of a plan? Is he there as backup?

But if he was backup, why would he drive straight up to the cabin? If he was backup, he'd be hiding in the trees like the man with the assault rifle below me.

I look over and realize that man has lowered his weapon. He is standing tall again and walks out into the pathway, waving as Boris climbs down from the large vehicle.

"Any movement?" Boris asks.

The man shakes his head. "Nothing yet. I've been here for an hour. No one has seen anything."

"Good, good," Boris nods, his hands on his wideset hips. "Aleksandr should be here soon."

Aleksandr is coming. Just like Cyrus says. He'll be here soon. I just have to wait. Just a little bit longer. He'll have a plan. I know it.

Only a few weeks ago, I would have climbed down at the sight of Boris. I would have run to him, begging for help. But now? After being fired and what he said to me in the kitchen, I'm not sure I even know who he is. So, I stay quiet and stay put, waiting for Aleksandr to arrive.

"Does he suspect anything?" the man asks.

Boris shakes his head. "Not a thing. My brother didn't, either. He trusted me until the moment I pulled the trigger."

My heart stalls in my chest. Once again, I feel like the earth is swaying beneath me.

Boris killed Vlad. He killed his own brother. Betrayed his own family.

I hear Cyrus again, complaining about the arrogance of Vlad and his sons. But never Boris. He never said a bad word about Vlad's second-hand man. Why? Because he was working for Boris.

Because Boris is the boss of the rival family.

I feel for the gun I stole from Cyrus, stashed in the waistband of my jeans, but I know I can't use it. As much as I want to, it would only bring more soldiers out of the trees. Even if I could manage to kill Boris, I would be overpowered or run out of bullets before I could escape. And still yet, that would do nothing to save Aleksandr when he arrives. No, I have to wait.

Boris instructs the man to hold his position and moves clockwise along the edge of the trees, probably going to talk to more of his men who are hidden there. More of his men who will certainly kill Aleksandr when he arrives.

The thought makes me feel nauseous and it takes every ounce of my remaining strength to keep down the acid in my stomach. I have to. Because I'm the only person here to help Aleksandr. I'm the only person here who is on his side.

If either of us want to get out of here alive, I have to keep my head.

I don't see Boris again until a second car pulls into the clearing.

This time, even with the darkly-tinted windows, I recognize the black car as Aleksandr's. And I recognize the crouching shape of Boris moving among the tall grasses towards the car.

When Aleksandr turns off the engine and steps out, his bright blonde hair reflecting the afternoon sunshine, I almost sob at the sight of him. His strong shoulders and square jaw. I can feel the memory of his hands gripping my waist, and I want nothing more than to feel that again. To feel the warmth of his chest against mine. But more than that, I want to scream at him to get back in the car. To flee. I would give away my own location in the process, but that doesn't matter. I would gladly give my life for his.

Because I love him.

The realization hits me like a kick to the chest. I pinch my lips together to keep from gasping.

I love Aleksandr Levushka.

Despite our dire situation, my mouth quirks up in a small smile. Warmth fills my chest for a second, taking away the tremors in my arms and legs from clinging to the rough branch for so long. But just as quickly as it washes over me, it is gone.

Because I can't save Aleksandr.

I could call out to him, but it won't matter. I don't know the exact number, but I know there are too many men hiding in the trees for him to have any hope of driving away unscathed. And me yelling at him might make Boris carry out his plan even faster than he intended, giving me no opportunity to step in and stop this madness. So, I bite my tongue and watch the events unfold.

Boris presses a gun to the back of Aleksandr's head, and I can practically feel the cold metal at the base of my own skull. Chills run through me as Boris circles Aleksandr like a predator, closing in on his prey.

When Boris swings the butt of his gun down, and Aleksandr drops to his knees, I have to bite down on my palm to keep from sobbing. I want to jump from the tree and run to him, but with the man standing guard beneath me, I wouldn't even make it out of the tree line.

Boris picks Aleksandr up, and I can tell he is hurt. His shoulders are slouched forward, and his head hangs at a slightly different angle than normal. But he is still standing, which is a victory in itself.

Then, Boris raises his arm over his head, and the man beneath my tree walks away, into the sunlight and towards the center of the clearing.

I look around the edges of the clearing and there are men stepping out from every direction. Twenty of them in total. Converging on where Boris is holding Aleksandr at gunpoint.

Whatever Boris's plan is, he just set it in motion, and I know I don't have much time.

Hoping all of the patrols are out in the clearing, I scale down my tree slowly with shaky limbs. By the time I reach the ground, my arms are shaking from the exertion, but I push onward, staying low to the ground.

I'm halfway to the cabin when I look out and see two of Boris' men walking towards me. I drop to the ground, making myself as flat as possible, and pull the gun from my jeans. I can hear the thrum of my heartbeat in my ears, and I lay there and wait for their footsteps to approach me. For them to find me.

But they never come.

Then, I hear a commotion coming from inside the cabin.

I lift myself on to my elbows and realize the men were coming for me, but not because they saw me crawling through the grass. Because they thought I was still inside the cabin. And instead, they've just found Cyrus handcuffed and bound.

Boris's plan is about to fall apart, and there is no telling what he will do next. I know I have to act quickly.

I look up and see Boris' Hummer parked just behind the cabin, and I crawl towards it. The door is unlocked, so I open it as quietly as I can, but the moment the door is cracked, the car begins to beep.

I jump backwards in surprise before I understand what the beeping means.

The keys are still in the ignition.

"Thank God," I whisper, adrenaline pumping into my veins, replacing my exhaustion with action. I clamber into the high front seat and wait. I'm waiting for a sign. Some signal that it is time to go.

Then, I get it.

The front door of the cabin slams shut, and I hear Boris's voice boom across the clearing.

"Where the fuck is she?"

I smile and turn the ignition.

∽

The men surrounding Boris and Aleksandr are still looking towards Cyrus and the two guards who found him when I come barreling around the corner of the cabin.

The engine of the Hummer roars beneath me. Even as I soar over bumps and dips in the landscape, the car remains steady, taking each shock and blow in stride.

The two men are cutting Cyrus free when I drive up on them. Cyrus is still handcuffed, but his feet are free, and like the rat he is, he runs the moment he sees me coming. The two guards who found him, however, are not as lucky. I see the twin expressions of horror on their faces as I plow into them and they fly up and over the hood of the car.

Before their bodies even hit the ground behind me, I turn and head for the men standing between me and Aleksandr. The more of them I can get rid of, the better.

They are standing in a line, mouths hanging open, shocked at what they are seeing. And then, they begin to scatter.

I study their ranks just long enough to note that Aleksandr isn't among them, and then I press the gas pedal to the floor.

Bullets ping off the sides of the Hummer, and I realize it is armored. They can't hit me.

I take down a line of guards in one fail swoop, knocking them around like black bowling pins. A few of them disappear beneath the tires, and I don't even feel the bump as I drive over top of them.

Then, I turn towards another group. More bullets zing past the car, a few denting the hood, but none of them touch me.

I try to look for Aleksandr, but with bodies flying in front of the windshield, I can't see him. I can only hope I've offered enough of a distraction for him to get away.

I run down another man, watching in the rearview mirror as he flies over the roof and then imbeds headfirst in the grass like a misfired arrow. I make a U-turn in the grass, heading back towards where a few of the men are running for the safety of the cabin, as if wooden walls are going to keep me from hunting them down, and I see Boris standing directly in my path.

Aleksandr doesn't appear to be anywhere nearby, and Boris has his gun aimed directly at me.

I press down on the gas as hard as I can, and the tires spin for a second before they find traction and the car launches forward.

Fire erupts from the end of Boris' weapon as he shoots at me again and again, and I can't wait to run him down. I can't wait until he is bloody pulp beneath the wheels of his own car.

And then, the windshield explodes.

20

ALEKSANDR

The car comes out of nowhere.

For a second, it is barreling straight towards me, and I think that this is how I'm going to die. Boris is going to run me down and leave me in this field to rot into the ground.

But then, I realize Boris and his men are standing between me and the car.

And Boris is screaming.

"Who is that? Shoot them! Get out of the way!"

Whatever is happening, it has nothing to do with his plan. It is the distraction I've been waiting for.

The car turns sharply and rams into the two men bringing Cyrus out of the house. They fly up in the air like human confetti. One of the men loses his shoes, and they fly through the air and land close to my car.

Boris is still barking orders at his men, and for the time being, he has forgotten all about me. His plan is unravelling, and he is trying his best to keep things on track.

I back away from him slowly, not wanting to draw too much attention to myself lest he decide to scrap his plan of torturing Zoya in front of me and just shoot me in the head to get it over with.

The car is crisscrossing all over the field, mowing down Boris' men like weeds, and I have no idea who is driving, but I'm grateful for them. As the car heads towards where Boris is standing, he begins looking around frantically, trying to find his escape, and that is when I find mine.

I dart behind the rear bumper of my car and pull my gun from the strap across my chest.

With Boris standing so close to me before, reaching for the weapon wasn't an option, but now I'm more glad than ever that I brought it.

"Where is he?" Boris blubbers, and I know he has realized I'm gone.

Shots are ringing out all around me, most of them aimed at the Hummer currently turning the guards into mulch, but I know it won't be long before they turn on me.

I crawl around to the passenger side of the car, putting as much space between myself and Boris as possible, and then I stand up and rest my shooting arm on the top of the car.

It has been a long time since I've been in a firefight, but the instinct is still there. I fire shot after shot, pausing only to take aim at the next thug before pulling the trigger again. Men start to go down all around Boris. As much as I want to put a shot in his head the way he put one in my father's, I also want to save him for last.

Just as he wanted to torture me with Zoya, I want to torment him by making him watch the destruction of all of his carefully laid plans.

The only problem is that there are more men than I realized.

The twenty men in the center of the field weren't Boris' only guards. More are pouring from the trees on the left side, and if I stay behind this car, they'll overpower me. Even with the help of the person in the Hummer, there are too many.

Boris breaks away from the group of men I'm currently aiming at and moves closer to the cabin. He is staring off towards the trees, and I think he is staring at his reinforcements making their way through the grass, but then I realize he is facing off with the Hummer.

The windows are too dark for me to make out the driver, but I watch as the car pulls a quick U-turn in the field and then comes to a stop.

Boris is standing in front of the vehicle, chest rising and falling like mad, and then he raises his gun.

At the same instant, the Hummer's engine revs, the sound echoing off the trees like a roll of thunder. For a second, the tires spin, dirt and grass flying into the air. But just as Boris pulls the trigger, the Hummer shoots forward.

I pause my own shooting to watch it happen, to have the satisfaction of seeing my uncle be demolished by the armored vehicle, but when the Hummer is still a good distance away, the windshield shatters.

The car swerves hard to the right, taking out a few guards, but leaving Boris unscathed. I watch as the car rumbles across the grass, losing speed with every second.

Whoever was behind the wheel, they aren't behind it anymore.

I have to fight this alone.

The men crossing from the other side of the field are too close for hesitation. I have to act now.

I run out from behind the car, staying as low and small as I can to avoid the bullets whizzing through the air. Apparently convinced the driver of the Hummer is no longer a threat, Boris' remaining men are looking for someone else to take aim at.

"There he is!" The shout comes from closer to the cabin, and I look up and see Cyrus jumping up in the air, his hands still handcuffed behind his back. The men turn to him, but because he doesn't have the use of his hands, he is just bobbing his head erratically, making it difficult for them to pinpoint where he is pointing.

I lift my gun and fire.

Cyrus takes the shot in the chest and falls to his knees.

It feels good to finally give that rat what he deserves, but the shot comes at a price. Boris' men trace the shot back to me and bullets start whirring past my ears. Still, I hunker down and keep moving.

Then, I feel searing heat rip through my leg.

I know I've been shot, but there is too much adrenaline for me to feel it yet. As long as I keep moving, I can distract myself. As long as I don't slow down, it won't hurt.

More heat tears across the back of my neck, but I know it is a graze. If it wasn't, I'd be dead right now. Or, at least, paralyzed.

So, I keep moving.

I can feel blood dripping down my back and soaking into my shirt. My pant leg is heavy like I stepped in a deep puddle, but I don't look down. Not yet. Not until I have my uncle's body at my feet.

By the time Boris takes in the scene around him and realizes how close I am, it is too late. Now I'm the one with a gun to *his* head.

"Drop your fucking weapon," I growl in his ear.

"My men will kill you," he snaps.

"Will they?" I spin us both around in a circle, taking in the blank faces of his men around us. "Because if they do, they kill you, too. Unless, of course, you trust their aim enough to take that risk."

We are standing almost cheek to cheek, and I can feel the sweat from his skin dripping down my chin. He is shaking with rage and exertion and adrenaline, and then, all at once, he drops his gun and lets it fall at his feet.

Sticking close to him, I take a few steps away from the weapon, doing my best not to limp because of my injured leg. The men standing around us back away to maintain their distance.

"Shoot me if you must," I shout to them. "If you do, you'll kill your boss, too."

A good leader would have told his men to fire. A good leader would have told his men to win at all costs.

But Boris is not a good leader.

He is selfish. He is out for himself with no real concern for the men around him.

If they realized how little he actually cares for him, they'd shoot us both dead on the spot. I have no intention of informing them.

Slowly, I lead Boris back towards the Hummer. The engine is still on, though I haven't seen the driver emerge yet. They are probably dead inside. But the bloody mess inside will be worth it because the Hummer will offer significantly more protection than my car as I drive away should Boris' men decide to shoot.

"What are you going to do with me?" Boris asks, trying to sound tough, but I know him well enough to know when he is scared.

He screwed me over, I fucked his plans, and now I am in control. There are very few scenarios in which this turns out well for him.

"That entirely depends on how well you cooperate in the next minute," I say calmly, adjusting the gun at the back of his head and keeping an eye on his men. Everyone is watching us helplessly as we move closer to the getaway car. "Resist me at all, and I'll pull the trigger and be gone before your body hits the ground."

"You are lucky, you know that?"

I snort. "I've been shot twice. I feel very lucky right now."

"I mean about Mikhail," he says. "He killed himself. You didn't have to fight for control the way I did."

"You think I would have killed my own brother?"

"Your situation was the same as mine," he says. "You just got lucky."

I'm tempted to pull the trigger right there. I'm tempted to blow his brains out just for suggesting my life is better now that Mikhail is dead.

"Fuck you," I whisper against the back of his ear. "That only goes to show what a heartless son of a bitch you really are."

"Maybe I am," he agrees. "But at least I tried to take control of my life. That is more than anyone can say about you."

I walk us around to the driver side of the Hummer, one arm wrapped around Boris' chest, the other holding the gun to his head. My hands are full, and I'm not sure how I'm going to get in the car and get out of here without making myself vulnerable. Plus, there is the matter of the likely deceased driver.

"Hello?" I call over my shoulder. "Anyone alive back there?"

"I lined the shot up perfectly," he says. "I saw it go in. I fucking killed her."

His words sink in slowly, but as they do, an icy chill fills my veins. The adrenaline that had been curbing the edge of my pain is gone. My leg is excruciating, the back of my neck is throbbing, but nothing compares to the ache in my chest.

"Who?"

"Who do you think?" Boris snorts. "Your bitch escaped. She was driving the car."

I feel stupid that it never even occurred to me that Zoya was in the car, but more than that, I'm enraged.

I pull the trigger without even thinking about it.

Boris goes limp immediately, falling back on me, and I have to fall against the side of the Hummer to avoid being crushed under his weight.

My left leg can barely hold any weight, so I grab the driver's side door handle for stability, and the door opens. That is when I see her.

Her hair is a tangled halo around her pale face, one hand still on the steering wheel. She is slumped in the seat, blood soaking into the cushions. But she is still Zoya.

The men across the field are screaming, and I know I have to move if I want to get out of here in time, but I feel frozen. Like I'm wading through a pond filled with molasses. I want to run, want to move, want to react that way I've been trained my entire life to react under pressure, but my brain isn't working. I'm sluggish and slow, still trying to process that Zoya is dead in front of me.

Then, I hear her voice.

Alek, go.

If she is dead, then she died to save me, so that is all the encouragement I need.

As gently and quickly as I can, I slide her across the console into the passenger seat, jump into the driver's side with my one good leg, and slam on the gas before the door is even closed.

The ping of bullets hitting the armored siding propels me forward and helps me keep my eyes on the road, but as soon as I'm out of the direct range of bullets, I reach across the console and caress her arm.

Her body is still warm but that could be because she so recently died. It doesn't mean she is alive.

"Zoya?" My voice breaks on her name, and I slam the gas pedal to the floor, pushing the car to the very edge of its capabilities. "Can you hear me?"

She doesn't move, and I stare through the shattered windshield and try to find the tiniest shred of hope to cling to.

"I love you," I say.

To Zoya.

To the universe.

To myself.

"I didn't know if I'd ever love another person, but I love you, and you can't die like this. I'm sorry for yelling at you the day I left. I'm sorry for leaving. None of it matters now. You just need to hang on. Because I love you."

I feel stupid, but Zoya is the only thing that pulled me through the last two weeks. She is the reason I'm alive, and I won't give up on her.

When I reach over and grab her hand, I think I feel her fingers flex in mine, but I can't be sure.

I can only hope.

21

ALEKSANDR

The nurses are concerned about my leg and the graze on the back of my neck, though the leg is their main concern. I could care less about it. My only concern is for Zoya.

"The bone could be broken," a red-headed nurse says. She is middle-aged and has mascara smudged under her eyes. "You could get an infection."

"It was cleaned when I arrived," I say.

As soon as I walked through the front doors of the hospital with Zoya in my arms, we were swarmed by emergency room nurses. They strapped her to a gurney and wheeled her away, and I took a seat in the waiting room. It took the woman at the front desk twenty minutes to realize that the blood on my clothes wasn't just from Zoya's wound. Since then, I've been fighting off nurses like a plague of locusts.

"And my leg isn't broken. I'm walking fine."

"We don't know that until we get an x-ray," she insists, growing more and more impatient.

I wave her away. "I'll worry about it later."

"You might as well worry about it now," she snaps. "That woman will be—"

"Zoya." I turn my full attention to her, eyes narrowed. "Her name is Zoya."

Though she doesn't lose her own look of determination, she softens slightly. "*Zoya* might be in surgery for a long time. When she wakes up, you won't want to leave her side to worry about your own wounds. It is better to do it now."

I know she is right, but the idea of patching up my own body while Zoya might be dying somewhere in this hospital makes me physically ill. If something happens to her, I want to be the first one to know. I want to be waiting for news. I don't want to be whacked out on pain killers.

"I want to be here in case she wakes up," I say.

"She isn't going to wake up anytime soon," she says. "Her wound was serious. They are doing everything they can to save her and the baby. Now let us help you."

My heart squeezes in my chest, and the force of it nearly knocks me over. I'm weak. I don't need to look at my pant leg to know I've lost too much blood. Still, I don't want to go.

"Aleksandr?"

I look up and see my mother walking towards me. She is in a pair of black slacks with a dark blue button-down shirt, but she might as well be in a ball gown compared to me. My pants are ripped down the seam and covered in blood, and my white shirt is now twenty shades of gray, brown, and red.

She rushes towards me, dropping into the chair next to me. "What happened? Are you all right?"

There is too much to tell her now, especially in front of a host of nurses, so I just nod. "I'm fine."

"He isn't," the nurses says, turning to my mother, clearly hoping she will be able to talk some sense into me. She quickly runs through my list of injuries and potential complications, and by the end of it, my mother is grabbing my arm and pulling me from my chair.

"I'll wait here. I'll come find you as soon as I learn anything about Zoya."

I hesitate, digging my good leg into the floor as a teenage intern rolls a wheelchair over to me.

"Go," she insists. "Everything will be fine."

I hope to God she's right.

~

Just as I suspected, the bone isn't broken, but the nurse wasn't entirely wrong, either. It has only been a few hours since I was shot, but already the wound in my leg is red and inflamed, infection setting in. The red-haired nurse offers me anesthesia, but I can tell by the roll of her eyes that she knows I won't take it. Instead, she gives me a mild painkiller and then gets to work.

I bite down on a rolled up wash cloth as they pull the bullet from my leg. Overall, I've endured worse, but there is a moment when she is digging in the wound for any fragments when my vision blacks out, and I have to lie back on the table.

Within an hour, my leg is bullet-free, cleaned, and bandaged, and the wound on the back of my neck is taken care of, as well.

I tell the nurse I'm fine to walk, but she shakes her head and points to the wheelchair. Usually, I'd insist, but I must be even more tired than I thought because I drop down in the chair without further complaint and let her wheel me back to the waiting room.

My mother is still there, alone.

"Any news?"

She shakes her head. "Nothing. Are you okay?"

"I'm fine." The nurse leaves, and I turn to my mother, trying to read her expression to see if she knows anything. I never realized exactly how much she and Mikhail looked alike. I suppose that means she and I look alike, too, but I didn't spend my entire life staring at my own face. I saw Mikhail's, and right now, I see his face in hers, too.

She has the same oval-face and high cheekbones, and her nose is thin and pointed up at the end. And right now, her forehead is wrinkled with one vertical line running between her brows, letting me know she is worried.

"Have you heard about father?" I ask.

Part of me hopes Boris was lying, and my father isn't really dead, but as soon as the words are out of my mouth, her eyes fall to the floor. She nods slowly.

"When I learned something was going on, I called the estate over and over again, but no one was answering," she says. "Finally, I drove there myself. I found him."

She leans forward, shoulders shaking, and I reach out and lay a hand on her shoulder.

"I searched for you, too," she says. "And Boris. I knew if Vlad was dead that you would be close by, but then I couldn't find anyone. The only reason I'm here now is because the hospital called me."

"I'm sorry. I should have called you."

She waves away my apology. "Maybe another day I'll be mad about that, but right now, I'm just glad you are alive."

I explain the events of the last few days and Boris' betrayal. I tell her about the fight in the field and how Zoya risked her own life to save mine. I tell her how we escaped, how I killed Boris before fleeing in the Hummer, and she listens with wide eyes, tearing up when I tell her I thought Zoya was dead.

"You really love her, don't you?" she asks, reaching out to grab my hand.

I shake my head. "It doesn't seem fair to talk about that right now. Not when so many people have died."

"That is exactly the time to talk about love," she argues. Then, she pauses, looking up towards the ceiling. "You know your father came to see me after Mikhail died?"

I do a double-take, surprised. "No, I didn't know that."

My parents rarely saw one another face to face. Throughout my entire life, they had lived separately, and as far as I knew, didn't even talk. I constantly wondered why they didn't just divorce.

She nods. "He came to see me because he was worried about you."

That really captures my attention. I turn to her, wincing as my injured leg shifts into the new position. "Why was he worried about me?"

"Really, he was worried about the two of you. Your relationship," she says. "I know you think your father loved Mikhail more, but as a parent, that isn't possible. You always love your children equally."

She can see I'm not convinced, and she sighs and then snaps her fingers, an idea forming. "Think of it like caring for plants."

"I've never cared for a plant," I say, smiling a bit when she narrows her eyes at me.

"But you can imagine it, I'm sure. Some plants are more trouble than others. They need specific amounts of light and water and pruning. They are constantly on the verge of catastrophe if someone isn't tending to them at all times. That was Mikhail."

I bob my head back and forth. It is a rather apt description.

"Whereas you," she says, running a hand across my cheek. I pull away from her, wrinkling my nose, and she smiles. "You are a hearty plant. You grow where you are planted regardless of the conditions, and you don't require much maintenance. Your father and I knew that from a very early age. But your father didn't realize until Mikhail was gone, exactly how much energy he had devoted to one of his sons and not the other. So, he came to me to talk about how to be better. To figure out how to be a father to you in the way you needed."

I'm a grown man, long past the age of needing parenting, but tears burn the corners of my eyes. I have to blink hard to keep them at bay.

My mother pats my knee and sits back in her chair. "He was trying, Aleksandr. I just want you to know that. Lord knows he was not a perfect husband or father, but when he died, he was trying to make things better."

We sit in silence for a few minutes, only the steady ticking of the clock on the wall above us filling the room.

Until, finally, my mom rubs me on the back. "Don't let death and grief stop your life. Your father was moving through his grief, using his love for you as a guidepost, and he would want you to find the same strength. He would want you to find happiness."

I know she is talking about Zoya, but I can't bring myself to picture her face or remember her warmth. I can't bring myself to daydream about something that might only be a daydream. For all I know, Zoya is dying on the operating table. I might never see her smile again, and if I anchor my future on her, I'll fall apart.

In a moment of unprecedented candor, I say as much to my mother.

"The fact that you can feel that way after everything you've been through means everything," she says. "Finding a place in your heart and mind for even a scrap of love after all off the pain and violence you have suffered—that you both have suffered—is enough to move forward on. Cling to the feeling, to the way she made you feel, and no matter what happens here tonight, I know you'll be okay."

I give her a sad smile, hoping I can one day have the clarity she does. Then, I frown. "Are you talking about what Boris did to Zoya? Is that the violence you are talking about?"

The line appears between her brows again, and she bites her lips. "I think that is something I should let Zoya share with you."

I want to argue and force the information out of her, but before I can, two of my father's brigadiers walk through the waiting room doors.

"Dmitry, Fedor." I nod to each of them. "Is something wrong?"

"Aside from the obvious?" Dmitry asks with a wry smile. "No, everything is fine. Boris's men seem to have fled for the time being, so we are just focusing on cleaning up and rebuilding."

"But we do need to talk with you," Fedor says.

"About?"

"Taking the oath," he says. "I know it isn't the best time, but now more than ever, we need to put forward a clear leader. And now that your father is gone, you are the boss."

The day has been so full of chaos and near-death experiences that I haven't given myself a moment to consider my own future in the family. When Mikhail died, I knew I would be next in line, but I failed to realize my father's death this morning made me the new boss. If I wanted the position, that is.

"We are ready to perform everything now," Dmitry says. "It would only take half an hour."

My mother leans forward, her hand resting between my shoulder blades. "You do have a choice, Aleksandr. Your father always wanted one of his boys to take over after him, but it is your life, and your decision."

I'd been content my entire life to let my brother take control even though I knew he wasn't suitable. Even my father was not the ideal leader. I'd watched mistakes be made and then do my best to clean them up, always working behind the scenes to keep things together. Now, however, I was being given the opportunity to be at the forefront. To take control and lead the Levushka family into the unknown future. And rather than dreading the position, I found myself looking forward to it.

I could run things the way I wanted, and more than anything, I'd be able to protect Zoya. She would have the entire Levushka family watching out for her.

So, holding my leg out to the side at a strange angle, I lift myself up to standing using the wooden arms of the chair, and nod to Dmitry and Fedor. "Lead the way, men. I'm ready to take the oath."

∽

The ceremony is short and simple, and although I trust the men are loyal to me and my family, I can see they aren't excited about handing over the leadership position. And I can't blame them. My father has only been dead a few hours.

As soon as it is finished, I rush back to the hospital and find my mother sitting in the waiting room. She shakes her head as I approach, letting me know the doctors haven't come in yet, but before I can even sit down, the double doors leading back to the operating room open, and a doctor in blue scrubs and a face mask walks out.

"Aleksandr Levushka?"

I hobble forward on my bad leg. "Is she okay? Can I see her?"

He pulls back his mask, revealing a soft jaw covered in dark stubble, and plants his hands on his hips. "She came through surgery just fine."

The weight that has been pressing down on my chest the last several hours lifts slightly, allowing me to take a deep breath. "She is alive."

"Yes, she is alive," he says.

"And the baby?"

His brows lower, shading his eyes, and he folds his hands in front of him. "As of now, the baby appears healthy."

"*Appears* healthy?" I ask. "What does that mean?"

"It means that she is still early in her pregnancy, and we can't be certain how this event will affect the remainder of her pregnancy."

"But the baby is healthy right now? It has a heartbeat?"

"Yes. As of now, she and the baby are both alive and well."

Once I'm certain Zoya is actually alive, I'm able to let the doctor explain what they were doing in surgery for so many hours. All of the information, however, flies right over my head. As he discusses the damage caused by the bullet and how close she was to death, all I can do is stare over his shoulder at the double doors, wondering when I'll be able to walk through them.

I just want to see her.

"She is a very lucky woman," he says. "A few more minutes, even, and she might not have made it."

"Can I see her?" I ask, taking a step towards the door in anticipation. "I need to see her."

"She is still under heavy anesthesia," he says before stepping aside and waving an arm towards the doors. "But you are welcome to wait in her room for her to wake up."

Walking down the hallway feels like moving through a dream.

I know there are other people around me. Other sounds and smells and rooms. But they all blur into the background. There is only one clear spot in my vision, and it is the step directly in front of me.

"Room 318," the doctor says, pointing to a room on the left. Once he sees I understand, he cuts away towards the nurse's station, leaving me alone.

I walk toward the door slowly.

The doctor told me Zoya is alive and well, but I can't get the image of her inside the car, pale and covered in blood, out of my head.

I can't stop seeing her slumped in the passenger seat, limp and lifeless.

I've dealt with a lot of painful things in the last few weeks, and a lot of blood and violence before that, but Zoya is different. I can't bear seeing Zoya like that again. I can't bear seeing her hurt.

The door is cracked partially open, and it seems to take me hours to lift my hand and push it inward. But when I do, the room inside is dark.

I walk through the narrow entryway and peek around the corner.

The electrical glow of the machines around her bed are the only source of light, but they are enough for me to navigate to her bedside. They are enough for me to see that her bloody clothes are gone and the color has returned to her cheeks.

The dim light is enough for me to see that she is warm and breathing and...

Alive.

I pull the upholstered chair from the corner closer to the bed and drop down into it. There is an IV taped to the back of her hand, so I carefully grab her fingers and lay them across my palm. I massage my thumbs across her knuckles, study her heart-shaped face.

And then I wait.

22

ZOYA

I feel my fingers first.

A soft, pulling pressure. It is warm and nice, and for a minute, I'm still too lost in the fog to realize I don't know where I am. And I can't see anything.

Slowly, though, I become aware of my other senses.

I feel the firm mattress beneath me, and I smell the generic lemon scent of clean tile floors. Then, I hear the soft beep of the machine behind me, and I know I'm in a hospital. The thought startles me for a moment, but then I realize the beeping means I'm alive.

And the tug on my fingers means I'm not alone.

I try to remember what happened, how I got here, but escaping the cloud of my thoughts is like untangling myself from a net. I make my way out through slow, torturous effort, freeing myself one thread at a time.

"Zoya?"

The voice is familiar but far away. Like I'm hearing someone's voice from underwater.

"Zoya, are you awake?"

Warmth wraps around my hand, and I know it is Aleksandr.

I fight against my heavy lids and the aching fatigue in my chest that wants me to give in and go back to sleep. I need to see him.

Then, I do see him.

Only, we aren't in a hospital room. He is standing in the middle of an open field, men circled around him.

And I see Boris.

Boris, standing in front of me as I rev a car engine.

Then, I see the gun.

The memories of the day—was it today? Or has it been longer? A week? A month?—come back all at once, overwhelming me. I try to sit up, but I can't lift my head, and I try to swipe away the blankets, but there is something sticking to the back of my hand.

I hear Aleksandr say something else, but the words are lost on me. I hear only the low timbre of his voice, and that is enough. Enough reason for me to keep fighting.

"Don't fight it, dear," a female voice says. "You'll feel like you can't breathe, but you can. Don't worry."

I don't know what she is talking about, but then there is a strange tugging on my throat, and I realize she is pulling a tube out of my throat.

The moment it leaves my lips, I move to inhale, but instead of sucking in air, my entire body freezes up. In that instant, my lips go dry, and my eyes, previously too heavy to lift, open wide.

The room is dark, but I still squint against the bright light coming from the hallway. Then, there is a figure standing in front of it, and I look up.

And see Aleksandr.

"Try again, honey. Breathe," the nurse says.

I listen, taking shallow breaths at first that grow deeper and deeper with each inhale.

She lets go of my arm and steps back, allowing Aleksandr to take her place.

He looks like hell. Dark circles under his eyes, a swollen bruise across the right side of his face, and his stubble thicker than I've ever seen it.

But he is still gorgeous.

Still square-jawed with blue eyes and full lips.

He is still Aleksandr, and I lift my hand, searching for his fingers. He smiles and wraps his hand around mine.

"Hi."

I move my lips around the word to respond, but nothing comes out.

"You don't have to say anything," he says, sitting down in the chair next to my bed. I wonder how long he has been sitting there. By the looks of him, a long time. "I'll be here when you're ready. I'll wait."

We sit in silence for a while.

Eventually, the nurses bring me water, advising me to drink it slowly, and then a red-haired nurse turns on Aleksandr.

"Have your bandages been checked recently?"

"Bandages?" My voice is hoarse and raw, but the nurse and Aleksandr both turn to me as though I just belted out an opera. "Were you hurt?"

"Not badly," he says.

"He was shot twice," the nurse says. "He almost wouldn't let me treat him; he was so worried about you."

Aleksandr rolls his eyes, but the nurse raises her eyebrows and nods, assuring me it is true.

"Get your bandages checked," I say, letting go of his hand. I don't recognize my own voice, but the nurse says it could be a few days before my throat isn't so raw.

If I wasn't so weak, Aleksandr might argue, but since I am, he sits down in the chair and allows the nurse to unwrap his leg. He winces as she pulls the final layer away from his skin.

I gasp. His calf is pale white, several shades lighter than the rest of his skin, and there are stitches running down the side.

"I'm fine," he says, smiling at me, though I see a flicker of pain as the nurse rewraps his wound. "If you are worried about me, you should have seen yourself."

I look down and realize I don't even know where I was shot. Or what happened. And as I run my hands down the front of my hospital gown, I pause on my stomach, and my heart lurches.

I don't know if the machines behind me start going wild or if Aleksandr could just see me beginning to spiral, but he leans over and grabs my hand. "The baby is fine, Zoya. The baby is healthy."

"They checked the heartbeat?" I ask through a sob.

He nods. "They did."

I take a shuddery breath in and let it out slowly, trying to calm the wave of panic that rose over me.

A few weeks ago, I may have counted an accident like this a blessing. It would have saved me from being a single mother.

But now, I can't imagine it.

I want this baby.

Regardless of how it came to be, I want to be a mother. I want to raise this child.

The nurse tells me to hit the button if I need anything and then leaves me and Aleksandr alone for the first time since I've woken up. He grabs my hand and brings it to his lips. "Zoya?"

"Yes?"

I regret answering him. I don't want him to speak. Because if he does, he might expand on what he said to me the last time I saw him.

He might admit that he only came here to make sure I'm alright, but he can't get over the fact that I'm pregnant with his brother's child. He might tell me that the wonderful, fleeting thing between us is over. And as weak as I am right now, news like that might kill me.

He lowers his head, looking down at the floor, and then lays his eyes on me again. They are the palest blue I've ever seen. "What happened with Mikhail?"

Another wave of panic washes over me. This one milder than the last, but I still feel my heart pick up speed. My fingers fidget with the edge of the scratchy hospital blanket.

What if he doesn't believe me?

What if he thinks I'm lying to protect my reputation? To keep myself from looking like the kind of woman who would sleep with two brothers? Twins, no less?

"I know I didn't let you explain before," he says. "I'm sorry about that, but you can tell me the whole truth now. I'm listening."

"Are you sure you're ready?" I ask.

He pauses to think, really weighing whether he is ready for whatever I might say, and then he nods. "I'm ready for the truth."

So, I tell him.

Thankfully, there isn't much to tell since my memory of that night is mostly a blank, but I tell him what little bit I can. I explain that I was out drinking by myself and then ended up back in my bed in the morning, sticky and sore.

I tell him what his mother told me she saw. About Mikhail helping me out of his car and walking me into the estate late in the evening.

"Why didn't she stop him?" he asks, his face paler than I've ever seen it. "Why didn't she do something?"

"She would have," I say quickly. "She didn't know, Aleksandr. She couldn't know."

I sit quietly while he processes, not wanting to burden him with too many details at once.

"So, when I told you I knew the baby was Mikhail's?" he asks, looking up at me from beneath lowered brows. "You didn't even know he was the father yet?"

I twist my lips to the corner of my mouth and shake my head. "I didn't have any clue."

He groans and lays his face in his hands. "God, I'm sorry. I'm so sorry, Zoya."

"It's fine. You didn't know." I rub a circle in the center of his back, massaging the bundles of tense muscles there.

"I should have asked you about," he says. "I should have started a conversation about it rather than flinging accusations."

"I don't blame you. Of course, you wouldn't think your brother could be capable of something like that, so there is no way you could have known."

His shoulders stiffen, and he sits up, his hands folded in front of him, elbows resting on his knees. "I'm not surprised, Zoya."

"What do you mean?"

"I mean," he says, taking a deep breath. "I should be shocked by what you are telling me...but I'm not. I loved my brother, but I am not surprised to hear that he did this to you. Does that make me a bad person?"

I slide my hand across his shoulder and down his arm, squeezing the corded muscle just above his elbow. "No."

"But I knew how he could get when he got drunk," he says. "I'd seen him make aggressive moves on other women, and I laughed it off. And I knew he needed serious help this last time, but I ignored it because I didn't want to deal with him on top of everything else. At what point does this become my fault?"

He hangs his head, and I can't stand the idea that Aleksandr is beating himself up for his brother's mistakes. I curl my fingers around his ear and down his neck, twining them through his blonde hair. "No, it does not make you a bad person. The only person responsible for Mikhail's actions is Mikhail. You do not need to carry his guilt."

Aleksandr looks up at me, and I press my palm to his cheek. "You are a good man and that is all that matters."

He opens his mouth to say something, but I cut him off.

"You are a good man, Aleksandr Levushka, and I won't let you feel responsible, okay? You are not responsible and neither am I."

His eyes widen. "Of course, you aren't, Zoya. You didn't do anything to deserve this."

I nod. "I know."

We sit in the moment, looking at one another, our hands tangling together, trying to figure out how to move forward.

"I'll take care of whatever you need," Aleksandr finally says. "Anything."

"I don't really need anything—"

"Therapy," he says quickly like he is ripping off a bandage. "If you ever need to talk to someone about this—about what happened—I'll take care of it. Or, even," he takes a deep breath. "Even if you decided not to have the baby, then that would be your choice, and—"

"No." I pull his hand across the railing, clutching his fingers to my chest. "I want the baby. And I know that could complicate things for you, and I understand if you can't stick around, but I really want this baby."

He stares at me blankly for a moment, blinking, and then relief washes over him. Color reenters his cheeks, and his eyes crinkle in a smile. "I do, too, Zoya. So much."

"You do?" My throat is so thick with unshed tears that I can hardly get the words out.

He nods. "Obviously now I realize Boris was just lying to screw with me, but at the time, I trusted him, and when we were leaving the estate he told me he heard you were going to get an abortion, and it devastated me. I know it isn't my place to make that decision for you, but even if my brother was…a monster, this baby—*your* baby—"

"Is the only piece of him you have left," I finish. "I understand."

He nods, glad I understand, and slides his hand from the center of my chest down to my stomach, being careful of my bandages. "I really want this baby."

I lay my hand over his and smile. "I'm glad because I want this child to be close to your family."

"Don't you mean *our* family?" he asks, tipping his head to the side.

His expression is so sincere and sweet that I start crying immediately. I cup my hands over my face, but immediately, Aleksandr pulls them away and looks into my eyes. "I want you, too."

I shake my head, unable to believe this is happening. Certain it has to be a dream.

"I don't want to help you raise this baby because it is a part of my brother," he says. "I want to help you raise it because it is a part of you."

"You don't have to," I choke out, face wet with tears. "I don't want you to do this because you feel bad. Or because you are guilty."

Aleksandr throws his head back and laughs. "You know, you are responsible for one of the only times in my life I've felt guilty. That is why I was at your apartment that night those men showed up. I felt guilty for getting you fired, and I came to see where you were living."

"You felt bad?"

He rolls his eyes and smiles. "Don't let it go to your head, but yes. I treated you unfairly, and I wanted to fix it."

He leans over the bed railing, his eyes on my lips, and I feel my entire body warm. I'm aware of every breath, every movement of my body when he is so close to me. He dips low, his lips hovering over mine, and I try to stretch up to him, but he moves out of the way.

"Did I?"

I'm dizzy, overwhelmed by the nearness of him, and I don't understand his question. "Huh?"

"Did I fix it?" he asks. "Did I make up for my bad first impression?"

I smile and wrinkle my nose. "Well, I mean, I suppose."

"You suppose?"

I grab the front of his white t-shirt—it is blood splattered and stained, and I can only imagine what the button-down he had on over it must look like—and pull him close to me. He could overpower me easily if he wanted to, but he lets me direct him.

"I mean, I love you," I say with a shrug. "So, I suppose you made up for it."

His pale blue eyes widen in surprise, and then his lips are on mine.

The aches and pains that had begun creeping in are washed away in a flood of endorphins as his kiss works its magic on me. Aleksandr curls his fingers in my hair and bites my lower lip. He caresses my cheeks with his thumbs and swirls his tongue with mine.

The kiss is gentle and hot, and I claw at his shirt, desperate to have his weight over me.

"Whoa," he whispers against my lips, his eyes crinkled in a smile. "We should probably hit pause on this until you are healed up."

I growl in frustration.

Aleksandr smiles and kisses the end of my nose. "I love you, Zoya."

I grab his shirt again and tug, but he resists this time, shaking his head. I let my head fall back on the pillows and groan. "Fine. I suppose that will have to do for now."

"You suppose?" he teases.

I nod. "I mean, if you wanted to do it in this hospital bed and give those nurses something out there to monitor, that would be fine. But for now, I suppose *I love you* will do."

"Good." He squeezes my hand and presses my knuckles to his lips. "I love you."

EPILOGUE

ALEKSANDR

Five Years Later

She smells like vanilla and sugar, and I bury my face in the brown curls spread out on her pillow.

"I'm sleeping," she murmurs, her voice soft and thick. It has been five years of waking up next to Zoya, and I'm still not used to the sight of her.

The morning sun is streaming through our sheer curtains, washing the bed in golden light, and Zoya looks like a fallen angel. The light brings out the red in her tangles, and I pinch them between my finger, admiring the beautiful complexity of something so ordinary.

"I have a meeting in the city this morning. I won't be able to come home for lunch."

She rolls over, eyes still closed, and frowns. Her full lower lip pouts out, and I can't stop myself from leaning forward and pressing a kiss to it.

As soon as my lips are on hers, she arches into me.

The sheets and comforter are in a tangle between us, and I kick them aside in one deft move to have better access to her body. When my hand lands on the curve of her warm, bare hip, I groan.

"This is why I've stopped wearing pajamas," she whispers, hooking her leg around mine and drawing me closer.

"They only get in the way."

She giggles. "If you knew how much money I spent on them, you wouldn't say that. You'd probably make me wear them on our next date night."

I wrap an arm around Zoya's lower back and roll over onto mine, bringing her with me. "Where are you buying pajamas that they cost so much?"

She sits up, her knees on either side of my body, and I can't believe how beautiful she is. I would pay double the amount of whatever she spent on her pajamas just to wake up to the sight of her naked body every day.

There is a scar across her chest where she was shot and another across her lower stomach where they performed the C-section after twenty-seven hours of labor, but she is perfect in my eyes. Utterly perfect.

I run my hands up her hips and grip her waist, rolling her body over me.

She circles her hips, taunting me, a wicked smile on her face. "They are less 'pajamas' and more...negligee."

A particular memory flickers in my head. "You mean the black lacy top from—"

"From the balcony," she finishes, biting her lower lip and nodding. "You took me from behind while we looked down on Paris. I paid a pretty penny for that one."

"Worth it," I moan, pulling her closer, desperate for more contact.

She lifts her hips and leans forward so her soft chest is pressed against mine and kisses my neck, her tongue swirling across my Adam's apple. "And then there is the red one from—"

"The limo," I gasp. "I can't believe I almost forgot about that."

Zoya sucks my earlobe into her mouth and trails her hand down my chest. "The driver had to make three trips around the block so we could finish."

I've always slept naked, so Zoya has no trouble reaching between us and finding my excitement. My entire body jerks when her warm little hand wraps around me.

"Do you want to know my favorite time?" she asks, her lips close to my ear.

I hum affirmatively, barely able to form words.

"It was the time I wore the navy-blue lace gown, and you took me against the wall," she breaths, kissing the neglected skin behind my ear at the same time her hand strokes me.

"And in the shower," she says with another stroke. "And bent over the side of the bed."

She is polishing my tip, her hand working faster and faster until my breathing is erratic and my hips are bucking upwards.

"I came three times in a row," she moans, stroking me until I think my eyes will be permanently crossed.

Then, suddenly, she stops.

My eyes snap open, the beast she unlocked searching for her.

"But," she says, lifting one of her legs as if there is any universe in which I'll let her crawl away from me and get out of bed. "You have a meeting, and we don't have time for that."

I growl and grab her arm, yanking her back on top of me. Her smile is mischievous, and I have every intention of pounding it off of her and replacing it with a satisfied one.

"We'll make time," I growl, lifting her hips and positioning myself at her opening.

I know Zoya was teasing about leaving because she lowers herself onto me eagerly. She is just as ready as I am.

In two strokes, I'm in to the hilt, and Zoya sits up and rolls her body on top of me. She arches her back, places her hands back on my thighs, and bucks her hips against me until our skin slaps together. Until I can't do anything other than grip her hips and hang on for the ride. Until the sight and the sensation are too much.

I sit up, wrapping an arm around her lower back, and press my face between her breasts. Then, in one move, I push her back on the bed and settle between her thighs.

I alternate deep thrusts with quick, shallow strokes until she is clawing at my shoulders and panting for more. She lifts her hips in time with my movements until we are in perfect sync, grinding together.

"Yes," she moans, digging her fingers into my shoulder blade. "Alek, yes."

I've been close since the moment I woke up and saw her naked in bed next to me, so I just need to make sure she gets there, too.

I reach down between us and let my thumb circle the rosebud between her legs.

She gasps, her entire body freezing up for a second, before she stretches up and bites my shoulder.

We both fall together.

Zoya curls her legs around mine when we are finished, clinging to me. "That was incredible."

I kiss the top of her head and roll onto my side. Her chest is still heaving, and I run my finger across her ribcage. "Another tick in the column against spending money on pajamas, don't you think?"

She nods. "Yes, absolutely. I'll stop buying negligee and maybe use some of that money on toys."

"Oh, Zoya," I growl, nuzzling her neck. "Don't tease me."

She throws her head back and laughs, her hands resting on her stomach. "I didn't mean toys for us. I meant toys for Maksim."

"Oh." I frown, and then lean over and check the clock by the bed. "He should be getting up soon."

Zoya stretches her arms over her head, arching her back and once again testing my dedication to my meeting. I kiss her stomach, pinning her to the bed, and work my way up to her breasts. "I need to get moving. Once he's awake, I won't have a moment to myself until I take him to visit his grandmas."

I swirl my tongue across her body, loving the way she moans under my touch, and then pull away. "I need to go, too. I'm going to barely make it to my meeting on time as it is."

Zoya stretches out to grab me and bring me back to bed, but I'm already out of reach, and she flops back on the bed with a sigh. "No fair."

"Always leave them wanting more," I say with a two-finger salute before I duck into the bathroom for a shower.

I'm only a little surprised when Zoya joins me thirty seconds later, dropping down onto her knees while the water washes all of our sins away.

One of the first decisions I made as the head of my family was to create an official office space.

My father hid away in his many homes spread across the country, and Boris utilized his estate as well as a smattering of hotel rooms around the city, but there was never a central location for business to be conducted. So, I remedied that by purchasing a loft above a small shoe shop in the city center.

Dmitry and Fedor are already there when I arrive, going over the contracts for our new weapons importer.

"Good morning, Mr. Levushka." Fedor stands tall, his hands behind his back.

Dmitry, always the more casual of the two, raises a silent hand in greeting and continues going over the paperwork.

Dmitry and Fedor were the two men who showed up at the hospital to swear me in to the position of boss for the Levushka family, and they've been by my side ever since.

My father always expressed the importance of having a confidante, a person you could trust with your life. But in the end, the person he trusted most abused his power and murdered him in cold blood. So, in an abundance of caution, I've opted for two right hand men.

Dmitry and Fedor both answer to me, and they both answer to each other. It is a system designed to make it more difficult for the same level of betrayal my uncle perpetrated on my father to happen again.

"Do we have any worries about the negotiations?" I ask, dropping down into the desk chair and folding my hands over my stomach. "I don't want to be surprised in the meeting."

"My only concern is the non-exclusivity clause," Fedor says.

"That is everyone's concern," Dmitry says. "No one likes it, boss."

"If no one is happy, then you know you've reached a good compromise."

Both men share a doubtful look, but this is the one thing I've refused to budge on. Keeping exclusive contracts is what created the hot bed of competition and frustration that led to our rivals rising up against us. Maintaining a fair market, even in the criminal world, is essential.

"Why do we want our weapons guy selling to other families?" Dmitry asks.

"More buyers means more weapons, which means more choices," I say. "Supply and demand."

"Sounds like someone is speaking my language."

I turn to see Leonid walking through the conference room door. He became one of the biggest weapons importers in St. Petersburg once Cyrus was dead. He serves our family as well as a number of other smaller operations in and around the city. Though, he isn't the only game in town. There are plenty of smaller dealers filling in the gaps, willing to step up and grow their business should Leonid fall out of favor.

I stand up and shake his hand, inviting him to sit down. Dmitry and Fedor maintain an air of suspicion, but I don't mind. It keeps Leonid slightly uncomfortable and ensures he'll treat us all with respect.

"Like I said last time, everything looks good with the paperwork," he says, picking up a pen and tapping it against his chin. "I do have one question, though."

"That's why we're here. Ask."

He pinches his lips together nervously. "Well, as you know, I'm working with other...clients, and I—I just want to make sure that isn't going to be a problem."

I tap my finger on the non-exclusivity clause. "It's in the contract."

"Right, but—" he sighs and leans forward on his elbows, voice low. "If I work with the Ivanovs on the west side of the city, I'm not going to be shot dead in the street by your men, right? I understand that you are pushing for looser restrictions on the businessmen you work with, which you know I'm in favor of. But I don't want to be murdered for dealing with another family on your turf."

I smile and raise an eyebrow. "Do you think I'd have you killed, Leonid?"

He hesitates and then bobs his head back and forth, an uncomfortable laugh bubbling out of him. "Kind of, Mr. Levushka. Yes."

I fold my hands on the table in front of me, letting them plop down on the wood with a loud smack. "Good. Because I would."

Leonid's smile fades, his eyes growing wide.

"However," I add, my tone softening. "We have graciously allowed the Ivanovs to work on the west side of the city."

"You have?" Leonid asks, shifting his gaze from me to Dmitry and Fedor behind me.

I don't need to turn around to know he is seeing a disapproving frown on Dmitry's face. He took the most convincing to agree to the deal with the Ivanovs. One of their men killed his cousin in a fight when they were all new recruits, and he has had a hard time letting it go.

"The Levushkas do not want to rule this city with an iron fist," I explain. "We want our boundaries to be respected, and we want peace. That is all."

Leonid lifts his brows in surprise. "Well, if you assure me I'm not going to be executed for doing business with them, then I'm ready to sign."

I slide the papers closer to him and wave for him to continue.

After the meeting, I have a few hours before I need to meet up with Zoya and Maksim, so I drive the familiar highway north out of town.

I don't get out to the old estate very often. After everything that happened there, my memories of the place are tainted, but the property has remained one of the Levushka holdings and it is a nice place to house recruits and guests of the family.

I drive down the long gravel road and through the wrought iron gates, passing the tiny cottage where Zoya spent her entire childhood. The new groundskeeper lives in the main house, so the cottage has been empty for the last few years and the neglect definitely shows.

The rest of the property, however, is well maintained. Not quite to the same standard Boris insisted upon, but I don't mind. Even when Boris lived here, he never spent any time out in the gardens or walking the paths, so that level of upkeep was an unnecessary expense. One of many such expenses he required that put a strain on the family.

There are a few cars in the drive to the left of the house, and I pull into the back corner furthest from the house. I get out and head out towards the line of trees rimming the property. I have no desire to speak with anyone inside.

After the funeral, my mother had Mikhail cremated. Doing so gave us time to decide where his final resting place would be. And when my father died just a few weeks later, I was glad for the decision. It meant we would be able to bury them together. To choose a spot that would suit them both.

My mother wasn't sure burying my father on the property of the estate where he died was appropriate, but I persuaded her that his final minutes on the estate shouldn't overshadow the happy memories we had of the property.

As children, coming to Boris's estate was one of the few times when my father would put down his role of head of the Levushka family and, for just a moment, become our father.

Mikhail and I would play soccer in the expansive lawn behind the house, and a number of times, my father came out and joined us. He would take off his jacket, roll up his sleeves, and run like I'd never seen him run before.

As we grew older and my father became more distant, those were the memories I thought about most often. That was the father I tried to remember. And, had he been given the chance, I think he may have become that man again. But he wasn't given that opportunity and so, I decided to bury him there. Just to the left of the field where he had played soccer with his boys.

The headstones are simple, just concrete markers bearing their names and the span of their lives, and I sit down on a bench that wasn't here the last time I visited. The groundskeeper must have added it for me. I make a mental reminder to thank him.

"Hey, guys," I say, feeling as dumb as ever talking to the open air.

I never wanted to visit the burial site at all, but Zoya pushed me to go a few months after we buried them. She thought I needed to get some things off of my chest. So, I came. Only to satisfy her. But then, to my surprise, I visited again. And again.

In the last five years, I've been here maybe ten times. And each time, a new emotion has ruled the day.

The first time, it was rage.

More anger than I thought I was capable of.

Zoya was days away from giving birth and the doctors were worried about her chances of a natural birth and her blood pressure. They were talking about inducing her, and I couldn't help but blame Mikhail. He was the reason she was pregnant. He was the reason she was in this position in the first place. And if I lost her, I'd never forgive him. And I told him as much.

The next time, I told him about my son. *My* son.

Not his.

Because Maksim is mine. He looks like me, he calls me Dad, and I am the one who changed his diapers, cleaned up his spit-up, and rocked him to sleep when he was sick.

Even if Mikhail had been alive, he wouldn't have done that. He would have left Zoya to handle things on her own. He never would have been a father to Maksim the way I am, and that makes Maksim mine.

After that, every visit became progressively easier.

The rage that burned inside at me because of what he did to Zoya began to fade as Maksim grew and amazed us more and more every day. Zoya had to work through things at her own pace, and I still don't think she has fully dealt with it all, but she has never regretted Maksim for a second. And I tell Mikhail that.

Not to ease his guilt—if he can feel guilt wherever he is—but to ease mine.

I've never stopped feeling responsible for what Mikhail did to Zoya. For not seeing that Mikhail was a danger to himself and others. Zoya has told me over and over again that it was never my fault, but my twin brother hurt her, and I couldn't help but wonder if that same tendency could live inside of me, too.

"Sorry it has been awhile," I say, wiping debris from the top of my father's headstone and kicking a fallen pinecone away from the base. "Things have been busy."

I update them on life. On how Maksim has started piano lessons and Zoya is getting cooking lessons from Samara. I tell them about the restructuring of the family and the new deals we are working on. And I tell them how much I love being a father.

"It is more satisfying than anything else I've ever done," I say. "It feels so cheesy to say that, but it is true. It is the best job in the world."

I haven't forgiven Mikhail. Not entirely. Not yet.

And maybe I never will.

But I still love him.

The part of me that grew up wanting to take care of Mikhail and watch his back is still there. When I think about him now, less and less do I see the strung out monster who hurt Zoya. Now, I see him as a cocky teenager, smoking his first cigarette behind our house in Moscow and trying to blow smoke rings. I see him smiling at me from the front seat of his first car, his hand held out the window like he is a bird soaring through the air.

Now, when I think about Mikhail, I see my brother in all of his messy complexities. And maybe that is the best I can hope for.

THE END

Thanks for reading! But don't stop now – there's more. Click the link below to receive the FREE extended epilogue to **KNOCKED UP BY THE MOB BOSS**. You'll also get a free sneak preview of another bestselling mafia romance novel.

So what are you waiting for? Click below!

https://dl.bookfunnel.com/xt73qpqpo2

SNEAK PREVIEW (BROKEN VOWS)

Keep reading for a sneak preview of my bestselling mafia romance, BROKEN VOWS!

∽

She's my fake wife, my property... and my last chance at redemption.

She's beautiful. An angel.

I'm dangerous. A killer.

She's my fake bride for a single reason – so I can crush her father's resistance.

But marrying Eve brings me far more than I bargained for.

She's fiery. Feisty. Won't take no for an answer.

She makes me believe that I might be worth redemption.

Until I discover a past she's been hiding from me.

One that threatens everything.

Now, I know that our wedding vows are not enough.

I need to make sure she's mine for good.

A baby in her belly is the only way to seal the deal.

In the end, the Bratva always gets what it wants.

∽

Luka

Their fear tingles against my skin like a whisper. As my leather-soled shoes tap against the concrete floor, I can sense it in the way their eyes dart towards and away from me. In the way they scurry around the production floor like mice, meek and unseen in the shadows. I enjoy it.

Even before I rose through the ranks of my family, I could inspire fear. Being a large man made that simple. But now, with brawn and power behind me, people cower. These people—the employees at the soda factory—don't even know why they fear me. Other than me being the owner's son, they have no real reason to be afraid of me, and yet, like prey in the grasslands, they sense the lion is near. I observe each of them as I weave my way around conveyors filled with plastic bottles and aluminum cans, carbonated soda being pumped into them, filling the room with a syrupy sweet smell.

I recognize their faces, though not their names. The people upstairs don't concern me. Or, at least, they shouldn't. The soda factory is a cover for the real operation downstairs, which must be protected at all costs. It's why I'm here on a Friday evening sniffing around for rats. For anyone who looks unfamiliar or out of place.

The floor manager—a Hispanic woman with a severe braid running down her back—calls out orders to the employees on the floor below in both English and Spanish, directing attention where necessary. She doesn't look at me once.

Noise permeates the metal shell of the building. The whirr of conveyor belts and grinding of gears makes the concrete floors feel like they are vibrating from the sheer power of the sound waves. A lot of people find the sights and smells overwhelming, but I've never minded. You don't become a mob underboss by shrinking in the face of chaos.

A group of employees in blue polos gather around a conveyor belt, smoothing out some kink in the production line. They pull a few aluminum cans from the line and drop them in a recycling bin, jockeying the rest of the cans back into a smooth line. The larger of the three men—a bald man with a doughy face and no obvious chin—flips a red switch. An alarm sounds and the cans begin moving again. He gives the floor manager a thumbs up and then turns to me, his hand flattening into a small wave. I raise an eyebrow in response. His face reddens, and he turns back to his work.

I don't recognize him, but he can't be in law enforcement. Undercover cops are more fit than he could ever dream to be. Plus, he wouldn't have drawn attention to himself. Likely, he is just a new hire, unaware of my position in the company. I resolve to go over new hires with the site manager and find out the man's name.

When I make it to the back of the production floor, the lights are dimmed—the back half of the factory not being utilized overnight—and I fumble with my keys for a moment before finding the right one to unlock the basement door. The stairway down is dark, and as soon as the metal door slams shut behind me, I'm left in blackness, my other senses heightening. The sounds of the production floor are but a whisper behind me, but the most pressing difference is the smell. Rather than the syrupy sweetness of the factory, there is an ether, chemical-like smell that makes my nose itch.

"That you, Luka?" Simon Oakley, the main chemist, doesn't wait for me to answer. "I've got a line here for you. We've perfected the chemistry. Best coke you'll ever try."

I pull back a thick curtain at the base of the stairs and step into the bright white light of the real production floor. I blink as my eyes adjust, and see Simon alone at the first metal table, three other men working in the back of the room. Like the employees upstairs, they don't look up as I enter. Simon, however, smiles and points to the line.

"I don't need to try it," I say flatly. "I'll know whether it's good or not when I see how much our profits increase."

"Well," Simon balks. "It can take time for word to spread. We may not see a rise in income until—"

"I'm not here to chat." I walk around the end of the table and stand next to Simon. He is an entire head shorter than me, his skin pale from spending so much time in the basement. "There have been nasty rumors going around among my men."

His bushy brows furrow in concern. "Rumors about what? You know we basement dwellers are often the last to hear just about everything." He tries to chuckle, but it dies as soon as he sees that I'm not here to fuck around.

"Disloyalty." I purse my lips and run my tongue over my top teeth. "The rumbling is that someone has turned their back on the family."

Fear dilates his pupils, and his fingers drum against the metal tabletop. "See? That is what I'm saying. I haven't heard a single thing about any of that."

"You haven't?" I hum in thought, taking a step closer. I can tell Simon wants to back away, but he stays put. I commend him for his bravery even as I loath him for it. "That is interesting."

His Adam's apple bobs in his throat. "Why is that interesting?"

Before he can even finish the sentence, my hand is around his neck. I strike like a snake, squeezing his windpipe in my hand and walking him back towards the stone wall. I hear the men in the back of the room jump and murmur, but they make no move to help their boss. Because I outrank Simon by a mile.

"It's interesting, Simon, because I have reliable information that says you met with members of the Furino mafia." I slam his head against the wall once, twice. "Is it true?"

His face is turning red, eyeballs beginning to bulge out, and he claws at my hand for air. I don't give him any.

"Why would you go behind my back and meet with another family? Have I not welcomed you into our fold? Have I not made your life here comfortable?"

Simon's eyes are rolling back in his head, his fingers becoming limp noodles on my wrist, weak and ineffective. Just before his body can sag into unconsciousness, I release him. He drops to the floor, falling onto his hands and knees and gasping for air. I let him get two breaths before I kick him in the ribs.

"I didn't meet with them," he rasps. When he looks up at me, I can already see the beginnings of bruises wrapping around his neck.

I kick him again. The force knocks the air out of him, and he collapses on his face, forehead pressed to the cement floor.

"Okay," he says, voice muffled. "I talked with them. Once."

I pressed the sole of my shoe into his ribs, rolling him onto his back. "Speak up."

"I met with them once," he admits, tears streaming down his face from the pain. "They reached out to me."

"Yet you did not tell me?"

"I didn't know what they wanted," he says, sitting up and leaning against the wall.

"All the more reason you should have told me." I reach down and grab his shirt, hauling him to his feet and pinning him against the wall. "Men who are loyal to me do not meet with my enemies."

"They offered me money," he says, wincing in preparation for the next blow. "They offered me a larger cut of the profits. I shouldn't have gone, but I have a family, and—"

I was raised to be an observer of people. To spot their weaknesses and know when I am being deceived. So, I know immediately Simon is not telling me the entire story. The Furinos would not reach out to our chemist and offer him more money unless there had been communication between them prior, unless they had some connection Simon is not telling me about. He thinks I am a fool. He thinks I will forgive him because of his wife and child, but he does not know the depths of my apathy. Simon thinks he can appeal to my humanity, but he does not realize I do not have any.

I press my hand into the bruises around his neck. Simon grabs my wrist, trying to pull me away, but I squeeze again, enjoying the feeling of his life in my hands. I like knowing that with one blow to the neck, I could break his trachea and watch him suffocate on the floor. I am in complete control.

"And your family will be dead before dawn unless you tell me why you met with the Furinos," I spit. I want nothing more than to kill Simon for being disloyal. I can figure out the truth without him. But it is not why I was sent here. Killing indiscriminately does not create the kind of controlled fear we need to keep our family standing. It only creates anarchy. So, reluctantly, I let Simon go. Once again, he falls to the floor, gasping, and I step away so I won't be tempted to beat him.

"I'll tell you," he says, his voice high-pitched, like the words are being released slowly from a balloon. "I'll tell you anything, just don't hurt my family."

I nod for him to continue. This is his only chance to come clean. If he lies to me again, I'll kill him.

Simon opens his mouth, but before he can say anything, I hear a loud bang upstairs and a scream. Just as I turn around, the door at the top of the stairs opens, and I know immediately something is wrong. Forgetting all about Simon, I grab the nearest table and tip it over, not worrying about the potential lost profits. Footsteps pound down the stairs and no sooner have I crouched down, the room erupts in bullets.

I see one of the men in the back of the room drop, clutching his stomach. The other two follow my lead and dive behind tables. Simon crawls over to lay on the floor next to me, his lips purple.

The room is filled with the pounding of footsteps, the ring of bullets, and the moans of the fallen man. It is chaos, but I am steady. My heart rate is even as I grab my phone, turn on the front facing camera, and lift it over the table. There are eight shoulders spread out around the room, guns at the ready. Two of them are at the base of the stairs, the other six are spread out in three-foot increments, forming a barrier in front of the stairs. No one here is supposed to get out alive.

But they do not know who is hiding behind the table. If they did, they'd be running.

I look over at one of the chemists. They are not our family's soldiers, but they are trained like anyone else. He has his gun at the ready, waiting for my order. I nod my head once, twice, and on three, we both turn and fire.

One man falls immediately, my bullet striking him in the neck, blood spraying against the wall like splattered paint. It is a kind of artwork, shooting a man. Years of training, placing the bullet just so. Art is meant to incite a reaction and a bullet certainly does that. The man drops his weapon, his hand flying to his neck. Before he can experience too much pain, I place another bullet in his forehead. He drops to his knees, but before he falls flat on his face, I shoot his friend.

The men expected this ambush to be simple, so they are still in shock, still scrambling to collect themselves. It makes it easy for my men to knock them off. Another two men drop as I chase my second target around the room, firing shot after shot at him. He ducks behind a table, and I wait, gun aimed. It is a deadly game of Whack-a-mole, and it requires patience. His gun pops up first, followed shortly by his head, which I blow off with one shot. His scream dies on his lips as he bleeds out, red seeping out from under the table and spreading across the floor.

There are three men left, and I'm out of bullets. I stash my gun in my pocket and pull out my KA-BAR knife. The blade feels like an old friend in my hand. I crawl past a shivering Simon, wishing I'd killed him just so I wouldn't have to see him looking so pathetic, and out from behind the table. I slide my feet under me, moving into a crouch. The remaining men are wounded, and they are focused on the back corner where shots are still coming from my men. They do not see me approaching from the side.

I lunge at the first man—a young kid with golden brown hair and a tattoo on his neck. It is half-hidden under the collar of his shirt, so I cannot make it out. When my knife cuts into his side, he spins to fight me off, but I knock his gun from his hand with my left arm and then drive the knife in under his ribs and upward. He freezes for a moment before blood leaks from his mouth.

The man next to him falls from multiple bullets in the chest and stomach. I kick his gun away from him as he falls to the floor, and advance on the last attacker. He is hiding behind a metal table, palm pressing into a wound on his shoulder. He scrambles to lift his gun as I approach, but I drop to my knees and slide next to him, knife pressed to his neck. His eyes go wide, and then they squeeze shut as he drops his weapon.

The blade of my knife is biting into his skin, and I see the same tattoo creeping up from beneath his collar. I slide the blade down, pushing his shirt aside, and I recognize it at once.

"You are with the Furinos?" I ask.

The man answers by squeezing his eyes shut even tighter.

"You should know who is in a room before you attack," I hiss. "I am Luka Volkov, and I could slit your throat right now."

His entire body is trembling, blood from his shoulder wound leaking through his clothes and onto the floor. Every ounce of me wants this kill. I feel like a dog who has not been fed, desperate for a hunk of flesh, but warfare is not endless bloodshed. It is tactical.

"But I will not," I say, pulling the blade back. The man blinks, unbelieving. "Get out of here and tell your boss what happened. Tell him this attack is a declaration of war, and the Volkov family will live up to our merciless reputation."

He hesitates, and I slash the blade across his cheek, drawing a thin line of blood from the corner of his mouth to his ear. "Go!" I roar.

The man scrambles to his feet and towards the stairs, blood dripping in his wake. As soon as he is gone, I clean my knife with the hem of my shirt and slide it back into place on my hip.

This will not end well.

Eve

I hold up a bag of raisins and a bag of prunes a few inches from the cook's face.

"Do you see the difference?" I ask. The question is rhetorical. Anyone with eyes could see the difference. And a cook—a properly trained cook—should be able to smell, feel, and sense the difference, as well.

Still, Felix wrinkles his forehead and studies the bags like it is a pop quiz.

"Raisins are small, Felix!" My shouting makes him jump, but I'm far too stressed out to care. "Prunes are huge. As big as a baby's fist.

Raisins are tiny. They taste very different because they start out as different fruits. Do you see the problem?"

He stares at me blankly, and I wonder if being sous chef gives me the authority to fire someone. Because this man has got to go.

"You've ruined an entire roast duck, Felix." I drop the bags on the counter and run a hand down my sweaty face. I grab the towel from my back pocket and towel off. "Throw it out and start again, but use *prunes* this time."

He smiles and nods, and I wonder how many times he must have hit his head to be so slow. I motion for another cook to come talk to me. He moves quickly, hands folded behind his back, waiting for my order.

"Chop up the duck and make a confit salad. We can toss it with more raisins, fennel—that kind of thing—and make it work."

He nods and shuffles away, and I mop my forehead again.

At the start of my shift, I strode into the kitchen like I owned the place. I was finally sous chef to Cal Higgs, genius chef in charge at The Floating Crown. After graduating culinary school, I didn't know where I'd get a job or where I'd be on the totem pole, and I certainly never imagined I'd be a sous chef so soon, but here I am. And now that I'm here, I can't help but wonder if it wasn't some sort of trick. Did Cal give into my father's wishes easily and give me this job because he needed a break from the insanity?

I've been assured by several members of staff that the dishwasher, whose name I can't remember, has been working at the kitchen for over a year, but he seems to be stuck on slow motion tonight. He is washing and drying plates seconds before the cooks are plating them up and sending them back out to the dining room. And two of the cooks, who were apparently dating, decided that the middle of dinner rush would be the perfect time to discuss their relationship, and they broke up. Dylan stormed out without a word, and Sarah, who should be okay since she was the dumper, not the dumpee, is hiding in the bathroom bawling her eyes out. I've knocked on the door once every ten minutes for an hour, but she refuses to let me in. Cal has a key, but he has been shut away in his office all night, and I don't want to go explain what a shitshow the kitchen is, so we are making do. Barely.

"Sarah?" I knock on the door. "If you don't come out in five minutes, you're fired."

For the first time, there is a break in the crying. "You can't do that."

"Yes, I can," I lie. "You'll leave here tonight without your apron. Single and jobless. Just imagine that shame."

I feel bad rubbing salt in her wound, threatening her, but I'm out of options. I tried comforting her and offering her some of the dark chocolate from the dessert pantry, but she refused to budge. Threats are my last recourse.

There is a long pause, and I wonder if I'm going to have to admit that I actually can't fire her—I don't think—and tell the staff to start using the bathrooms on the customer side, when finally, Sarah emerges. Mascara is smeared down her cheeks, and her eyes are red and puffy from crying, but she is out of the bathroom. As soon as she steps through the doorway, one of the waitresses darts in after her and slams the door shut.

"I'm sorry, Eve," she blubbers, covering her face with her hands.

I grab her wrists and pry her palms from her eyes. When she looks up, her eyes are still closed, tears leaking from the corners.

"Go to the sinks and help with the dishes," I say firmly. "You're in no state to cook right now. Just focus on cleaning plates, okay?"

Sarah nods, her lower lip wobbling.

"Everything is fine," I say, speaking to her like she is a wild animal who might attack. "You won't lose your job. Cal never needs to know, okay? Just go wash dishes. Now."

She turns away from me in a daze and heads back to help the dishwasher whose name I can't for the life of me remember, and I take a deep breath. I've finally put out all the fires, and I lean against the counter and watch the kitchen move around me. It is like a living, breathing machine. Each person has to play their part or everything falls apart. And tonight, I'm barely holding them together.

When the kitchen door swings open, I hope it is Makayla. She has been a waitress at The Floating Crown for five years, and while she has no formal culinary training, she knows this kitchen better than anyone. I've asked her for help tonight more times than I'm comfortable with, but at this point, just seeing one, capable, smiling face would be enough to keep me from crying. But when I turn and instead see a man in a suit, the tie loose and askew around his neck, and his eyes glassy, I almost sag to the floor.

"You can't be back here, sir," I say, moving forward to block his access to the rest of the kitchen. "We have hot stoves and fire and sharp knives, and you are already unstable on your feet."

Makayla told me a businessman at the bar had been demanding macaroni and cheese all night between shots. Apparently, he would not take 'no' for an answer.

"Macaroni and cheese," he mutters, falling against my palms, his feet sliding out from underneath him. "I need macaroni and cheese to soak up the alcohol."

I turn to the nearest person for help, but Felix is still looking at the bags of raisins and prunes like he might seriously still be confused which is which, and I don't want to distract him lest he ruin another duck. I could call out for help from someone else or call the police, but I don't want to cause a scene. Cal is just in the next room. He may have hired me because my father is Don of the Furino family, but even my father can't be angry if Cal fires me for sheer incompetence. I have to prove that I'm capable.

"Sir, we don't have macaroni and cheese, but may I recommend our scoglio?"

"What is that?" he asks, top lip curled back.

"A delicious seafood pasta. Mussels, clams, shrimp, and scallops in a tomato sauce with herbs and spices. Truly delicious. One of my favorite meals on the menu."

"No cheese?"

I sigh. "No. No cheese."

He shakes his head and pushes past me, running his hands along the counters like he might stumble upon a prepared bowl of cheesy pasta.

"Sir, you can't be back here."

"I can be wherever I like," he shouts. "This is America, isn't it?"

"It is, but this is a private restaurant and our insurance does not cover diners being back in the kitchen, so I have to ask you—"

"Oh, say can you see by the dawn's early light!"

"Is that 'The Star-Spangled Banner'?" I ask, looking around to see whether anyone else can see this man or whether I'm having some sort of exhausted fever dream.

"What so proudly we hailed at the twilight's last gleaming?"

This is absurd. Truly absurd. Beyond calling the police, the easiest thing to do seems to be to give in to his demands, so I lay a hand on his shoulder and lead him to the corner of the kitchen. I pat the counter, and he jumps up like he is a child.

I listen to the National Anthem six times before I hand the man a bowl of whole grain linguini with a sharp cheddar cheese sauce on top. "Can you please take this back to the bar and leave me alone?"

He grabs the bowl from my hands, takes a bite, and then breaks into yet another rousing rendition of "The Star-Spangled Banner." This time in falsetto with accompanying dance moves.

I sigh and push him towards the door. "Come on, man."

The dining room is loud enough that no one pays the man too much attention. Plus, he has been drunk out here for an hour before ambushing the kitchen. A few guests shake their heads at the man and then smile at me, giving me the understanding and recognition I sought from the kitchen staff. I lead the man back to the bar, tell the bartender to get rid of him as soon as the pasta is gone, and then make my way back through the dining room.

"She isn't the chef," says a deep voice at normal volume. "Chefs don't look like *that*."

I don't turn towards the table because I don't want to give them the satisfaction of knowing I heard them, of knowing they had any kind of power over me.

"Whatever she makes, it can't taste half as good as her muffin," another man says to raucous laughter.

I roll my eyes and speed up. I'm used to the comments and the cat calls. I've been dealing with it since I sprouted boobs. Even my father's men would whisper things about me. It is part of the reason I chose a path outside the scope of the family business. I couldn't imagine working with the kind of men my father employed. They were crass and mean and treated women like possessions. Unfortunately, the more I learn of the world beyond the Bratva, the more I realize men everywhere are like that. It is the reason I'll never get married. I won't belong to anyone.

I hear the men's deep voices as I walk back towards the kitchen, but I don't listen. I let the words roll off of me like water on a windowpane and step back into the safe chaos of the kitchen.

The kitchen seems to calm down as dinner service goes on, and I'm able to take a step back from micro-managing everything to work on an order of chicken tikka masala. While letting the tomato puree and spices simmer, I realize my stomach is growling. I was too nervous before shift to eat anything, and now that things have finally settled into an easy rhythm, my body is about to absorb itself. So, I casually walk over to where two giant stock pots are simmering with the starter soups for the day and scoop myself out a hearty ladle of lobster and bacon soup. Cal doesn't like for anyone to eat while on service, but he has been in his office all evening, and based on the smell slipping out from under his door, he will be far too stoned to notice or care.

The soup is warm and filling, and I close my eyes as I eat, enjoying the blissful moment of peace before more chaos ensues.

The kitchen door opens, and this time it really is Makayla. I wave her over, eager to see how everyone is enjoying the food and whether the drunk patriot finally left the restaurant, but she doesn't see me and walks with purpose through the kitchen and straight to Cal's office door. She opens it and steps inside, and I wonder what she needed Cal for and why she couldn't come to me. Lord knows I've handled every other situation that arose all night.

I'm just finished the last bite of my soup when Cal's office door slams open, bouncing off the wall, and he stomps his way across the kitchen.

"Eve!"

I shove the bowl to the back of the counter, throwing a dish towel over top to hide the evidence, and then wipe my mouth quickly.

"Yes, chef?"

"Front and center," he barks like we are in the military rather than a kitchen.

Despite the offense I take with his tone—especially after everything I've done to keep the place running all night—I move quickly to follow his order. Because that is what a good sous chef does. I follow the chef's orders, no matter how demeaning.

Cal Higgs is a large man in every sense of the word. He is tall, round, and thick. His head sits on top of his shoulders with no neck in sight, and just walking across the room looks like a chore. I imagine being in his body would be like wearing a winter coat and scarf all the time.

"What is the problem, Chef?"

He hitches a thumb over his shoulder, and Makayla gives me an apologetic wince. "Someone complained about the food, and they want to see the chef."

I wrinkled my forehead. I'd personally tasted every dish that went out. Unless Felix managed to slide another dish past me with raisins in it instead of prunes, I'm not sure what the complaint could be. "Was there something wrong with the dish or did they simply not like it?"

"Does it matter?" he snaps. His eyes are bloodshot and glassy, yet his temper is as sharp as ever. "I don't like unhappy customers, and you need to fix it."

"But you're the chef," I say, realizing too late I should have stayed quiet.

Cal steps forward, and I swear I can feel the floor quake under his weight. "But you made the food. Should I go out there and apologize on your behalf? No, this is your mess, and you will take care of it."

"Of course," I say, looking down at the ground. "You're right. I'll go out there and make this right."

Before Cal can find another reason to yell at me, I retie my apron around my waist, straighten my white jacket, and march through the swinging kitchen doors.

The dining room is quieter than before. The drunk man is no longer singing the National Anthem at the bar and several of the tables are empty, the bussers clearing away empty plates. Happy plates, I might add. Clearly, they didn't have an issue with the food.

I didn't ask Makayla who complained about the food, but as soon as I walk into the main dining area, it is obvious. There is a small gathering at the corner booth, and a salt and pepper-haired man in his late fifties or early sixties raising a hand in the air and waves me over without looking directly at me. I haven't even spoken to the man yet, and I already hate him.

I'm standing at their table, staring at the man, but he doesn't speak to me until I announce my presence.

"I heard someone wanted to speak with the chef," I say.

He turns to me, one eyebrow raised. "You are the chef?"

I recognize a Russian accent when I hear one, and this man is Russian without a doubt. I wonder if I know him. Or if my father does. Would he be complaining to me if he knew my father was head of the Furino family? I would never throw my family name around in order to scare people, but for just a second, I have the inclination.

"Sous chef," I say with as much confidence as I can muster. "I ran the kitchen tonight, so I'll be hearing the complaints."

His eyes move down my body slowly like he is inspecting a cut of meat in a butcher shop. I cross my arms over my chest and spread my feet hip-width apart. "So, was there an issue with the food? I'd love to correct any problems."

"Soup was cold." He nudges his empty bowl to the center of the table with three fingers. "The portions were too small, and I ordered my steak medium-rare, not raw."

Every plate on the table is empty. Not a single crumb in sight. Apparently, the issues were not bad enough he couldn't finish his meal.

"Do you have any of the steak left?" I ask, making a show of looking around the table. "If one of my cooks undercooked the meat, I'd like to be able to inform them."

"If? I just told you the meet was undercooked. Are you doubting me?"

"Of course not," I say. *Yes, absolutely I am.* "It is just that if the meat was undercooked, I do not understand why you waited until you'd eaten everything to inform me of the problem?"

The man looks around the table at his companions. They are all smiling, and I can practically see them sharpening their teeth, preparing to rip me to shreds. When he turns back to me, his smile is acidic, deadly. "How did you get this position—sous chef? Surely not by skill. You are pretty, which I'm sure did you a favor. Did you sleep with the chef? Maybe—" he moves his hand in an obscene gesture —"'service' the boss to earn your place in the kitchen? Surely your 'talent' didn't get you the job, seeing as how you have none."

I physically bite my tongue and then take a deep breath. "If you'd like me to remake anything for you or bring out a complimentary dessert, I'm happy to do that. If not, I apologize for the issues and hope you will not hold it against us. We'd love to have you again."

Lies. Lies. Lies. I'm smiling and being friendly the way I was taught in culinary school. I actually took a class on dealing with customers, and this man is being even more outrageous than the overexaggerated angry customer played by my professor.

"Why would I want more food from you if the things you already sent out were terrible?" He snorts and shakes his head. "I see you do not have a ring on. That is no surprise. Men like a woman who can cook. Men don't care if you know your way around a professional kitchen if you don't know your way around a dinner plate."

The older gentleman is speaking, but I hear my father's words in my head. *You do not need to go to culinary school to find a husband, Eve. Your aunties can teach you to cook good food for your man.*

My entire life has been preparation for finding a husband. The validity of every hobby is judged by whether it will fetch me a suitor or not. My father wants me to be happy, but he mostly wants me to be married. Single, I'm a disappointment. Married, I'm a vessel for future Furino mafia members.

Years of anger and resentment begin to bubble and hiss inside of me until I'm boiling. My hands are shaking, and I can feel adrenaline pulsing through me, lighting every inch of me on fire. This time, I don't bite my tongue.

"I'd rather die alone than spent another minute near a man like you," I spit, stepping forward and laying my palms flat on the table. "The fact that you ate all of the food you apparently hated shows you are a pig in more ways than one."

In the back of my mind, I recognize that my voice is echoing around the restaurant and the chatter in the rest of the room has gone quiet, but blood is whirring in my ears, and I can't stop. I've stayed quiet and docile for too long. Now, it is my turn to speak my mind.

"You and your friends may be wealthy and respected, but I see you for what you are—spineless, cowardly assholes who are so insecure they have to take their rage out on everybody else."

I want to spin on my heel and storm away, making a grand exit, but in classic Eve fashion, my heel catches on the tablecloth, and I nearly trip. I fall sideways and throw an arm out to catch myself, knocking a nearly full bottle of wine on the table over. The glass shatters and red wine splashes across the tablecloth and onto the guests in the booth like a river of blood.

I pause long enough to note the old Russian man's shirt is splattered like he has been shot before I continue my exit and head straight for the doors.

I suck in the night air. The evening is warm and humid, summer strangling the city in its hold, and I want to rip off my clothes for some relief. I feel like I'm being strangled. Like there is a hand around my neck, squeezing the life out of me.

Breathing in and out slowly helps, but as the physical panic begins to ebb away, emotional panic flows in.

What have I done? Cal Higgs is going to find out about the altercation any minute, and then what? Will he fire me? And if he does, will I ever be able to get another chef position? I was only offered this position because of my father, and I doubt he will help me earn another kitchen position, especially since I'm no closer to finding a boyfriend (or husband) since I left for culinary school.

Despite it all, I want to call my dad. He has always made it clear he will move heaven and earth to take care of me, to make sure no one is mean to me, and I want his support right now. But the support he offered me when a girl tripped me during soccer practice and made me miss the net won't apply here. He will tell me to come home. To put down my apron and knife and focus on more meaningful pursuits. And that is the last thing I want to hear right now.

I pull out my phone and scroll through my contacts list, hoping to see a spark of hope amidst the names, but there is nothing. I've lost touch with everyone since I started culinary school. There hasn't been time for friends.

This is probably the kind of situation where most girls would turn to their moms, but she hasn't been in the picture since I was six years old. Even if I had her number, I wouldn't call her. Dad hasn't always been perfect, but at least he was there. At least he cared enough to stay.

I untie my apron and pull it over my head, leaning back against the brick side of the restaurant.

"Take it off, baby!"

I look up and see a man on a motorcycle with his hair in a bun parked along the curb. He is waggling his eyebrows at me like I'm supposed to fall in love with him for harassing me on the street, and the fire that filled my veins inside hasn't died out yet. The embers are still there, burning under the skin, and I step towards him, lips pulled back in a smile.

He looks surprised, and I'm sure he is. That move has probably never worked for him before. He smiles back at me, his tongue darting out to lick his lower lip.

"Is that your bike?" I purr.

He nods. "Want a ride?"

My voice is still sticky sweet as I respond, "So sweet of you to offer. I'd rather choke and die on that grease ball you call a man bun, but thanks anyway, hon."

It takes him a second to realize my words don't match the tone. When it hits him, he snarls, "Bitch."

"Asshole." I flip him the bird over my shoulder and start the long walk home.

∼

Click here to keep reading BROKEN VOWS.

MAILING LIST

Sign up to my mailing list!
New subscribers receive a FREE steamy bad boy romance novel.

Click the link below to join.
https://readerlinks.com/l/1057996

ALSO BY NICOLE FOX

Kornilov Bratva Duet

Married to the Don

Til Death Do Us Part

Heirs to the Bratva Empire

Can be read in any order

Kostya

Maksim

Andrei

Tsezar Bratva

Nightfall (Book 1)

Daybreak (Book 2)

Russian Crime Brotherhood

Can be read in any order

Owned by the Mob Boss

Unprotected with the Mob Boss

Knocked Up by the Mob Boss

Sold to the Mob Boss

Stolen by the Mob Boss

Trapped with the Mob Boss

Volkov Bratva

Broken Vows (Book 1)

Broken Hope (Book 2)

Other Standalones

Vin: A Mafia Romance

Printed in Great Britain
by Amazon